"I find it hard," the captain said, "to believe you would flee from the prospect of becoming a countess, when you walked to my house in the pouring rain, thinking you were about to become a mere governess."

Countess?

"Not that it makes any difference now," he said in a tone of chilling finality.

"Oh, but…" she began, but he had turned away. His shoulders stiff with affront, he stalked from the room, shutting the door behind him with the exaggerated care of a man who would have got a great deal more satisfaction from slamming it hard.

Aimée rolled onto her back, thumping the counterpane at her sides. Yes, why had he gone to such lengths to get her to his house? Why had he placed an advertisement in a London newspaper that made it sound as though he wanted to employ a governess when what he really wanted was a wife?

* * *

Captain Corcoran's Hoyden Bride
Harlequin® Historical #330—April 2012

Author Note

The Earl of Caxton has two granddaughters. One of them, Miss Aimée Peters, has grown up in exile, knowing only poverty and hardship. She is desperate to find some security. To put down roots.

To the outside world the other, Lady Jayne Chilcot, has been her family's pampered darling. But she feels suffocated by the stultifying propriety that hems her in on all sides, and longs for adventure.

These cousins have one thing in common. Their mothers were proud women, who instilled that pride into their daughters, teaching them that a lady will always rise to the occasion, and to look upon adverse circumstances as a test of character.

At the moment I am still writing about how Lady Jayne finds her adventure, but first you can read about Aimée.

In this story Aimée goes looking for the respectability she craves in a job as a governess. What could be safer for a single woman than living quietly in the country, teaching children all the things she has learned in her so far turbulent life? She does not dream that in her new employer, Captain Corcoran, she will face the greatest challenge of all. A challenge to her heart…

Captain Corcoran's Hoyden Bride

ANNIE BURROWS

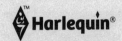

TORONTO NEW YORK LONDON
AMSTERDAM PARIS SYDNEY HAMBURG
STOCKHOLM ATHENS TOKYO MILAN MADRID
PRAGUE WARSAW BUDAPEST AUCKLAND

Recycling programs
for this product may
not exist in your area.

ISBN-13: 978-0-373-30639-8

CAPTAIN CORCORAN'S HOYDEN BRIDE

Copyright © 2011 by Annie Burrows

First North American Publication 2012

www.Harlequin.com

Printed in U.S.A.

ANNIE BURROWS

has been making up stories for her own amusement since she first went to school. As soon as she got the hang of using a pencil she began to write them down. Her love of books meant she had to do a degree in English literature. And her love of writing meant she could never take on a job where she didn't have time to jot down notes when inspiration for a new plot struck her. She still wants the heroines of her stories to wear beautiful floaty dresses, and triumph over all that life can throw at them. But when she got married she discovered that finding a hero is an essential ingredient to arriving at 'happy ever after'.

Available from Harlequin® Historical and ANNIE BURROWS

Captain Corcoran's Hoyden Bride #330
One Candlelit Christmas #919
"The Rake's Secret Son"
The Earl's Untouched Bride #933
*The Viscount and the Virgin #1012
A Countess by Christmas #1021
Gift-Wrapped Governess #1063
"Governess to Christmas Bride"

**Silk & Scandal

Other works include:
Harlequin Historical *Undone!* ebooks

Notorious Lord, Compromised Miss

To my editor, Sally Williamson, for all your patience
with me on this one and your insightful revision suggestions,
but most of all for reminding me to write from the heart.

Chapter One

*Wanted: For Gentleman's family in Yorkshire.
A Healthy Young Person from good family, to
supervise education of young children. She will
not be expected to dine with servants or do any
menial work. Any person able to provide proofs
of their pedigree, education and character may
call at the Black Swan, Holborn, on Tuesday, 6th
June, between the hours of three and four in the
afternoon.*

Miss Aimée Peters sighed as the church clock of
Beckforth chimed the half-hour.

Again.

It meant she had been sitting on her trunk in the
coaching yard of the King's Arms for well over an hour.

Of course, no governess could expect her employers
to send one of their other servants to *wait* for the stage
to come in, and to meet her as though they regarded
her as a significant member of the household. There

was not a creature on earth of less significance than a governess.

Which had been the whole point of going to such lengths to secure this position. Nobody ever looked twice at a governess. Her background and education separated her from the servants, and her status as paid employee kept her apart from the family. She would belong neither above nor below stairs.

To all intents and purposes she would be invisible.

Which was exactly what Aimée wanted.

Though—she shivered as the wind skirled round the corner of the yard in which she was sitting—it was one thing to have pulled off such a successful disappearing act, but where on earth was Mr Jago?

He had left a letter for her at the Black Swan, telling her that if she still wanted the position for which she had undergone that rather cursory interview, it was hers. All she had to do was go to the Bull and Mouth and collect the tickets he had purchased for her transport as far as this inn in Beckforth, which was the closest village to her employer's home.

But what if the letter she had sent, along with the requested references, to tell him she was indeed accepting the post, and would be travelling to Yorkshire immediately, had gone astray? What if nobody was expecting her to arrive today at all? She could not just sit on her trunk in this ramshackle inn yard indefinitely!

She gripped her overnight bag, which she had kept on her lap the entire way, a little more firmly, stood up, and brushed a few stalks of dried, muddy straw from her skirts.

It was not as though she was not perfectly used to fending for herself. Her lips twitched into a wry smile. Her willingness to travel—nay, her *experience* of travelling had been, she was convinced, the deciding factor in landing her this post. Mr Jago had scarcely asked anything about her pedigree, but had sat up and looked very interested once she had told him how she had spent her childhood becoming fluent in Italian and French by flitting from one European city to the next. Naturally, she had not mentioned that these moves had usually occurred at dead of night, with outraged creditors in hot pursuit.

Mr Jago, after pursing his lips and looking her up and down with those keen blue eyes of his, had unbent far enough to tell her that his employer, the man who had placed the advertisement in the London papers and had sent him to conduct interviews, was a naval captain who was looking for a woman with backbone. Aimée had only briefly been puzzled by his choice of words, for she perceived that a naval officer would probably need to uproot his family regularly, depending on where he was to be stationed. She saw that she would adapt to a peripatetic lifestyle more readily than any of the other applicants, and so had proudly replied that she had a backbone of steel.

Aimée picked her way carefully through the piles of droppings, refuse and puddles that made up the surface of the yard, to the half-open inn door. If Mr Jago really had hired her because he had thought nothing would daunt her, she had better prove him right! Beginning by finding out how far it was to The Lady's Bower, the charmingly named house where her new employer and his family now lived, and making her own way there.

She might have cheated her way into this post, but she was so grateful for the chance to earn her living doing honest work that she was utterly determined that neither Mr Jago nor the naval officer whose children she would be caring for would ever have cause to be sorry they had hired her.

The smell of spilled ale, tobacco fumes and unwashed working men hung over the threshold like a thick curtain. She had to mentally push her revulsion to one side before she could go inside.

'Can you tell me, sir, how far it is to The Lady's Bower?' she asked the stringy individual who was leaning on his elbows on the far side of the bar. 'And whether it is practical for me to walk there?' She could probably hire some form of conveyance from this inn, if not. She had enough coin in her purse, tucked into a side pocket of her overnight bag, to provide for such contingencies.

He sucked air in through his teeth. 'You don't want to be going there, miss,' he said, shaking his head. 'You want to put up here for the night, and take the stage back to London in the morning. I'll have a room made up for you, shall I?'

'No, thank you!' Aimée drew herself up to her full height and glared at the slovenly landlord. She had enough experience of his type to tell from the state of the yard and his clothing that his bedrooms too would be dirty, the sheets damp, and any food on offer poorly cooked.

'I most definitely do not want to return to London. I just want to reach The Lady's Bower before nightfall!'

The landlord's patronising expression hardened into a sneer.

'On your own head be it, then,' he said, eyeing her in a way that made her even less inclined to sample the dubious quality of his lodgings. 'T'aint more than three, mebbe four miles across Sir Thomas Gregory's lands. Course, a stranger to these parts, taking the direct route across his land would like as not run foul of his game-keeper...'

'You expect me to believe this area, being so far from London, is so savage that people go around taking pot-shots at strangers?' she scoffed.

'Poachers, aye...'

'Do I look like a poacher?' she exclaimed, indicating her neat little bonnet, deep green travelling dress and serviceable cloak. She had chosen each item carefully, from second-hand dealers that stocked a better class of cast-offs, so that the entire outfit made her look exactly what she thought a governess ought to look like.

'Or an imbecile?' It had suddenly dawned on her that her outfit actually made her look fairly well off, as well as eminently respectable. The man was obviously trying to scare her into giving him her custom. Just because she was a stranger to the area, he thought he could hoodwink her into staying the night, then hiring some overpriced conveyance from his stables in the morning to take her on a journey that would probably turn out to be hardly any distance at all!

He sucked air through his teeth again, running his eyes over her slender frame with a decidedly hostile expression.

'You *could* go by the roads, I dare say. If you're so set on going there.'

'I am,' she snapped, her initial plan, of asking if he could provide some form of transport evaporating in the heat of her increasing irritation.

The directions he then gave her were so complicated, with a couple of left turns by the corners of beet fields, followed by right turns after blasted oaks, and making sure to take the right fork after Sir Thomas's beech plantation, that she was half-convinced she was going to go round in a great big circle and end up right back where she started.

In this benighted inn yard.

Having left instructions as to the care of her trunk, she strode off with her head held high, her overnight bag gripped tightly in her left hand, and a confirmed dislike of the inhabitants of Yorkshire simmering in her breast.

She eyed the fields to either side of the lane, wondering if the funny-looking reddish leaves within them belonged to beetroots. If they did, then she had to turn left at the end of the next one, then left again once she had crossed the little footbridge over the stream.

That she found a stream, complete with a footbridge, did not encourage her as much as it might have, had she not suspected the innkeeper was sending her on a wild goose chase. She had annoyed him, by not immediately falling in with his suggestions, and surely this was her punishment! She ought to have been more conciliatory, she supposed.

Her mother always used to say that there was never any excuse for forgetting her manners. Or surrendering to displays of emotion in front of vulgar persons.

How right, Aimée sighed, her mother had been. Vulgar persons did not waste time in getting their own back. Vulgar persons took great delight in sending you out on six-mile hikes. When rain was on the way.

She hefted her bag into her other hand, and glanced warily at the sky. When she had set out, the clouds had not looked all that noteworthy, but now they were building into a decidedly threatening mass. And there were no other buildings in sight. She was right out in the countryside now.

But she could, at last, see the woodland that the inn-

keeper had told her belonged to Sir Thomas Gregory.
A stone wall delineated the boundary of his property,
but if it really came on to rain hard, she would have no
trouble nipping over it and seeking shelter under the
trees.

She could only hope that the gamekeeper was the
type who stayed at home on wet afternoons.

She shrugged down into her travelling cloak, flicking up the large shawl collar over her bonnet, forming
it into a hood, as it began to rain. The shopkeeper had
promised her that the cloak, though lightweight, would
keep out the wet.

And had she been walking back to her lodgings from
the shops, through city streets, it might well have done
so. But the kind of rain that gusted across open fields,
building up speed and force by the acre, could not be
halted by one layer of merino wool, no matter how
finely woven.

She eyed the wall uncertainly. And the trees on the
other side. They did not look, now she was up close,
as though they would offer that much shelter after all.
Every time a gust of wind shook the branches, great
cataracts of water flowed from the leaves, as though
a million tiny housemaids were emptying buckets out
of invisible upstairs windows. And the wall that from
a distance, when it had been dry, had looked so easy
to climb, looked positively treacherous up close, now
it was slick with rain.

She had no wish to turn up on the first day of her new
job looking like a drowned rat. But it would be far worse
to look like a drowned rat in torn and muddy clothes.
The only thing that could have been worse was to have
stayed huddled on her trunk, in the inn yard, looking

like the kind of helpless female that required the services of a nursemaid to so much as wipe her nose!

She stayed on the road. It was not as if she could get much wetter, anyway. The unmannerly Yorkshire rain sneered at cloaks fashioned for city dwellers, using its playmate, the wind, to flick it aside so that it could soak her dress directly. And because she was having to clutch her makeshift hood to her throat, to keep it in place, it also managed to trickle down her cuffs. Not to mention the way it alternately splashed up under her skirts, and dragged her hem down into the mud. And although her sturdy brown boots were watertight, it did her feet no good, because her stockings were soaked, which meant that the water oozing down her legs had no means of escape. She should have purchased a coat, she sighed, that buttoned fast all the way down the front. Had she had more experience of weather in the north of England, she would have known that labelling the season between June and September 'summer' was no guarantee that light clothing would suffice.

And to cap it all, she could hear a distant rumble that sounded as though a thunderstorm was approaching. She shivered. The way her luck was going today, that probably meant hailstones.

But then she spotted the fork in the road that the innkeeper had mentioned about halfway through his convoluted directions. Hopefully, that meant she was geographically halfway to her destination.

She changed her bag to her left hand, clutched her hood to her throat with her right and strode out a little faster.

The sound of thunder grew steadily louder; in fact, so steadily it began to sound more like carriage wheels.

She glanced over her shoulder, and, sure enough,

cresting the brow of the undulating lane behind her came a carriage and pair at a spanking pace. Such a spanking pace that she had to leap nimbly over the ditch that flanked one side of the road to escape being run down.

She managed to stay upright, even though the stubby crops made for a most uneven surface. Though naturally, given the way her day was going, she landed ankle deep in mud. She looked up from the quagmire in which she stood in some surprise when the driver hauled on the reins, drawing the carriage to a halt abreast of her, and shouted, 'Miss Peters?'

When she nodded, he pointed his whip at her and bellowed, 'Do you have any idea how long I've been driving up and down these lanes attempting to find you?'

His words sent a shiver of dread coursing through her. Surely he could not be a Bow Street Runner? Not after she had taken such pains to cover her tracks. Nobody could possibly know she was in Yorkshire.

Though how could he know her name, if he was not a paid investigator of some kind? She eyed him with trepidation, rapidly taking in the many-caped coat and tricorne hat of a typical coachman. His appearance was no consolation. A really good thief taker would naturally be a master of disguise. If he was masquerading as a coachman, then he would take care to handle the ribbons nonchalantly, as well as dressing the part so convincingly!

With the tip of his whip, he pushed back the hat that had been pulled low down over his forehead, sending a shower of water cascading over his broad shoulders, and revealing the fact that he wore an eyepatch. It gave his harsh, weatherbeaten features such a sinister touch that she promptly abandoned all thought of either begging him for mercy, or offering him double whatever he had been paid to capture her to let her go.

Then he tugged down the muffler that had covered the lower half of his face, and said, 'What the devil do you think you are doing out in this weather?'

She had been cautiously feeling her way backwards with her feet, but the incongruity of the question halted her. Why on earth would a man paid to hunt down fugitives care what kind of weather she was out in? Unless it was on his own account. That must be it. He resented having to be up on that exposed box, in such foul weather.

Well, it served him right! As she surreptitiously tried to ease one foot out of the mud that held it fast, she glared right back at him, the villain! What kind of man took on such work?

He watched her freeze, then frown up at him in bewilderment. And felt as though somebody had reached into his chest and squeezed hard. It was as though somebody had cast a spell on the figurehead from *The Speedwell*, bringing her to life and casting her ashore in that muddy beet field. Dripping wet, confused and somewhat afraid, she still had sufficient spirit to lift her chin and square her shoulders, as though daring him to do his worst.

'Mr Jago!' he bellowed. Behind him, he heard the coach window come rattling down. Miss Peters tore her eyes from her appalled perusal of his wreck of a face. He saw the moment she recognised Mr Jago, then closed her eyes, her whole body sagging with what looked like profound relief.

Just who the hell had she thought he was? And what was she doing out here anyway?

He half-turned, and roared over his shoulder, 'Did your letter not specify that we were coming to fetch Miss Peters from the King's Arms?'

Aimée wanted to kick herself. Of course this vehicle and its driver were the transportation arranged for her by her new employers. It was just because her nerves were in tatters that she had immediately jumped to the conclusion that Bow Street Runners or thief takers must have caught up with her.

Thank heaven she had honest work now! She was not cut out for a life of crime. Her guilty conscience had left her fearing arrest every minute these last couple of weeks.

Perversely, the stupidity of her mistake made her absolutely furious with the coachman for giving her such a fright.

'Don't you yell at him!' she yelled at the piratical-looking driver. 'The letter offering me this job did say someone was coming to fetch me, but I had been waiting for an age in that filthy inn yard, and assumed that my arrival must have been forgotten. So I decided to walk.'

'In this weather?'

'It was not raining when I set out,' she replied tartly. 'Besides, I am not made of spun sugar, you know. I will not melt.'

Mr Jago opened the carriage door fully and clambered down. 'Well, never mind who thought what,' he said, crossing the road. 'The thing is to get you out of this rain now.' He extended his hand to her across the ditch.

A fleeting look of chagrin flickered across Miss Peters's face as she regarded Mr Jago's outstretched hand. Then her mouth compressed into a thin, hard line. She looked as though she wished she could consign the pair of them to perdition. But in the end, he saw a streak of practicality overcome her pride. He nodded to himself in approval as she reluctantly took hold of Mr Jago's outstretched hand. The former bosun had come back from London telling the rest of the crew that he'd found a woman who boasted she had a backbone of steel. Which was just as well, considering what lay in store for her. But even better, her swift suppression of that little flash of temper showed him that she was sensible enough to know when to bow to the inevitable.

He could not help grinning when she consoled herself by pausing to bestow one last, fulminating glare at him before accepting Mr Jago's assistance into the carriage.

Coxcomb! Aimée fumed, gathering the folds of her sopping wet cloak around her as she settled herself into the seat. It was his fault she was covered in mud now. And the shaft of pure terror that had lanced through her when she had thought he had come to arrest her and haul her back to London had left her shaking like a leaf.

'Captain Corcoran intended to pick you up in the gig,' said Mr. Jago, his face creasing with concern as she knotted her fingers together on her lap in a vain attempt to conceal how badly they were shaking. 'But seeing the weather likely to blow up a storm, he went to his neighbour, Sir Thomas, to see if it would be possible to borrow his carriage, so you would not get wet.'

His eyes slid to the little pool of water that was forming around her boots, and added, with a faint tinge of reproof, 'It all took a bit longer than we anticipated. But you really should have waited.'

Aimée's chin went up. She absolutely hated being

criticised for showing some initiative. Looking Mr Jago
straight in the face, she considered telling him exactly
why she had set out on her own across unknown ter-
rain. How could she possibly have known what this
Captain…whatever his name was, had arranged? It was
not as if anyone had bothered to inform her. Why, the
Captain had not even deigned to put his name to the
letter his man of business had left for her at the Bull
and Mouth.

And was she supposed, then, to just meekly accept
any arrangements he might or might not have made on
her behalf? As though she had no brain in her head?

However, she reined in her impulse to inform him
exactly what she thought of him and his employer. It
would not be a good start to her new life, to spend the
journey to The Lady's Bower arguing with a man who
seemed to be very much in her employer's confidence.

The fact that the carriage, with her in it, was even
now rattling into the very yard of the King's Arms she
had hoped never to see again almost overset her good
intentions. All the time and energy she had wasted,
getting thoroughly soaked into the bargain, and here
they were, back in the King's Arms, presumably in
order to collect her trunk.

She seethed. If anybody had thought to inform her
of their intentions, she need never have set out in the
rain at all!

And Mr Jago was still looking at her with that faint
air of reproof as though he expected her to be grateful
to his employer!

For one moment, just one, she admitted to herself
that perhaps she ought to feel grateful. She could not
remember anyone going to such trouble to see to her
well-being, at least not since her mother had died.

But on the very day of that wretchedly pathetic little funeral, she had discovered that it was no use sitting about waiting for somebody else to look after her. Her father had taken to the bottle; if she had not swiftly learned to shift for herself, she would have starved.

And half a lifetime of facing neglect, of having to be self-reliant, was not going to dissipate under the meagre weight of Mr Jago's disapproving frown!

The coach lurched to a halt, rocking as the driver jumped down from his box. She tore her eyes from Mr Jago's disapproving ones to follow the driver's progress across the yard to the inn door.

He had one of those voices that carried. Even from this distance, she could hear him berating the landlord for not stopping lone females from going wandering about the countryside in foul weather—in such highly colourful terms that she wondered whether she ought to be covering her ears. She was quite sure she ought not to know what half those terms meant. And Mr Jago, to judge from the way he shifted in his seat and cleared his throat loudly, was alive to her embarrassment, but at a complete loss to know what to do about it.

He ought, of course, to have got out and told the man to mind his manners.

Although perhaps not. She was merely a governess now, and not worthy of much consideration. She had to content herself with displaying her disapproval by glaring out of the window at the driver as he instructed the ostlers to stow her trunk in the boot at the back of the carriage.

She hoped she would not have to have too many dealings with this bad-tempered man. She thought it unlikely. A governess would not have much to do with the outdoor staff.

Thank goodness.

Having strapped the trunk in place with a violence that had the whole carriage jerking, and which to her mind seemed completely unnecessary, the driver whipped up the horses and the carriage lurched out of the yard at a cracking pace. She grabbed for the strap as they rattled down the lanes she had so recently trudged along, with a speed that had both passengers bouncing around the interior.

Wonderful. She was going to arrive at her first proper job in a state of bruised, chilled exhaustion! She had so wanted to impress her employers with an image of neatness and competence. Instead, she had the feeling that if this nightmare ride continued for much longer she was going to tumble out of the carriage looking like something the cat had dragged in.

What was more, if she had been a delicate sort of female, she had the notion she would promptly go down with a severe chill and take to her bed. The Captain might well have taken some pains to procure a closed carriage for her, to prevent her from getting the wetting that her independence of mind had ensured she got anyway, but he had not thought to equip it with a hot brick. No, there was not so much as a blanket to keep off the chill that was seeping through to her bones.

She had been far less uncomfortable outside! At least the activity of walking had kept her warm, whereas now, sitting still in her wet clothes in the unheated confines of the carriage, she was starting to shiver.

Yes, if she were not as tough as old boots, the incompetent Captain would be summoning a doctor for his new governess, within hours of her arrival.

Perversely, cataloguing the fallibility of her new employer went a great way to consoling her for her uncomfortable physical state. Like all men, he had decided he knew what was best, without either consulting, or informing, her what he was about. And his plans, like the plans of every man she had ever met, had been woefully inept. As well as being deleterious to the health of the female they intended to dominate.

She gripped the strap a little harder, bracing her feet against the opposite seat as they flew over the potholed, rutted road.

Oh, how she hoped some of his children were girls. She would thoroughly enjoy teaching them to think for themselves. To warn them that though men thought they were the superior sex, they were not to be trusted, never mind depended on!

She had cheered herself up no end with a series of similarly subversive plans by the time the carriage finally slowed down, to make a sharp turn between two gateposts topped with stone acorns. And the smooth glide along the short, but impressively maintained, driveway came as a welcome respite to her bruised posterior.

Mr Jago opened the door, got out and extended his arm to help her alight.

Aimée found herself standing on a neatly raked gravel turning circle in front of a three-storeyed, slate-roofed house.

The front door opened, and three men in a livery that consisted of dark blue short jackets, and baggy white trousers, which made them all look vaguely nautical, came tumbling out. One of them, a bow-legged, skinny man with eyes that each seemed to work totally independently of the other, came scampering up with an umbrella, which he unfurled with a flourish, and held over her head.

Far too late, of course, to do her any good, but it was a lovely gesture. She smiled her thanks and the man grinned back, revealing a set of teeth that appeared to have been stuck into his jaws at random.

'I am taking the carriage straight back to Sir Thomas,' the driver bellowed, shattering the feeling of welcome that had briefly engulfed her.

'Get Miss Peters's trunk and see her settled!' he barked at nobody in particular. Yet one of the men ran directly to the boot of the carriage, unstrapped her trunk, hefted it on to his shoulder and trotted with it to the house. Her eyes widened in amazement. It had taken two sweating ostlers to manhandle it into the rear boot of the stage when she had left London, yet he was treating it as though its weight was negligible.

Mr Jago waved his arm in the direction of the front door. 'Welcome to your new home,' he said.

With the bow-legged man holding the umbrella over her, the support of Mr Jago's arm, and the way the other two men stood each to one side like a guard of honour as she trod up the three shallow steps to the front door, Aimée almost felt like a queen being escorted into her palace.

She shook her head at the absurd notion. It was only the latest in a string of strange fancies that had popped into her head today. The certainty that she had been forgotten, when in fact her new employer was going out of his way to help her, the conviction that the piratical-looking coachman he'd sent was a Bow Street Runner, and now, the odd feeling that had not Mr Jago frowned at them so repressively, the oddly liveried staff here would have burst into applause as she alighted from the coach.

She raised her hand to her brow. Perhaps she was

sickening for something after all. Her nerves had been strained almost to breaking point over the last few weeks. And her journey from London had seemed never-ending, because of the persistent feeling that at any minute, somebody was going to point at her, and cry 'There she is!' and drag her ignominiously back again.

And yet, here she was, her muddy boots staining the strip of carpeting that ran down the centre of the highly polished wooden floor of The Lady's Bower. And the front door was closing behind her.

Shutting her off from her past.

Oh, they would keep on looking for her for a while, she had no doubt of that. But nobody, surely, would ever guess she had managed to get herself employment as a governess. Or if they did, by some peculiar quirk of fate, pick up her trail, she was surely not worth following this far north. Not all the way into the wilds of Yorkshire!

She had done it.

She had escaped.

And suddenly, the realisation that, against all the odds, she had reached her chosen hiding place came over her in such a great rush that she began to shake all over. The room shimmered around her, the heat, which had seemed so welcome only seconds before, now stifling her.

Tugging at the ribbons of her bonnet, she tottered to the staircase, sat down heavily on the bottom tread and bowed her head down over her damp knees.

She was not going to faint! There was absolutely no need to.

Not now she was safe.

Chapter Two

Somebody, no, two somebodies took her by one elbow each, and hustled her across the hall and into a small parlour. They removed her wet cloak, her undone bonnet sliding from the back of her head in the process. And then they lowered her gently on to an armchair in front of a crackling fire. Again, she leaned forwards, burying her face in her hands to counteract the horrible feeling that she was about to faint.

'Get some hot tea in here!' she heard Mr Jago bark, swiftly followed by the sound of feet running to do his bidding. 'And some cake!' She heard another set of feet pounding from the room.

Eventually, the lurching, swimmy sensations settled sufficiently for Aimée to feel able to raise her head. Mr. Jago and the wall-eyed man who had held the umbrella over her were watching her with some anxiety.

'I will be fine now,' she murmured, attempting a smile through lips that still felt strangely numb.

'Yes, you heard her,' Mr Jago said, starting as though coming to himself. 'And the sight of your ugly mug is not going to help her get better. Be about your business!'

'Looks like a puff of wind would blow her away,' she heard the man mutter as he left the room.

'Aye, far too scrawny…' she heard another man, who had apparently been lurking just outside the door, agreeing.

And then there was just Mr Jago, assessing her slender frame with those keen blue eyes.

As if she was not nervous enough, that comment, coupled with Mr Jago's assessing look, sent a new fear clutching at her belly.

'I am far stronger than I look,' she declared. 'Truly, you need have no fear that I am not fit for work!'

Indeed, she did not know what had come over her. She could only assume that the strain she had been under recently had taken a deeper toll on her health than she had realised.

She knew she had lost quite a bit of weight. To begin with, she had felt too sickened by what her father had done to feel like eating anything. And then flitting from one cheap lodging house to another, whilst racking her brains for a permanent solution to her dire predicament, had done nothing to counteract her total loss of appetite.

And the people she'd been obliged to approach, in the end—people nobody in their right mind would trust! She had not been sure they had not double-crossed her until she'd boarded the stage, and it was actually leaving London.

'I am just tired,' she pleaded with Mr Jago. 'It was such a long journey…' And it had begun not the day before, in the coaching yard of the Bull and Mouth, but on the night she'd had to flee from the lodgings she shared with her father. When she had to finally accept she needed to thrust aside any last remnants of obligation she felt towards the man who had sired her.

For he clearly felt none towards her!

To her relief, Mr Jago's expression softened.

'You must rest, then, until you have recovered,' he said. 'Do not worry about your position. It is yours. Quite secure.'

The door opened, and the burly man who had taken her trunk upstairs came in with a large tray, which he slapped down on a little side table at Aimée's elbow, making the cups rattle in their saucers. Mr Jago shot him a dark look, which the man ignored with an insouciance that immediately raised him in her estimation.

Once she had drunk two cups of hot sweet tea and consumed a large slice of rich fruitcake, Mr Jago led her up the stairs to a charming little bedroom on the first floor. On the hearthrug, before yet another blazing fire, stood a bath, already filled with steaming, rose-scented water.

'You will feel much better for getting out of those wet clothes and having a warm bath,' said Mr Jago, and then, going a little pink in the cheeks, added, 'I hope you will be able to manage unassisted.'

'Naturally,' she replied, determined to erase the impression of a helpless, weak and foolish woman she was worried might be forming in his mind, after the way she had behaved today. 'A governess has no need for a maid.'

He cleared his throat, going a tinge deeper pink, then said briskly, 'Have a lie down, after your bath. There is nothing for you to do until this evening, when the Captain requests the pleasure of your company at dinner.'

Mr Jago had phrased it like an invitation, but, of course, it was an order. Her new employer would want to look her over. And find out what kind of creature his man of business had hired to take care of his children.

'Thank you. I shall be ready,' she assured him.

She wasted no time, after he had left, in slithering out of her wet clothes and slipping into the warm bath with a sigh of contentment. She could not recall the last time somebody else had drawn a bath for her! Several large, soft towels had been draped over an airer before the fire to warm. Having dried herself, she wrapped one round herself, toga style, and set about getting herself organised. The first thing she did was to drape her chemise, petticoat and stays over the frame that had been used to warm the towels. Then she went to her trunk, which somebody—the burly man, she assumed—had placed at the foot of the divan bed, which was up against the far wall. She unpacked the silver-backed hairbrush first, an item she had purchased for the express purpose of placing in a prominent position on her dressing table. She did not know much about being in service, but she did know that a governess had to establish that she was no ordinary servant from the outset, by employing such little ruses as this.

Then she took out the gown she had bought in case she ever had to dine with the family. It looked almost new. And not too badly creased, either. She had pressed it again before packing it. She had got a laundress to carefully run a hot iron over the seams the very day she had purchased it, as she was in the habit of doing with every item of second-hand clothing she ever bought, to make sure that no lice the previous owner might have carried could survive to plague her. It was not a very flattering style, and the dove-grey silk did not suit her colouring, but apart from the fact that it was the only thing she had been able to find that struck the right balance between decorum and style, it added to the impression she wished to give, of being in mourning.

She grimaced as she hung it from two pegs on the back of the door. The day she had bought it was the day she had decided her father was dead to her. She had fulfilled her filial duty by making sure he was free of debt before she left town. And paid for one more month's rent on his lodgings. But that was it. She would have nothing more to do with him.

Her stays and petticoat were still slightly damp when she put them back on later, upon rising from her nap, but she could not leave them lying about her room! The coins she had sewn into the hem of her petticoat bumped reassuringly against her calves, reminding her that the safest place for the amount of money she was carrying was on her person. And that it was where it must remain, no matter what.

Having dressed, and brushed, braided and pinned up her hair in the style she had decided made her look the most severely governess-like, Aimée lifted her chin, straightened her back and left her room.

The burly servant was lounging against the wall opposite, his brawny arms folded across his massive chest.

'Evenin', miss.' He grinned at her, straightening up. 'They call me Nelson.' He shrugged in a way that suggested it was not his real name at all, but that he was not averse to the nickname.

'I'm to take you down to the front parlour, where the Captain is waiting,' he explained.

'Are you the footman?' she asked as he led the way

along the corridor to the head of the stairs. She knew that as governess, her position would be outside the hierarchy that governed the rest of the staff, which she did not mind in the least. No, so far as she was concerned, if the only people she spoke to, from one end of the day to the next, were her charges, the safer she would feel. Nevertheless, it would be useful to ascertain the status of every person working in this household, so that she did not inadvertently tread on anyone's toes. Mr Jago was easy enough to place. He was in a position of some authority. But Nelson was something of a puzzle. He had hefted luggage about like a menial, but then served tea with an air of doing Mr Jago a personal favour, and had come to fetch her as though he had a fairly responsible position himself.

He turned and looked at her over his shoulder, his leathery, brown face creasing even further as he frowned.

'In a manner of speaking, just now, aye, I suppose I am,' he said. 'Down to minimum complement of four side-boys, just now, on account of—' He stopped short, his eyes skittering away from hers. 'And, well, we all do whatever's necessary,' he finished, crossing the hallway and flinging open the door to the parlour.

She could not help noticing his rolling gait, which, coupled with his nautical outfit, and the incomprehensible jargon he used, confirmed her belief that this man was an ex-sailor. In fact, now she came to think of it, all the men who had gathered at the front door, upon her arrival, looked more like the crew of a ship, loitering on the dockside, than formally trained household servants.

And when he announced, 'Miss Peters, Cap'n!' before bowing her into the room as though she were a duchess, she wondered if Mr Jago had hoped all her years of travel had rendered her broad minded enough to deal with what was looking increasingly like a very eccentrically run household. Because, from what Nelson had just said, it sounded as though the Captain expected all his staff to adapt themselves to the circumstances, rather than rigidly stick to a narrow sphere of duty.

Well, that did not bother her. She could cook and sew, manage household accounts and even clean out the nursery grates and light the fires if necessary. As long as her wages came in regularly, and nobody asked too many questions about her past, she would not mind taking on duties that were, strictly speaking, not generally expected of a governess.

A tall man dressed in naval uniform was standing with his back to the room, gazing out of the rain-lashed windows. His coat was of the same dark blue as that of his staff, though cut to fit his broad shoulders and tapering down to his narrow waist. Gold epaulettes proclaimed his rank. And instead of the baggy trousers of his men, he wore knee breeches and silk stockings.

He swung round suddenly, making her gasp in surprise. For one thing, though she could not say precisely why it should be, she had always imagined her employer would be quite old. Yet this man did not look as though he was much past the age of thirty.

But what really shocked her was the scarring that ran from one empty eye socket to his right temple, where a substantial section of his hair was completely white.

What a coincidence! His coachman, too, had worn an eyepatch over his right eye.

No, wait… Her stomach sinking, she studied his face more closely.

Earlier on, she had only glimpsed the coachman's features fully for a few seconds, when he had pulled his muffler down, the better to berate her. And the hat had concealed that thick mane of dark blond hair.

But there was no doubt this was the same man!

Her stomach sinking as she recalled the way she had shouted right back at him, she sank into a curtsy, hanging her head.

He must have had a perfectly good reason for driving the coach himself. Nelson had said the household was short of staff at present. Perhaps that accounted for it. Perhaps that accounted for him coming to fetch her so late, too. Nelson's ambiguous comments indicated the place was in turmoil, for some reason he did not care to divulge to her, the newcomer.

But did that excuse Captain Corcoran from not introducing himself properly? Or shouting at her, and scaring her half to death?

Oh, if he were not her employer she would…

But he *was* her employer. And he had every right to shout at her if she angered him. And since she needed this job so badly, she would just have to bite back the remarks she would so dearly love to make.

She clenched her fists and kept her eyes fixed on the floor just in front of the Captain's highly polished shoes, knowing that it was a bit too soon to look him in the face. Not until she had fully quenched her ire at being so completely wrong-footed could she risk that!

She had never imagined how hard this aspect of getting a job as a governess would be. She supposed it came from not having to submit to anyone's authority for so many years. Not since her mother had died. Though she had never had any trouble doing exactly as *she* had told her.

At least she would not have to resort to asking a few of the questions she was sure this man would think impertinent, to work some things out. For one thing, she could see perfectly why Mr Jago had said he wanted to hire a woman with backbone. This Captain Corcoran clearly had a hasty temper, as well as a completely unique way of organising his household. She had been on the receiving end of it herself already, as well as witnessing his treatment of the slovenly landlord in Beckforth. A more sensitive female would wilt under the lash of that vicious tongue, let alone the force of the blistering glare she could feel him bending upon her now!

As she continued to stand, with her head down, the Captain emitted a noise that was just what she guessed a bear, prematurely roused from its hibernation, would make before devouring the hapless creature that had woken it.

It surprised her into looking up. She caught him fumbling a patch into position over the empty eye socket, his lips drawn into a flat line as though he was experiencing some degree of discomfort.

He might have known the sight of it would turn her stomach, he thought as her eyes skittered away from the ruined right side of his face. Mr Jago had said she did not seem to be the squeamish sort, but you never could tell what was going on inside a woman's head, not unless you shocked them into revealing it.

'C-Captain Corcoran?' she stammered, wondering how on earth to get past this awkward moment.

'Miss Peters,' he said crisply, as though her mere presence in the room was causing him intense annoyance. Though she could not imagine why it should.

He was not the one who had made a complete fool of himself out there in the road!

'Shall we go in to dine?' he said, holding out his arm. 'Unless you are not hungry?' She would not be the first woman to find his features so repellent they robbed her of her appetite.

Just then her stomach rumbled so loudly that even the Captain must have heard it, for he looked down at it in surprise, at the exact moment her hands fluttered to her waist. Though she was appalled at such a loss of dignity, she swiftly decided that it had at least gone some way towards dissipating the tension that thrummed between them.

'There is no point,' she said with a rueful twist to her lips, 'trying to pretend that I am not completely famished!'

It was quite true. The nausea that had been roiling in her stomach ever since the night she had learned her father had attempted to auction off her virginity in some noisome gambling hell in a last-ditch attempt to escape his crushing debts had completely vanished the moment she had crossed the threshold of The Lady's Bower. She had enjoyed every mouthful of that cake, and now she felt as though she could eat a horse.

The ferocity of the Captain's frown abated by several degrees.

'Then let us go in,' he said.

She laid her hand upon his arm, and he led her through a door into a generously proportioned dining room. The floor-to-ceiling windows looked out over a terrace, and thence to grounds that were obscured by the driving rain.

There was an oval table in the centre of the highly polished floor, beautifully set out, with a centrepiece of artistically arranged roses that filled the air with their perfume.

It was only as a servant came to pull out one of the chairs for her that it struck her how odd it was that it was only set for two.

Where was the Captain's wife?

She darted him one curious glance as he took his own place and signalled for service to begin.

She toyed with her napkin in her lap, as she bit back the thousand-and-one questions she wanted to ask. It was so frustrating, having to constantly remember her place! He would only tell her whatever he thought she needed to know, in his own good time.

He sat stiffly, eating his soup in brooding silence. But it was so delicious that before long she no longer cared that her new employer was turning out to be a bit of an autocrat. A man would not have risen to the rank of Captain, she decided, at such a relatively young age, without having a forceful personality. Nobody would put a man in charge of a fighting ship if he were not extremely capable.

The navy was not run in the same way as the army, where a man could rise through the ranks merely by buying commissions. In the navy, a man had to earn his promotion. Even pass exams in seamanship, she seemed to recall having heard somewhere.

And he definitely looked intelligent. It sparked from that one, steely grey eye. There had been an uncomfortable moment, just before dinner, when she had felt as though he was looking into her very soul. But then, fortunately, her stomach had rumbled. And although that hard mouth had not curved into a smile, she had seen a flash of humour lighten his expression somewhat. And if he was capable of seeing the funny side of things, perhaps he would not turn out to be a complete tyrant.

It was a shame, she mused, about his scars. Because without them, he would be quite handsome. Though even before he had lost that eye, she did not think he would have had the sensuous kind of good looks that had some women practically swooning with desire. No, he would have had...still had, in fact, the rugged features of a man with plenty of character.

She laid her spoon aside, astonished to find she had devoured her soup in complete silence, whilst musing over the Captain's looks and character.

'So, you spoke no less than the truth,' the Captain remarked as the servant whisked her empty bowl away. 'I do not think I have ever observed any female eat with such gusto.'

Though he looked faintly amused, again, she felt rebuked by his remark. Her mother had taught her better than this! She ought to have sipped at her soup daintily, not revealed she was utterly famished.

She folded her hands in her lap, pulling herself upright as more servants bustled about with dishes containing the next course.

She had not forgotten her table manners entirely, thank goodness. She had not slurped her soup, or grabbed a couple of the rolls and stuffed them into her pocket for later. But she felt as though she might just as well have done.

A lady, her mother had always insisted, should never betray the fact that she was starving. Not even when her clothes hung in rags from her skinny shoulders, and they were obliged to subsist on handouts from friends.

'Adverse circumstances,' her mother had been fond of saying, 'are only a test of character. Never forget you are a Vickery,' she would say, while her father had rolled his eyes in exasperation at the way she continually reminded Aimée of that side of her heritage. 'A Vickery will always rise to the occasion.'

Oh, Mama, she thought, a guilty flush heating her cheeks. *How I have let things slide, of late! Today, especially. Losing my temper with that innkeeper, and shouting at my employer in the road! Even though he was disguised as a coachman, I had no business letting my emotions get the better of me. I will do better*, she vowed. *I will rise to the occasion.*

'You are blushing,' the Captain startled her by observing. 'Directness of my speech too much for you?'

She turned her head to look directly at him. The pugnacious set of his jaw made her wonder if he was deliberately trying to unsettle her. Perhaps he was. Had she not expected her new employer to want to test her mettle for himself? When a woman was to be put in charge of a man's children, he would want to be quite sure of her character.

If she really wanted to retain this post, it was past time to swallow her pride and account for her earlier, inappropriate behaviour.

She cleared her throat.

'I have no objection to speaking directly. So, while we are being direct with one another, I would like to take the opportunity to clear the air between us. There is still some awkwardness, I believe, resulting from my earlier reaction to your appearance.'

If she had thought his face had looked harsh before, it was as nothing to the expression that darkened it now. Hastily, she explained, 'You see, the first time we met, I was under the impression you were merely a coachman. And I believe I may have been somewhat impolite...'

'May have been?' For a moment, he glared at her so intensely she thought she had seriously offended him. But then he flung back his head and barked with laughter.

'You gave as good as you got, and you damn well know it! Mr Jago promised me he had found me a woman of spirit, and you certainly have that, Miss Peters.'

He took a sip of wine, then added, 'But you are not too proud to apologise, when you know you are in the wrong, either.'

'Not quite,' she agreed with a rueful smile, reflecting how hard it had been to broach the topic of her folly.

'Ah, you'll do.' He leaned back in his chair. And smiled back.

It was amazing how drastically the change of expression altered his appearance. She had already thought he looked like a man used to command. But now there was such a compelling aura about him she could well believe men would follow him slavishly to their deaths.

'Yes, you'll do nicely!' he said again. 'You really are tough enough to take on the task I chose you for.'

'Ah, yes!' Finally, they were going to put aside any personal feelings and discuss her professional role within his household. She had been so nervous during her interview with Mr Jago. She had been too busy looking over her shoulder, at what she was escaping from, to ascertain *exactly* what he expected from her. She had not asked nearly enough questions. Why, she did not even know how many children she was to take charge of, nor their ages!

'When will I be meeting the children?' she asked. 'And your wife?'

The young man with eyes like a spaniel, who had

been carving the duck, dropped the knife on to the table with a muffled clunk.

'Give me that, Billy,' Captain Corcoran snapped, getting to his feet, retrieving the knife and setting about skilfully carving the bird himself.

Oh, dear. From the young man's nervous start, and the Captain's set jaw, she could tell she had somehow put her foot in it. After rapidly reviewing the events of the day to see if she could work out in what way, it occurred to her that she had seen no sign that any children lived in this house at all. Surely, if they did, the first thing that would have happened, upon her arrival, would have been a visit to the nursery. Though she had been unwell...

'My wife is dead,' he bit out, as he placed a slice of duck on to her plate.

'I am so sorry,' she gasped, her heart going out to his poor little motherless children. No wonder he had sent as far afield as London to find just the right woman to take charge of them! She would be the primary female influence upon their lives.

'You need not be,' he said, pausing in his dissection of the duck for a while, before continuing, in a lighter tone, 'Since I took up the lease on this house, not a single female had crossed its threshold. Until today. The locals think it a great joke, since it is called The Lady's Bower.'

From his abrupt change of topic, she deduced that he did not wish to discuss his deceased wife. She completely understood. Though his comment made her wonder if perhaps the landlord of the King's Arms had not been trying to fleece her after all. He might just have thought that The Lady's Bower was not the kind of place into which a lone female ought to stray.

She lifted the lid of the tureen that Billy had placed beside her plate and helped herself to a portion of peas.

'And your children? I take it, they are all boys?'

'I have no children.'

No children? No children!

She replaced the lid of the tureen carefully and reached for the dish of cauliflower. She was *not* going to fly into a panic. Just because he had no wife. Or children.

And because she was the only female in the household. The only female who had *ever* been in this household.

But her will, it seemed, had no control over her heart, which began to stutter uncomfortably in her chest.

'You need not worry about my men, Miss Peters,' said the Captain, who was clearly aware how nervous she felt, despite her attempts to conceal it.

'Not one of them will lay so much as a finger on you. They would not dare.' His face darkened.

'I would not have taken a single one of them in if they were not completely loyal to me.' He gestured with the carving knife to emphasise his next point. 'Every man jack of them has served under my command at some time or another, and knows I don't hesitate to flog a man who transgresses.'

When her eyes flew wide, he added, 'They also know I won't do so without good reason.' Abruptly, he tossed the knife aside, sat down and picked up his knife and fork. 'Not that I need to flog a single one of them to ensure their good behaviour.' He began to saw away at the meat on his plate. 'Any infringement of the rules here—' he impaled a piece of duck on his fork '—and they would be back on the streets where I found them. Each of 'em damn lucky I took him on. No, you need have no worry about being a lone female in a household of men. Besides, it won't be for long.' He raised the fork to his mouth and began to chew his meat.

'Oh?' She ladled a generous helping of béchamel sauce over the cauliflower on her plate, noting with a detached sense of pride that her hands were scarcely shaking at all.

Though all his talk of flogging was hardly comforting. And what had he meant, it would not be for long?

Unless...

'Are you intending, perhaps, to marry again?'

He looked up from his plate, a strange smile playing about his lips.

'You are very perceptive.'

Though it did not fully explain why he had hired a governess...unless his new bride already had children from a former marriage.

Yes, that must be it! She gave a sigh of relief, gripped her knife and fork tightly and forced herself to cut up her vegetables as though she saw nothing bizarre about the whole situation.

There must be a perfectly logical reason for the Captain to have had her brought here. She was being extremely foolish to assign nefarious motives to everything *every* man did. She had already jumped to far too many wrong conclusions today.

'We did not get off to a very good start,' he commented. 'But I was pleased to see the way you weathered that storm.'

'Thank you,' she said, accepting a slice of tongue from the plate the Captain nudged in her direction, along with the compliment.

'You find me somewhat rough around the edges, I dare say,' he observed.

'Not at all,' she murmured mechanically. It was not her place to comment on her employer's manners, or lack thereof. Besides, working for somebody who was 'rough around the edges', as he put it, would be a great improvement on habitually dealing with men who were rotten to the core.

'Hmmph,' he grunted, clearly unconvinced by her reply, then went on, in a conversational tone, 'I have spent most of my life at sea, in the company of men such as Billy and Jago. Not used to females at all.'

She could not help raising just one eyebrow as she lifted another forkful of food to her mouth. With the kind of rugged good looks he still possessed, in spite of the scarring round his empty eye socket, she was sure he must have had his flings. She knew what sailors were like when they got shore leave. Particularly the young officers, who got more liberty when a ship was in dock than did the ratings. Besides, he had been married!

'At least, not society females,' he amended, confirming her opinion that a man as brim full of vitality as him would have had plenty of experience with women.

'Not that I ever really understood my wife, either, and she was merely a chandler's daughter. She did not mind…did not *seem* to mind my ways. I thought she saw marrying a lieutenant as a step up the social ladder.' He frowned. 'I know better now. Once bitten, twice shy. Besides which, my needs now are nothing like the expectations I had when I was a callow youth. And I've a sight too much self-respect, at my age, to try to play the suitor to a succession of society beauties in Almack's or some such place. I have neither the time, nor the inclination, to go down that route.'

Though Aimée was somewhat baffled by the turn

the conversation was taking, she smiled politely, and took a sip of her wine.

'But Mr Jago said you would suit me down to the ground. You have lived much harder than most gently born ladies, have you not?'

Her eyes flickered back to him uncertainly. When she had been a little girl, her mother had shielded her from knowing about their constant financial hardships. Living within the orbit of Lady Aurora Vickery was like being on a grand adventure. She had even managed to make fleeing lodgings where the rent was overdue, at the dead of night, into a game. A game of hide-and-seek, she smiled sadly, that had been played out over an entire continent, from an ever-increasing army of creditors. It was only once she had died that reality had set in with a vengeance. Her father had always been a little too fond of drinking and gambling, but without her mother's restraining influence, he shed any veneer of decency. Then the man she had called father had progressively crumbled away, until even Aimée had been forced to admit there was nothing left of the man who had inspired her mother to elope with him.

So it was pointless to quibble about how *she* regarded her past. She just nodded her head, murmuring, 'Yes.'

'Then it is about time we came to terms,' he said.

'T-terms?'

He shifted position, as though his chair had suddenly become very uncomfortable. 'Yes, terms. I was not planning to lay my cards on the table quite this soon, but you have already guessed that I got you here under false pretences, have you not? I knew, of course, that a woman applying for a job as a governess would have a certain level of education, but you really do have a quick mind, Miss Peters. I admire that about you.'

He looked her over, in a way that made her very aware of her body.

'As well as being every bit as pretty as Mr Jago told me. I could not find,' he said, with evident satisfaction, 'a woman more suitable for my purposes if I were to trawl society ballrooms for a month.'

She bent her head over her plate, carrying on eating as though nothing troubled her. Thank heavens she had already reminded herself of what her mother would have expected of her, and buckled her manners in place like armour!

She had begun to suspect the Captain was up to something when she had discovered he had no wife or children here. Really, she ought to have been put on the alert by the fact he had been so coy about revealing his identity until *after* she was already committed to travelling up here. No wonder the interview had been so cursory. Captain Corcoran did not need a governess for his fictitious children!

No, now he was freely admitting that he had lured her to this isolated spot under false pretences. And had then gone on to tell her that he found her pretty. Put that together with the way he had said he admired her spirit, but was relieved to see she was not *too* proud... She felt the soup curdling in her stomach. Even though he had no desire to remarry, and he was discerning enough in his tastes now to want a well-born, intelligent woman to warm his bed whilst he was ashore, it was not the least bit flattering to hear that he was so delighted with her that he could not wait to offer her *carte blanche*.

'Miss Peters, I am, nowadays, such a wealthy man

that you can have as many fancy clothes and jewels as you wish,' he said, confirming her worst fears. 'And servants. Though I will not have you trying to lay off any of the men who have served under my command at sea,' he warned her sternly. 'Apart from that one proviso, you may have a free hand. Yes, a completely free hand.' He sat back and regarded her expectantly.

She laid her knife and fork down with precision, reaching for her wine glass and taking a ladylike sip. Thank heavens she had grown so adept at remaining outwardly calm. That she had so many years' practice in keeping up appearances, no matter how severe the strain she endured.

Even if, as now, real fear was gripping her.

'Well, what is your answer?' Captain Corcoran said impatiently after she had remained silent for several moments. 'Surely you must see the advantages of the position I am offering you? It is not as though you can have anything to go back to London for, or you would not have applied for work as a governess in the first place!'

No, nothing awaited her in London except certain degradation. For her father's career there had followed the same path as it had in every other city they had ever visited. An initial flourish to persuade the citizens he was wealthy, entrée into several of the less select gaming clubs, and then the rapid descent into horrendous debt. Only this time, her father had been so lost to any sense of decency, he had attempted to sell her to some…lecher.

Had sold her!

Lord Matthison had sent his servant to her lodgings with the money, and instructions that she was to deal with him directly in future. So much money, there was no mistaking his intent.

It had been the last straw. The final outrage that had made her sever all ties from her scandalous father for ever.

She had vowed then and there that she would *never* trust a man again.

How right she had been. She lifted her head and regarded Captain Corcoran coldly. She had escaped from London's sewers, only to fall into the clutches of another such as Lord Matthison.

In fact, worse. At least Lord Matthison had been completely open about his intentions. *This* man had as good as kidnapped her, then taken pains to inform her that all his staff were utterly loyal to him. And that he would have them flogged and dismissed should any of them take pity on her, and help her escape!

Her heart beating fast, she patted her lips with her napkin. She was not going to let him see how scared she was. That would be fatal. She had learned long ago, given the numerous precarious positions to which her father had so frequently exposed her, that nothing inflamed a potential predator more than the knowledge his victim was afraid.

'Your proposition has taken me by surprise,' she said, proud of the even tone of her voice. 'May I have some time to think about it?'

When he frowned, her heart beat so fast that she began to go light-headed. If he was the type of man who was not averse to using violence in his dealings with women, her appeal would go unheeded. He could swing her over his shoulder, heave her upstairs to one of his bedrooms, and...

She flinched from picturing the awful deed. She

had to fill her mind with something other than the fear that threatened to blot out all ability to reason. *Think, Aimée, think!* How on earth was she to get out of this?

She took a deep breath, reminded herself she had escaped from sticky situations before. Ever since her shape had first started to change from that of a girl to a woman, she'd had to evade the groping hands of the drunken lecherous men who made up her father's coterie.

Though the Captain was not drunk. Nor was he simply an opportunist, trying to make sport of a defenceless girl who had strayed into his path. No, he had coldly, calmly, planned this seduction!

But his mistake would be the same as all other men made: in underestimating her determination to thwart his vile schemes.

'Very well,' he grudgingly conceded. 'You may have until the morning. But no longer. I have no time to waste.'

Outwardly calm, she got to her feet. Captain Corcoran did so too. Aping the gentleman, she mentally sneered.

'Thank you, Captain,' she said graciously, inclining her head as though she fully intended to think about his disgusting proposition.

The moment she left the dining room, she saw her way to the front door barred by Nelson. Lounging against the far wall, his arms folded across his chest, he no longer looked like the amiable, salt-of-the-earth character with whom she had fleetingly felt a connection. His stance, and then the over-familiar grin he bestowed upon her, put her in mind of the kind of men employed to guard the doors at brothels.

And he *insisted* on escorting her upstairs.

But she refused to give him any indication that she resented him guarding her, and her ruse was so successful that, the moment she was inside the room with the door shut, she heard him go straight back downstairs.

Probably to report back to his master, she thought, opening the door a crack, and peeping out. But the Captain did not hold all the cards. She could still employ the element of surprise.

Since nobody else seemed to be about, she darted out of her room and leaned over the banister rail to check that the downstairs hall was clear. It was! *Now or never, Aimée*, she told herself, her heart pounding with terror of discovery. And she ran swiftly back down the stairs and straight to the front door.

She had no need to waste time collecting anything from her room. Long before leaving London, she had sewn most of the banknotes Lord Matthison had sent to her into her stays. And the hem of her petticoat was weighted down with guineas. She could buy anything she needed later. If only she could get well away from her captors!

To her intense relief, when she clawed at the handle, she found the front door was neither bolted, nor locked, and it swung open easily on well-oiled hinges.

The cold wet air that gusted into the hall made her gasp. But she did not regret the lack of a coat. Retaining just enough presence of mind to shut the door quietly behind her, to prevent her flight being detected for as long as possible, she slipped out into the rain and ran. And ran.

Only for a few seconds on the gravel drive, because it made too much noise. Then along the grass verge, though it was treacherously slippery. She made it to the twin stone pillars at the end of the drive. Then, with her tortured breath rasping in her throat, across the lane and into the woods, where a branch promptly slapped her in the face. As she recoiled with a yelp, it raked over the crown of her head, tearing the pins from her oh-so-carefully-arranged hairstyle. Her braids came tumbling over her face, but she kept on running. It was almost pitch black under these trees in any case. It was only after she had been crashing through the undergrowth, heedless of the branches snagging at her hair, and the brambles tearing at her skirts, that it occurred to her she had no idea where she was running to.

She had long been prepared to take flight at a moment's notice.

But she had thought her flight would be in London. From Lord Matthison.

Not out here in the howling wilderness, where there were no signposts to tell her which way to go. No convenient alleys to duck into. No rooms to rent with no questions asked if the price was right. Just trees, she panted, and brambles and rain and wind and mud.

She stopped. And bent over slightly from the waist to get her breath back. And her powers of reasoning.

The lane.

If she kept close to the lane, she could probably make her way back to the King's Arms. The innkeeper had tried to warn her to stay away from Captain Corcoran and his henchmen. And, after the way Captain Corcoran had berated him, the man would be only too pleased to do him an ill turn.

It was only a matter of finding her way out of the woods and back to the lane. And praying that her absence would not be noticed for some considerable time.

Chapter Three

But her luck was out.

The shadowy blackness surrounding her resolved itself into distinct shapes as light streamed into the woodland. From the opened front door of the house.

She heard somebody shout, 'This way, lads! I saw her dart in amongst the trees!'

And then several somebodies were crunching along the gravel path, straight towards her!

How could they have discovered her flight so quickly? Had Captain Corcoran posted a lookout? Or, worse, had he followed her straight up to her room? Oh, he might have *said* he would give her until morning, but what reliance could she, of all people, place on what a man said?

Thank heavens she had followed her instincts and just got out of the place as fast as she could!

She pressed her hands to the stitch in her side. She was still not out of the woods yet—not in any sense! She was already panting from her dash for the trees, and now that she knew the pursuit was hot her heart began pounding even faster than ever. Her eyes darted wildly from side to side, hating the trees that were stopping her from just picking up her heels and running.

But then a vision flashed into her mind of a deer, hotly pursued by a pack of slavering hounds, closely followed by the chilling awareness that dogs always ran their quarry to earth in the end. She could tell exactly how close the pack was getting already by the amount of noise they made crashing through the undergrowth.

If she ran, *they* would hear *her*, and outrun her, and then…

Think, Aimée, think! She had no chance of outrunning them. Not even if she was out in the open. But here in this dense woodland…well, she might run smack into a tree in this darkness. Or trip and fall flat on her face.

But then…if she could barely see her way, then nor could they. Still half-crouching, she stretched her hands out in front of her and began to inch her way forwards, as quietly as she could, searching for the nearest tree. It would make an effective shield in this darkness. Her questing hands soon grazed against rough bark, and not a moment too soon. Her pursuers were closing fast. She straightened up to flatten herself against the massive trunk.

And a slim branch struck her right in the face.

She recoiled, her heel caught in a tree root and she went flying, landing upon her back so hard that all the wind was knocked out of her. The smell of damp earth and crushed bracken was like a hand pressing down on her chest, smothering her.

She thrashed like a fish on a riverbank, desperately trying to gasp in air. At last, it went whooping back through her constricted throat, but with such force that she knew Captain Corcoran's pack must have heard it. She could hear them all veering from their random search patterns and converging in her direction.

And then it was no further use telling herself to keep calm. Wild panic had her leaping to her feet, but agonising pain, tearing from her ankle and up her leg, had her falling to the ground again with a shocked yelp.

And it was all over.

Shadowy figures encircled her, breaking ranks to allow Captain Corcoran himself to come striding through. He alone of the men had taken a few moments to provide himself with a lantern before setting out after her. He held it aloft now, the shadows it cast over his face making him look positively demonic.

'What on earth possessed you, you damn fool woman?' he yelled.

He looked so angry that Aimée could not help emitting a frightened little whimper as she clutched at her ankle.

'I told you I would wait for your answer until morning. Do I give you such a disgust that you must run out into the night?'

He thrust the lantern into the hands of one of the men lurking behind him, and bent over her.

She could not help cowering deeper into the bracken, the look on his face was so murderous.

'For God's sake,' he muttered, 'I may look like your worst nightmare, but wouldn't you rather *I* carried you back to the house than one of my men?'

She looked past him to the shifting shadows, imagining the hands of Nelson on her, or that one with the bow legs and splayed teeth, and shuddered. What choice did she have? She had hurt her ankle so badly, there was no escape now. With a faint moan, she nodded her assent.

'Brace yourself, then,' he sneered, crouching down

and sweeping her up into his arms. Rain dripped from the ends of his long, shaggy hair on to her face, making her blink.

'Just shut your eyes if you can't bear the sight of me!'

How could he mock her terror like this? Had he no pity? No, she whimpered, or he would not have lured her up here, hand-picked his accomplices…set the whole thing up so…meticulously!

He set his jaw as he settled her into the cradle of his arms before striding back through the woods to the lane. Oh, God, he was so strong! The shoulder under her cheek was like a rock, the arms that held her against him bulging with muscle. She did not stand a chance!

As he carried her back through the gateposts, it was all she could do to hold back the tears. How could she have been so stupid as to fall into his trap?

The fear that had been her constant companion since she'd had to flee from her father had clearly addled her wits, as well as robbing her of her appetite and prodding her awake, night after night, with sickening visions of what the future held in store. It had escalated to such proportions that she could think of nothing but escape. Clinging on to the slim hope that if only she could get out of London, and away from her father, she would be safe, she had entirely overlooked the fact that men could be as wicked in the wilds of Yorkshire as they were in the gambling hells and back alleys of town.

At least in London, she would have known places to hide!

But now Captain Corcoran was carrying her into the house, and up the stairs, shouldering the door to her room open with barely suppressed fury. And for the first time in her life, Aimée felt real despair. In spite of all her cunning, she had ended up falling prey to the very type of man she had gone to such lengths to evade.

It really was a case of out of the frying pan, into the fire, for he was bound to make her pay for trying to foil his plans.

He flung her on to the bed and reared back, swiping the rain from his face with the palm of his hand. The way he had dropped her jolted her ankle, sending a fresh wave of pain shooting up her leg. She could not help wincing and gingerly trying to move it into a less painful position, though she did not dare take her eyes off his face as she awaited his next move.

His mouth flattened into a grim line. He turned and strode to the door, leaned his head out, and roared, 'Billy! Fetch some wet cloths to strap up this woman's foot!'

Then he turned and strode back to the bed, swiftly pulling off her sodden indoor shoes. Oh, how she now regretted not pausing to change them for sturdier boots!

How she regretted so many of her choices.

She swallowed nervously, then lifted her chin. She might be completely in his power, but she was a Vickery. No man would break her spirit!

Her flash of defiance lasted just as long as it took him to reach up under her dress and untie one of her garters. She scuttled back up the bed so quickly her shoulders slammed into the headboard.

'Stop looking at me as though I am about to rape you, damn your eyes!' he snarled at her. 'Do you think I would get any satisfaction from forcing a woman to endure my unwelcome attentions?'

What? Breathing hard, she blinked up at him, pushing the straggling hanks of wet hair away from her face.

And really looked at him.

To her amazement, she realised he was not leering at her. There was not even the faintest trace of lust mingled with the scalding anger blazing from his one eye.

He was not, she suddenly perceived, another Lord Sandiford, the man who, according to her informant, had started the bidding for her virginity. *He* would not have cared whether she was willing or not. On the contrary, Mr Carpenter had warned her that he would have enjoyed making her suffer as much as he possibly could.

It felt like a reprieve. She was still in considerable danger, but having the threat of violence removed from the equation left her feeling weak with relief.

As she slumped down into the pillows the Captain's lips twisted into a sneer.

'Though how on earth you could think that a skinny little half-drowned rat like you would be capable of rousing any man's lust is beyond me.'

He looked so full of contempt that her whole perspective suddenly changed. She was little more than skin and bone these days. Skin and bone, clad in a sodden, torn, stained dress, wild-eyed with panic, and her hair all over the place. Though earlier he had said he found her pretty, that had obviously been a piece of idle flattery, intended to win her over. Now that she had angered him, the truth was out.

It set the seal on her humiliation when he said, 'God only knows what Jago was thinking to bring you here. I told him to pick a woman who could at least *look* as though she belonged in society.'

He bent down and yanked the wrinkled stocking over her rapidly swelling ankle, making her gasp with the pain.

She thought she caught a look of remorse flicker

across the Captain's face, but it was swiftly replaced by a glare so fierce, she decided she must have imagined it. Particularly when he swore colourfully, and said, 'It is your own fault! Now you won't even be able to leave in the morning, like as not, which you could have done had you told me to my face that you did not want to marry me!'

He turned away from her abruptly then, as Billy came in carrying a bowl of crushed ice, and a pile of what looked like somebody's neckcloths. And so he missed her soundlessly gasping, 'Marry you?' The shock of hearing him speak of marriage was so great her voice had dried up completely.

'Tell me what I need to do,' he was saying to Billy, while she pressed one hand to her forehead.

Aimée's mind was reeling. When had he ever said one single word to her about marriage?

Surely that proposition he had made to her, outlining his willingness to shower her with jewels and servants, had not been one of marriage? Why, it had sounded exactly like every single one of the many other dishonourable propositions she had received since her mother died.

Could she really have just fled, in total panic, from the only proposal of marriage she had ever had?

Or was ever likely to have.

There had been only one occasion before, when she had thought she stood a chance of marrying, and thereby crossing the boundary that existed between her precarious existence and that of a decent, respectable woman.

Young Mr Carpenter had professed himself wildly in love with her. He had written her odes, comparing her to 'Beauty enmeshed by poverty' in which her father figured as a bloated spider. He had declared he would be her champion, and took to following her father to some of the lowest haunts he frequented, in a vain attempt to put a brake on his downhill slide.

Instead, he had returned with the tale so vile she'd had nightmares about it ever since. Lord Sandiford and Lord Matthison had only just begun the bidding when Mr Carpenter left the Restoration Club and ran to warn her she must flee.

'Where will we go?' she had naïvely asked him, assuming that the time had come to stop holding him at arm's length and accept his protection, even though she did not love him.

'Oh, but, ahh…d-don't exactly have the blunt to set you up. Not right now,' he had blustered.

'Take me to your mother's house then. Just until we are married—'

'Married?' he had squeaked, actually taking a step back and going pale.

And she had seen that in spite of the number of times he had declared he would do *anything* for her, that *anything* did not encompass making the ultimate sacrifice of giving her his name.

'N-not that I don't adore you, sweet one, but…bring a man like your father into my family?'

The scales had fallen from her eyes. When Mr Carpenter married, it would be to a fresh-faced, innocent débutante with a handsome dowry and a cast-iron pedigree, not the daughter of a pair of vagabonds whose escapades had scandalised half of Europe.

He had fled from her lodgings, with the air of a man making a narrow escape, and she had finally seen that she would never have anyone to rely on but herself.

Nobody would ever come riding to her rescue on a white charger. She was on her own.

And so she had pocketed the down payment Lord Matthison had sent to ensure her compliance, God forgive her, and used it to go into hiding.

That was when she had seen Captain Corcoran's advertisement. It had seemed like the perfect solution. If she could persuade the man who interviewed her that she had what it took to be a governess, she could support herself, honestly, and in total anonymity. Or so she had thought.

Billy brought the bowl and towels to the nightstand beside the bed. She closed her eyes while he gave the Captain detailed instructions about how to form a compress, and the best way to strap it on, shutting him out while she rapidly reviewed the only lengthy conversation she'd had with Captain Corcoran.

Where, or when, had there ever been any hint that what the Captain was seeking was a wife? All he had said upon the topic of marriage was that his needs now were very different from the expectations he'd had as a callow youth. Naturally she had assumed he meant he saw no need to actually *marry* a woman he wanted to bed.

Her eyes flew open in shock as the Captain applied the first, icy cold layer of bandages to her ankle. But then, this seemed to be a night for shocks. First of all in hearing him admit he had no wife or children, followed by what she had thought was an indecent proposition. And now finding out that he had been speaking of marriage. To her.

She could still not quite believe it. She looked at him closely, not as a prospective employer, or a would-be ravisher, but for the first time as a suitor.

And her heart turned over. His hair was dripping wet, and so was his coat. Yet he was selflessly tending to her injury before making himself comfortable. She had already discovered how strong he was, yet now his fingers were gentle as he deftly wrapped layer after layer of ice-cold cloth round her swollen joint.

He was handsome, in spite of his scars, and strong and affluent.

And capable of reining in his anger. It was a rare thing, in her experience, to see a man exercise any self-control, let alone to such a degree. He had been furious with her. Completely furious. Yet even though he had shouted, and, yes, sworn at her, he had still managed to consider how she would have felt if he had delegated the task of carrying her back to the house to one of his men.

'You'd better give 'er some of this, too,' Billy was saying, pulling a small brown vial from his pocket.

'No...' she whispered, shaking her head as Billy unstoppered what was clearly a bottle of laudanum.

In a voice as cold as the iced water in which Billy had soaked the towels, Captain Corcoran said, 'She clearly suspects that you are offering it only so that I can tear her clothes off and ravish her the moment she loses consciousness.'

It was probably just as well she did not want to marry him. The woman affected him far more than he would like. It was not just that her beauty appealed to him, though God knows it did. Too much. Though he had railed at her, telling her she looked like a drowned rat, in truth she resembled nothing so much as a mermaid, with all that ripped grey silk streaming over her luscious little body. The image had started the moment he had seen her thrashing around in the undergrowth, as though she was unable to walk on land, with her hair flowing like so much deep-brown kelp down to her waist. And men, he reminded himself, got snared in such weed. It tangled round their legs and drowned them.

Just as he was drowning in the reproach in those sea-green eyes of hers. The sight of her tears coursing down her cheeks had made him want to drop to his knees, and kiss that tiny, perfectly formed foot, and beg her forgiveness, even though he was utterly determined he would never let another woman bring him to his knees. When he married again, *he* would be the one in control.

'No!' she said again, this time pulling herself together and sitting up straight. There had been quite enough misunderstanding between them already. One after the other, from the very moment she had read that confounded advertisement! Maybe she could do nothing about the others, but this one, at least, she could nip in the bud.

'The fact that I do not wish to take laudanum has nothing to do with you, sir. It is just that I prefer not to take it. It makes me feel so sick, and leaves me feeling so confused—'

'You do not need to worry about keeping your wits about you,' he bit out. 'I have never taken a woman against her will, and I am not about to start upon one who has injured herself whilst under my care.'

He straightened up to his not inconsiderable height, clasped his hands behind his back, and said, pacing over to the window, 'Moreover, you need not worry that I shall importune you with repeated requests that you consider my proposal, since you find the idea so repugnant.'

Billy, his head lowered, began to tidy up the scattered

towels, bowl and the stockings the Captain had tossed to the floor.

'In the morning,' he continued, 'Jago will make whatever arrangements are necessary for your transportation back to the slums he plucked you out of.'

'No, please,' said Aimée, aghast to think of being sent straight back to London.

'I find it hard,' he said, not even breaking his stride, 'to believe you would flee from the prospect of becoming a Countess, when you walked to my house in the pouring rain, thinking you were about to become a mere governess. Am I so repulsive to you?'

Countess? Mr Jago had told her that he was a naval officer. Not that a man could not hold a title, as well as a post in the navy, but…

He strode to the end of her bed, his large hands clenching on the footboard, and glared at her while Billy scuttled out of the door.

'Not that it makes any difference now,' he said in a tone of chilling finality.

'Oh, but…' she began, but he had turned away. His shoulders stiff with affront, he stalked from the room, shutting the door behind him with the exaggerated care of a man who would have got a great deal more satisfaction from slamming it hard.

Aimée sank back into her pillows.

'Oh, no,' she moaned, curling up into a ball and covering her face with her hands.

If only he had not used the very words Hincksey had employed when she had gone to him to request the services of one of his underlings, to forge her some convincing-looking character references!

'Are you sure you want to go through with this?' Hincksey had said, as he handed the documents to her.

'It's a miserable business, being a governess. You'd have a lot more fun sticking with me. And better conditions. You could have fancy clothes and jewels. Even set up your own house with servants, if you was clever about the way you worked your clients…'

'Oh,' she moaned, rolling on to her other side. No wonder she had jumped to the wrong conclusion, after the way her own father and that weasely Mr Carpenter had let her down.

Especially after his admission that he had lured her to Yorkshire under false pretences!

She rolled on to her back, thumping the counterpane at her sides. Yes, why had he gone to such lengths to get her to his house? Why had he placed an advertisement in a London newspaper that made it sound as though he wanted to employ a governess, when what he really wanted was a wife?

Men! They were all so untrustworthy. No wonder she had not recognised his meanderings about the glowing future he could provide as an honest proposal of marriage.

'Marriage,' she groaned, pressing the heels of her hand to her eyes. If she had not been so suspicious, so very frightened of the man, she might be an engaged woman by now. Not that marriage necessarily meant safety for a woman. Her mother's marriage had been a mistake of monumental proportions.

But Captain Corcoran was not a penniless charmer like her father had been in his youth. He was not attempting to get his hands on her fortune, for she hadn't one. Quite the reverse. He was offering to provide for her in a style she had hitherto only dreamed of.

'Jewels and servants,' she moaned.

Not that she was tempted by them, as such. If they were all she cared about, she could have become some man's mistress years ago! Or thrown in her lot with Hincksey.

It was just…what would it have been like to never have to worry about where the next meal was coming from? Or what means she might have to employ to procure it?

What would it have been like to have had a home of her own? Somewhere she could put down roots? To be able to make friends with neighbours, rather than keeping everyone at arm's length lest they see through the latest story her father had fabricated to explain their current mode of life?

Above all, to have become respectable.

No, more than that. The Captain had told her she might have been a Countess. She could have screamed with frustration. Her mother had always insisted she should set her sights on that kind of rank, should she ever consider matrimony.

She groaned again. She could not believe she had thrown away such a golden opportunity!

Not that the marriage would have been a great success. He thought she was too plain. Too thin and ragged to rouse his desire. She brushed a tear from her cheek.

What was she to do?

As ever, when faced with a dilemma, Aimée wondered how her mother would have reacted in similar circumstances.

Well, to start with, her mother would not have panicked, and run from the house without a bonnet and coat. She would have remained calm and dignified. Lifted her chin, and told Captain Corcoran to his face that he was a cad who ought to be ashamed of himself.

Instead of which, it was Aimée who felt ashamed of herself. She curled into a ball and wrapped her arms round her waist, burying her face in the sodden pillow. She might have had everything she had ever wished for. Instead of which, tomorrow, she would end up right back where she had started. No, she would be even worse off, because she would not even have the hope of being on her way to a decent job!

Oh, how she wished she had never met Captain Corcoran!

Chapter Four

Damn the woman!

Captain Corcoran slammed his bedroom door behind him with satisfying force. Give him cannon fire or a howling tempest any day in preference to crossing swords with a woman!

It was no use telling himself that he was still in charge of the situation. That she was in his domain, guarded by his devoted crew. That, beyond that, he was rich and she was poor. He had felt anything but victorious when he had felt her shivering in his arms as he carried her back to the house. It had been one of the lowest moments of his life, because she was injured and it was all his fault.

But, dammit, how could he have guessed she would do something as crazy as run away in the middle of the night, without so much as a coat to keep the rain off her?

He rubbed one hand wearily over his face, his fingers snagging on the eyepatch.

He tore it from his face, hurled it at the mirror and glared at his reflection.

Was it any wonder she'd fled, screaming, into the woods, rather than ally herself to that?

He turned from the sight that, truth be told, made his own stomach heave every time he looked at it, went to a side table where he kept a bottle of good brandy and poured himself a generous measure. Of late, he had begun to think the scarring was less revolting than it had been when he had first lost his eye and the suppuration and swelling had made him look truly monstrous.

But back then, he had never thought he would be contemplating matrimony again! Matrimony. He shuddered. Very soon after coming into the title, he had learned that one of his primary duties was to marry and produce an heir. And he was a firm believer in doing his duty. As a naval officer, he had often expected to die in the performance of his duty.

He emptied a second glass and slammed it down on the side table.

The kind of battle he was used to was child's play, in comparison to tangling with the woman upstairs.

Aimée was up and dressed by the time Nelson brought her breakfast tray to her room. There had been no point lying in bed any longer. Not when she had scarcely slept all night anyway.

She had dressed for travel as far as she was able, though she could not yet bear to lace her walking boots up over her swollen ankle. Instead, she had slipped her feet back into the shoes she had worn to dinner the night before. They were still a bit damp, even though she had got up at some point during her restless night, stuffed them with paper and propped them up against the fender. Her ruined dress was too wet to pack, so she had left that draped over the clothes airer. What would become of it, she could not begin to guess.

Nelson slapped the tray down on a table just inside the door.

'When you've eaten, the Captain wants a word with you,' he said curtly.

'He…he does?' Aimée's heart began to thud unevenly. She did not know what on earth he could want to speak to her about. Last night he had made it quite plain he never wanted to clap eyes on her again!

'Please, miss,' said the burly servant, 'just listen to what he has to say, will yer?' He took a step towards her, his face creasing anxiously. 'Don't go hurting him no more. You might not like the look of him much, but you won't find a decenter gent. Got a heart of gold, he has. I served the Crown for years, I did, after being pressed into the service. Fought during campaigns that made many of the officers on the ships I served in into national heroes. Then got cast adrift when we beat France to flinders. And what with stoppages and one thing and another, I washed up ashore homeless and penniless. Would've ended up at the end of a rope, if the Captain hadn't sprung me from jail and given me this job.'

Aimée was somewhat taken aback by the man's passionate plea on behalf of his captain. 'Well, of course I will listen to whatever it is he wishes to say to me. And as for hurting him—' she frowned, a little puzzled, for she could not see how that might be possible '—I have never deliberately hurt anyone in my life. But I shall offer him an apology for my behaviour.' She had misjudged him terribly. And from what he had said, made him think she had fled from him because she found him repulsive.

Nelson's face cleared. 'You could marry him, then, couldn't yer? Now you've had a chance to mull it over? He wouldn't never hurt a lady. Not a man what's done all he's done for me.'

'I know.' She had already worked that out for herself. The care he had taken of her, in spite of being so angry, had told her more about his character than he probably realised. So it was with great sadness that she shook her head, and said, 'But he does not intend to renew his offer.'

The man's face fell. Without another word, he turned and left the room.

Aimée did not waste a moment wondering what reason the Captain might have for wishing to speak to her before sending her away. All night, her thoughts had been running round and round like a dog chasing its tail. She had not reached any sensible conclusions about anything. All she had done was wear herself out, worrying about the hopelessness of it all. Instead, she went to the table and pulled up a chair. By the time Nelson returned, she had demolished every scrap of food on the breakfast tray, and regained at least an outward semblance of composure.

The brawny servant stood for a moment in the doorway, tears in his eyes, before heaving a sentimental sigh and offering her his arm to help her hobble along the landing and down the stairs.

Captain Corcoran was sitting behind his desk when Nelson ushered her into his study, but he got to his feet and waited until she was seated before sitting back down.

Though it was a little late for him to be playing the gentleman, considering how rudely he had spoken to her the night before, she appreciated the gesture.

He cleared his throat.

'How is your ankle this morning?' he asked gruffly. It was *not* weakness to want to see her one last time, before bidding her farewell for ever. He could not just let her leave, without ensuring she came to no lasting harm from this encounter. 'Do you think you are fit enough to travel?'

For one wild moment, Aimée considered telling him she was in such pain that she could not endure the prospect of a lengthy journey by public stage. But it would only postpone the inevitable for perhaps a day, at most. All he would have to do would be to examine her to see that the swelling had gone down considerably. And he would discover she was a liar, on top of everything else.

'I shall manage,' she said stiffly.

He frowned. 'I have no doubt of that.' Mr Jago had told him she was a plucky little thing. And he had no sooner clapped eyes on her than he had seen his former bosun was right. Nothing would break this woman. Not the most humiliating of ordeals.

Even last night, soaking wet, clothing torn and hair tumbling from its moorings, she had somehow managed to maintain her dignity.

'Do you have any family to take care of you?' No, Jago had told him she had nobody, which was why she was obliged to seek work to support herself. He had thought this was a point in her favour. But now it appeared he might be totally responsible for her, even though it was clearly the last thing she wanted. 'Or is there anyone you will need to contact, to inform them of your imminent return?'

She barely repressed a shudder as she thought of

her father, from whom she had gone to such lengths to escape. 'Nobody,' she said grimly.

'Then I should be happier if you stayed here and rested, until you are no longer in any pain at all.'

He could not quite believe he had made her that offer. Especially since happy was the last thing he would feel while he knew she was somewhere in the same house as him! She had only to turn those lustrous green eyes on him, or utter one softly spoken phrase, to provoke the kind of yearning that had him believing in the legend of the siren's song. Though it would be fatal to let her know the power she could have over him, should she decide to deploy it.

He deliberately hardened his face, hoping she would interpret a stony silence as a sign of strength, not debilitating uncertainty. He had no intention of opening his mouth and stuttering and stammering, making himself look a bigger fool than he already felt.

Aimée twisted her hands together in her lap. The way he was glaring at her made her feel like a butterfly skewered on a pin. He was clearly waiting for her to thank him for the kind offer and leave him alone. Which she would do, of course, once she had apologised. Though it was not going to be easy. He was already angry with her. How much more angry would he be when she explained what she had thought?

Yet she could not let him carry on thinking she had fled into the night in response to a proposal of marriage from him. That would be even more insulting.

'To be honest,' she said, blushing hotly, 'I am glad you sent for me. Before I leave, there was something I wanted to say to you. Well, no, actually, I do not want to say it. But I must. Oh, heavens,' she said, darting a nervous glance at him, 'I feel like such a fool!'

He blinked, and sat up straight. It was the very last thing he might have expected her to say.

'In what way do you think you are a fool, Miss Peters?'

Her eyes skittered away from his face, before returning to him with renewed resolve.

He wondered what game she was playing now. If this was all an act, to rouse his curiosity and make him feel protective of her, it was a damn fine one. It was giving him the uncomfortable feeling that it was not her, caught in his nets and hauled ashore, but *he* that was slowly becoming more and more deeply entangled by her.

Then she took a deep breath and plunged right in.

'Just…well, to be truthful, I was not aware you had asked me to marry you.'

'Not aware I had asked you to marry me? What nonsense is this?'

'I know now that this must sound rather insulting.' Her blush deepened and her eyes skittered away once more. 'But at the time, I really, truly thought you were offering me, well…*carte blanche.*'

'You thought I what?' He leapt to his feet. 'What the hell kind of mind have you got to suppose that I, an officer in his Majesty's navy, would stoop to such… such…?'

He shook his head in disbelief. Why on earth would she say such a thing? Women were so unpredictable. More unpredictable than the sea. At least the sea could not help but give warnings that a storm was brewing. The glass dropped. Clouds gathered. But women? He knew from bitter experience that there was no telling what a woman might do or say next!

He had been quite frank with her last night. Had

told her far more than he had intended to at this stage. He had explained that he was new to the ways of society, and did not think he would fare well trying to get himself a wife the way other nobly born men did—by going to London, and doing the rounds of the marriage mart. He had also confided in her that he did not want to have the kind of marriage he'd had as a young man, either. One based on fleeting emotions. That had been a disastrous mistake. Far better, this time round, to recruit a woman fit for the role she had to play. Besides, persons of his rank nearly always chose wives with their heads, not their hearts.

Though, naturally, he had paid her a few compliments, too. Told her he admired her perspicacity, as well as her looks.

He had then pointed out the advantages to her of being his wife, rather than a governess, which is what she had come here expecting to be.

So how could she have so misunderstood him? She needed a job. And he needed a wife. It was all perfectly straightforward!

She was sitting with her head bowed, twisting her fingers together in her lap. He had assumed she had run, in disgust, from the prospect of marrying him. But what if she was telling him the truth this morning?

Now he came to think of it, it had not been revulsion he had seen on her face when he had stooped to pick her up off the woodland floor, but terror.

Stark, abject terror. My God… He ran his fingers through his hair, ploughing great furrows through it. The moment he had said, point blank, that he had no intention of ravishing a defenceless woman, a guest under his roof, she had calmed down considerably. She really had thought that he…

'Although, try as I might,' she suddenly said, lifting her head and looking straight at him with a mutinous glint in her eyes, 'I cannot recollect you ever mentioning the word *marriage*. And after the way you went about getting me to The Lady's Bower,' she said truculently, 'which, you have to admit, was downright underhanded, surely you can see that you yourself laid a groundwork of suspicion!'

All of a sudden, he wanted to laugh. The little minx could not quite stop herself from pointing out that though she acknowledged she had been in error, she held him entirely to blame! Just as, last night, she had referred to the blistering rebuke she had delivered when she'd thought he was just a coach driver as being *somewhat impolite*. Twice in as many days she had made him want to laugh out loud, when he could not remember even having anything to smile about for the last few years.

'I do not think,' he said, finding it hard to keep his face straight, 'I have ever heard anybody apologising in one breath, and taking it back with the next.' Whereupon she looked so anxious that, after maintaining a stony expression for only a few more seconds, he relented and said, 'But I accept it. Such as it is.' For he could see now that she'd had such a profound effect on him, he had obviously made a total mull of his proposal.

She sighed with relief.

He sat down.

'What do you expect from me now?'

She must have delivered that apology for a reason. She could have just left, and let him think she simply could not face marrying him. But, no, she had forced herself to apologise, even though she had found it highly embarrassing to admit to her mistake.

'Expect?' For a second she looked surprised. But then a cynical look swept across her pretty face. 'Nothing,' she said crisply. 'You have already made it quite plain that you have changed your mind about my suitability as a wife. Although if you had only explained things properly—'

She broke off, looking so aggrieved that he felt hope surge through him. If she had understood he was proposing *marriage*, she was implying, she might have reacted completely differently. He swivelled his chair round, so that he was staring out of the window and not at her.

He wanted her. By God, how he wanted her! The very first time he had seen her for himself, dripping wet and leaning into the wind as though she scorned the elements, something inside him had leapt with a kind of recognition. If ever there was a woman destined to be the wife of a sea captain, he had thought, then this was that woman. Within minutes of crossing his threshold he had seen that not only did she appeal to him as a man, but that she had that indefinable something that would convince anyone she ever met that she was every inch a lady. In short, she was not just suitable, she was perfect.

Which made her dangerous. When she had fled from him, it had been like Miranda, all over again. When you cared too much about a woman, every word, every gesture had the power to cause unbelievable pain.

But only if you *let* yourself care too much in the first place.

'Are you saying that now you have calmed down,' he said, turning his chair towards her again, 'and have realised that my proposal was one of marriage, you wish me to renew it?'

'I…umm,' she fidgeted in her chair, her eyes clouded with uncertainty. 'Not exactly,' she eventually confessed. Then, drawing herself upright, she looked him straight in the face, took a deep breath, and said, 'I would not want to marry any man who was engaged in something…underhand. Illegal. Or immoral.'

It was all he could do to remain seated. He could not think of any way she could have insulted him more comprehensively. He could, just, see how she might have misunderstood the situation last night. But now she *knew* it was marriage he was offering, and she was still trying to paint him as the villain of the piece!

She held her hand out to him, in a placatory gesture, saying hastily, 'You see, all my life I have struggled to remain within the limits of the laws of whatever country I have lived in.' In spite of her father's increasing disregard for any kind of moral code. 'I could have had a much easier life, financially speaking, if I had not had such…rigid morals.' She flung up her chin. 'I could have become some man's mistress years ago, and been kept in the lap of luxury, if I could have abandoned all the principles that my mother instilled in me. But I would rather have starved.'

His anger abated. '*That* is why you leapt to the wrong conclusion about my proposal last night.' It was *not* completely his fault. 'You have been propositioned before.' And her determination to escape it certainly put her in a different league from his first wife. Miranda had thought nothing of entertaining a lover while he was away at sea. Had, in the end, run off with her fancy man, for far less money than he had brought to the table last night.

She nodded. 'And in my experience, a man will always take advantage of a woman without adequate protection. I do hope you will forgive my error of judgement. I had no notion of your character then. Though,' she continued with a perplexed frown, 'if you cannot give me a sensible reason for putting an advertisement in the papers for what sounded like a governess, when really you wanted a wife, what was I supposed to think? I have explained why I tried to run away,' she said, her eyes snapping with irritation. 'If you had made it clear you were offering marriage, rather than—' She broke off, huffing in exasperation. 'And you still have not explained why you went to such lengths to…to…lure me here!'

'There are perfectly good reasons why I was not willing to advertise openly for a wife,' he replied, amusement tugging at him yet again. She had started off that little speech in penitence, but before she had taken her first breath, she was one step away from rebuking him.

'Well, that is not going to help me make up my mind, is it?' she said in vexation. 'I need to know—'

'Why the devil do you *think* I picked a woman who answered an advertisement for what sounded like a job as a governess? Any woman who would rather earn her living honestly when she is pretty enough to do so on her back has to have at least a modicum of integrity. And I told Mr Jago to be on the lookout for a pretty woman. If I was planning something illegal, or immoral, do you think I would want such a woman at my side? As my partner in crime?'

'Put like that, no, I suppose not.' Very well, he might not want to go down the more conventional route of finding a bride, but he had mentioned she would become a Countess if she married him. He must have known that there would have been dozens of applicants for such a position! 'But why did you not just advertise openly for a wife?'

He laughed mockingly. 'The kind of woman who would offer herself up as a wife under those conditions is precisely the kind of wife I don't want—a woman who would sell herself for wealth and a title! And before you tell me I could go about it in the more usual way, doing the Season and courting some milk-and-water débutante...' His lips twisted in derision.

'I have not the time for all that nonsense. Besides, I have already told you that I have a sight too much self-respect to go grovelling to a succession of society beauties, in Almack's or some such place. I have no address, fewer manners, and you have already learned that I have a damnable temper! I would probably just scatter them all like a flock of silly geese. And I have absolutely no intention of ending up with a vapid creature who would shrink from me.'

She regarded the clenched fists that he'd slammed on to the desk top to illustrate his point, then raised her eyes to his face. They seemed to linger over his scars, and a troubled frown knotted her brows. The intensity of her scrutiny was hard to bear. His instinct was to put up his hands and conceal his ugliness. Instead, he forced himself to sit completely still and bear that vision of perfection studying the wreckage of a face that had never been worth looking at in the first place.

What was she thinking while she studied him so intently? She had flinched the first time she had seen him without the eyepatch. He had left it off deliberately, to see how she would react. He had vowed not to subject any female to the close proximity marriage would entail, if it was clear it was beyond her. It had seemed like a good omen when she had overcome her initial revulsion so swiftly. There were not many women who could cope with a sight like that.

It seemed like a very long time before she blinked, and shook her head as though coming out of a trance.

'I still do not quite see...'

'Can you suggest a better way of finding the kind of woman I want than this? From what I have heard of the Season, it brings out all the worst traits of your sex. They smile and simper and lie to trap you into making an offer, and only then do you find out what they are really made of. Well, Miss Peters, I have a clearer idea what you are made of now, after getting you to apply for an honest job and being in your company only one day, than I had of my first wife after two years of being married.'

Granted, he had been away at sea for almost the entire period. He supposed it was hardly surprising she had found somebody else. And that the sight of him, when he had returned home to be nursed back to health after the injury that had robbed him of his eye, had precipitated her final flight.

'And do not make some foolish remark about it being too soon to fall in love with each other. I warn you now, I am done with love,' he declared, looking straight at her. 'I married for love before, and it was a disaster from start to finish. This time, I want a rational, sensible union of two beings who both know exactly what to expect from one another. For I must marry. It has been made quite clear that it is my duty to produce heirs.'

'Heirs,' she repeated weakly.

'Make no mistake, if you marry me, it will be a full marriage. I shall expect you to welcome me into your bed. And I shall demand fidelity from you.'

'And what,' she retorted, her eyes sparking with indignation, 'may I expect from you, sir?'

His face hardened.

'Go back to London, then, if you do not want such a marriage!' he snapped. 'I am not keeping you a prisoner!'

Her stomach lurched. She could not return to London! Not after scheming and striving so hard to escape. She knew what awaited her there—men who wanted to use and humiliate her. She might be able to evade them again, but...

She gripped the arm of the chair, shivering at the possibility of falling into the clutches of any of those men who had thought it sport to bid for her virtue.

All that awaited her in London was degradation and horror.

At least if she stayed here, and married the Captain, she would know a measure of security. Last night, she had been in despair, believing she had ruined her one and only chance at marriage and respectability. But now he was offering her a second chance. A slim chance...

She looked at him, sitting stony faced behind his desk. Unmoving. Intractable.

Could she really marry a man she barely knew? A man who admitted he had a fiery temper, and vowed he would never love her?

'I...I need time to consider,' she eventually managed to whisper.

'I will grant you one day, no more,' he grated harshly. 'You may stay here today and rest. Allow your ankle to recover. But do not regard me as an easy mark, Miss Peters. Don't think I have not noticed how thin you are. Or how you clean every plate that is set before you. This is not an asylum for the waifs and strays of

London's gutters. You will tell me your decision tonight at dinner. And if it is a refusal, make no mistake, the free meals and board will cease tomorrow morning. And this interview,' he said, pulling a sheaf of papers across the desktop towards him, 'is at an end. I have work to do. Nelson!' he bellowed.

The man must have been lurking just outside the door, because he burst in at once. 'Miss Peters will not be leaving today after all. See that she has whatever she needs to make her stay with us comfortable. Send Mr Jago in to me, but keep *her* out of my way. And above all,' he growled as she got to her feet, 'see that she does not get into any more mischief.'

Chapter Five

Nelson held out his arm, and, once more, she allowed him to support her as they crossed the hall, back to the parlour where she had sat—had it only been the night before?—on her arrival.

Yes, that was all it had been. Though so much had happened, she reflected as Nelson led her to the self-same armchair, that it seemed like a lifetime ago! She had come here, expecting to become a governess, had run away, fearing the Captain meant to make her his mistress, and now…

Now, she sighed, sinking back against the cushions, she was seriously contemplating marrying the man— For what was the alternative?

Billy came barrelling into the room then, and, after exchanging a nod and some meaningful grimaces with Nelson, he swept all the clutter from a low table under the window, brought it to her chair, grabbed a cushion, and said, 'You just put your foot up, here, miss.'

Rather bemused, she did as she was told.

'Billy was a loblolly boy on *The Speedwell*,' Nelson explained.

Feeling even more bewildered by the strange terminology on top of everything else, she said, 'A...lob... What is one of those?'

'I 'elped the ship's surgeon,' Billy explained.

'Oh, so that is how you knew exactly what the Captain needed to do with my ankle, last night, to make it feel so much better,' she mused aloud.

She went back in her mind to how gently Captain Corcoran had bound up her ankle, even though he had been absolutely furious with her.

And how this morning he had sent for her to enquire after her health, even though he had thought she found him so repulsive she had run out into the night to escape him. Just to make sure she had somewhere to go.

He might say he had a fiery temper. But she had already discovered he was not the kind of man to cause deliberate pain. Or turn an injured woman out on the streets, no matter how badly she had behaved.

Billy and Nelson were still standing there, staring down at her as though they were taking the Captain's orders to watch her quite literally, when the door opened and the bow-legged man with the dreadful teeth came in, a bunch of wild flowers clutched in his hands.

'This is to say sorry for scaring you last night,' he said, thrusting them at her. The mashed stems were tied together with string that had been plaited, then tied into some kind of complicated knot that was far more skilfully put together than the selection of flowers. 'Nelson says you've got over your fright, and you're gonna stay,' he added, shifting from one leg to the other.

'I am not quite yet decided,' she said, taking the

flowers from his knobbly hands. Their faces all fell dramatically.

Aimée looked from one man to the other. They all seemed so keen for her to stay, and marry their precious Captain! Even after all the trouble she had caused them the night before.

'You can't go holding it against him just coz he impressed you,' blurted Jenks, his face full of woe.

Nelson swatted him round the back of the head, making the poor fellow's eyes water.

'What?' he said, swinging round with an injured air.

'You're supposed to be helping, not making things worse!' hissed Nelson angrily.

Jenks turned on Nelson, his expression belligerent. 'I am helping! We all know what it feels like first time you get pressed. Everyone resents it! Till you get used to being on board ship and find the life ain't so bad if you've got officers like Cap'n Corky…'

For a few minutes, the three men seemed to forget all about Aimée as they engaged in a heated argument about whether the way the Captain had acted to secure her presence at The Lady's Bower could truly be construed as impressment. It was a fascinating insight into a world of which Aimée had no previous experience. She learned that almost any healthy man who lived within sight of British shores faced the constant threat of being plucked from his home and livelihood, to serve in his Majesty's navy.

'But she come 'ere of her own free will,' argued Nelson hotly, 'like a volunteer answering to a recruitment poster.'

'Well, you know what a pack of lies they tell,' Jenks said. 'Promising you beer and beef, and fiddlers and dancing every night…'

'Aye, but being a wife is a sight better than being a governess,' protested Billy. 'She signed up to work for the Captain, and got instant promotion. She ought to be grateful!'

At that point, Nelson darted her a troubled look, as though suddenly recollecting she was sitting there listening to every word. He clouted Jenks once more for good measure, and it might have got ugly had not the door opened again, to reveal a man who was almost as wide as he was tall, with greying, greasy hair and a florid complexion. He was bearing a tray.

'Jenks tells me how much you enjoyed my cake, miss,' he said, attempting, she thought, to make a bow, though his girth prevented him from doing much more than inclining the upper half of his body slightly. 'And that you are having a bit of a think about whether to marry the Captain or not. And so I thought I'd come and add my own weight to the argument.'

Though it was an unfortunate turn of phrase, Aimée managed not to laugh at the company's cook. Besides, she was not going to be swayed into making any decision merely because Captain Corcoran inspired devotion amongst his followers. Why, even Hincksey, who was a moneylender and a brothel-keeper, inspired loyalty in his minions. And that, merely because he did not break a man's legs without provocation!

Though what they had said had given her a revealing glimpse into the lives of a class of men she'd never really thought about before. She had, occasionally, encountered members of the officer class, strutting about the salons of places like Naples. They never mentioned the men who served under them. She did not suppose many officers, once ashore, spared a single thought for the welfare of the inhabitants of the lower decks.

No, from what Billy and Jenks and Nelson said, they just treated them like criminals. They wrested them from their homes, denied them liberty, flogged them, kept them half-starved, and then expected them to fight like demons whenever they came across an enemy ship.

The poor wretches!

Though she was still perplexed by their eagerness to see her marry their wonderful Captain.

'There is nothing special about *me*, you know,' she said, splashing just a dash of milk into her teacup. 'I am beginning to wonder why you are all so keen to see me, in particular, marry him. If I were to leave—'

'No, you can't do that, miss!' cried Jenks. 'Not and leave him to the mercy of the likes of Lady Frog Face! Not after all he's been through!'

The other men rounded on him, their faces equally furious.

'Get him back to the kitchen, where he can't do no more damage,' Nelson growled.

'With pleasure,' replied the cook, taking the hapless man by one ear and tugging him out of the door.

Aimée looked from Billy to Nelson, her eyes narrowed.

'What did he mean? And who is Lady Frog Face?'

They shifted uncomfortably. Then Nelson said, 'Look, we just want to see him happy, that's all. It were wicked, the way his wife ran off and left him, when he come home half-dead with fever after losing of his eye.'

'It weren't even that bad,' muttered Billy. 'I seen a lot worse…'

'Mr Jago found him this place, and we came here and looked after him till he was strong enough to return to duty, just like he helped all of us when we was washed ashore without friends. And now he wants to marry you, miss. And we don't care what you're like, if you're the woman he's fixed his sights on, that's good enough for us!'

Well, it wasn't good enough for her. She could not agree to marry a man just because these former mariners could tell a heart-wrenching tale or two.

'Would you mind leaving me now, please?' she said as firmly as she could. She needed peace and quiet so that she could make the decision, a decision that would affect her whole future, in a cool, calm, rational manner.

'I hope you enjoy your tea,' said Nelson, backing towards the door.

'And the cake,' added Billy, pointing to it as though reminding her there would be plenty more where that came from, should she stay at The Lady's Bower and marry Captain Corcoran.

Lady Frog Face? Aimée watched the door close behind their hasty departure, and took a sip of her tea. Surely, Captain Corcoran had not sent all the way to London for her, to avoid marrying some lady with the facial features of a frog? He struck her as being far too forceful a personality to do anything so feeble.

Still, the little chat she'd just had with his servants had made some things clear. It had given her a glimpse of a world utterly alien to her own. No wonder the Captain's outlook on life was very different from hers. He probably saw nothing wrong with pressing innocent people into service. He must have recruited dozens, nay, hundreds of men to fight and die on his warships during his career in the navy in a like manner. He was so used to having his word treated as law that virtually kidnapping a woman before proposing to her probably seemed perfectly logical to him.

She reached for a slice of cake. Had he done her any actual, physical harm? No. Nor had he intended to. Aimée was not too proud to admit that much of what she had suffered had been entirely her own fault. She need not have got soaked if she had waited at the King's Arms for him to fetch her in the carriage he had borrowed especially. She would not have twisted her ankle if she had listened to his proposal calmly, instead of assuming he was the kind of brute she had encountered in the past and panicked. In spite of his gruff manner, he had not crossed the line many men she had known in the past would have done with alacrity. She was stranded in his house, surrounded by his fanatically loyal crew. He could have done whatever he wished with her. And tossed her aside afterwards, had he felt so inclined. Many women would consider he was a cruel beast for putting her through the ordeal she had undergone. But she had met truly, brutally cruel men before. And the Captain was nothing like any of them.

During the course of just one day, she realised, as she took a bite of fruit cake, she had learned as much about him as, probably, any woman ever learned about a man before she married him. That he was given to good works. He had told her, rather angrily earlier on, that this place was not a home for waifs and strays, but she had since learned that was exactly what it was. He had given each of his men a home, and work here, whether he was in residence, or away at sea.

Yes, he was autocratic, and quick-tempered. Grew affronted when she doubted his integrity.

But he was also quite handsome, if you overlooked his scar. Was actually quite appealing, in spite of it. For he had a certain vitality…

He might not make her very happy, she reflected as

she took another large bite of cake, but then, the truth was, marriage was something of a lottery.

There were no guarantees of happiness for a woman, whether she ran away with someone she was wildly in love with, as her mother had done, or bowed to family pressure and submitted to an arranged marriage as, apparently, her aunt had done.

Or took a chance on a complete stranger, as she was considering doing.

She rubbed her finger round the plate, sweeping up every single crumb, as she asked herself exactly what she did want of marriage.

Captain Corcoran had said he did not want love to form a part of it.

He said he had done that once, and it had been a disaster. She could believe it, having witnessed her parents' own turbulent match.

Now all he seemed to want was a woman who would not disgrace him by running off with some other man, or having adulterous *affaires* behind his back.

She almost dropped the cake plate as she suddenly realised that it was right after he'd realised she had run off into a storm rather than submit to being his mistress, in spite of all the money he had offered her, that he had begun to speak of marriage again. As though she had passed some kind of test.

Why had she not seen it before? Behind that take-it-or-leave-it attitude, she had detected a certain tension. It was because he was trying to hide how very keen he was for her to stay.

She had watched enough men playing cards, gambling for ruinous stakes, to be able to read the signs of suppressed emotion.

And the way the crew were all trying to persuade

her to stay…was it because they knew he really, really wanted her? Was that a bargaining chip? Could she use that, somehow, to her own advantage?

She leaned back into the cushions, her mind a whirl. How, exactly, did learning all this help her to make up her mind?

Aimée gazed sightlessly into the blazing fire, and before long, what with being replete from tea and cakes, and being so comfortable with her foot propped up, her eyelids began to grow heavy. It was hardly surprising. She had barely slept the night before, so furious had she been with herself for so badly misinterpreting the situation. And for days before that, she yawned, she had not been in any dwelling where she had been able to so much as lie down without first checking that the door was securely barred and there was a means of defending herself close at hand.

As her eyes drifted shut, she thought she saw the door open, but when she opened her eyes fully, there was nobody there.

Captain Corcoran shut the door softly, so as not to disturb her. He had thought he might as well join her for tea, since he had been totally unable to concentrate on the mountain of correspondence he ought to have been attending to. How right he had been to liken her to a siren. She drew him to her, just by being in his house. He stood in the hallway, the image of her lying on the sofa emblazoned on his mind. She looked so lovely, her cheeks flushed with sleep and her hair escaping its pins so that it spread all over the cushions. But for some reason, it was seeing that empty plate still clutched in her fingers that clawed at his conscience.

She was always hungry. But she must have been

exhausted, too, to fall asleep in that position. She could not have slept very much last night, he thought, rubbing absentmindedly at the scarred side of his face. She had been scared, and confused, and in a great deal of pain. But she had refused the laudanum, which might have helped her get some rest.

His mouth firming into a grim line, he marched upstairs to the linen closet and fetched a blanket. There was not much he could do about what had happened last night, but he could at least ensure she was comfortable now.

He went back into the parlour as quietly as he could, detached the empty plate from her lax grip and gently draped the blanket over her.

The slight noise he made putting the plate on the table had her half-opening her eyes. But they drifted shut again almost immediately, and she snuggled down, one hand under her cheek.

He straightened up abruptly. She needed somebody to look after her. She might not want to admit it, but she did. If she married him, she need never go hungry again. Nor would he let anyone harm so much as a hair on her head.

Rather stunned by the ferocity of his determination to protect her from imaginary enemies, as well as potential draughts, he stalked to the door and made for his study. He had work to do. Important work. And she had already proved far too much of a distraction for one day.

Even without opening her eyes, Aimée had known Captain Corcoran was the person creeping about the room, making her comfortable. She recognised his unique scent, from when he had carried her from the woods to the house. Besides, he would not permit any of his men to perform so intimate a task as tucking a blanket about her person, like this.

It was only later, when she awoke, that she fully understood the significance of what had just happened.

Somehow, she had begun to trust the Captain. She knew he meant her no harm, or she would not have been able to lie there, quite relaxed, and allow him to tuck that blanket round her. Or snuggle down again afterwards, completely unperturbed by his presence.

It was not much to go on, perhaps, but it was more than most women got. If she were to marry the Captain, she knew he would take good care of her, in his own way, the same way as he looked out for the welfare of the other members of his crew.

She sat up, folded the blanket neatly, and draped it over the arm of the chair, smiling at the image she had conjured up. Of herself swabbing the decks, whilst Captain Corcoran stood, legs braced, on the poop deck, bellowing orders at her like any other of his crew members.

Her smile faded abruptly as she reminded herself that marriage was not like a grand adventure in some storybook. In fact, she had no idea what marriage to a man of the Captain's temperament might bring. When she tried to picture it again, all she could see was an endless stormy sea and her in a little boat with the Captain, heading who knew where.

She did not have to marry him, of course. He had said she could leave as soon as her ankle was better.

And at the very prospect, her stomach lurched as though she really was in a boat on a storm-tossed sea. It had been something of a miracle that she had escaped

London the last time. Was her luck likely to hold if he sent her back?

Because, it struck her, although she had passed all the tests the Captain had set her, and though he was keen to bend her to his will, he was not so set on her, and her alone, that he would feel all that much of a qualm if she left.

He would probably rant and rave a bit, then go out and pressgang some other unsuspecting female into service. She imagined him sitting at that beautifully set dining table, offering this imaginary woman jewels, and servants, and his title. Her mouth tightened as she heard her replacement cooing that she would be delighted to accept. And as she pictured him sweeping the sly minx up in those steely arms of his, and carrying her out into the woods, she discovered that her fingers had formed claws and were digging into the weave of the blanket.

Taking a deep breath, she uncurled them, and smoothed away the creases her spurt of irrational anger had put there.

It seemed her choice was already made. She had no idea whether it would prove to be a good choice. Only time would tell. But the one thing she knew was that she could not permit some other woman to become Captain Corcoran's bride!

She got to her feet and limped to the door. It was time she was changing for dinner. The Captain had asked her to dine with him this evening, when he would expect her answer.

She clung to the banister rail as she hobbled up the stairs, her mouth set with grim determination.

She might live to regret this. But the alternative, of leaving his home and trying to fend for herself again… She gave an involuntary shudder. She knew that life all too well. And she would be a fool to go back to it, when the Captain was offering her the kind of security she had always longed for.

Her travelling dress was horribly creased from having dozed in it. Her best gown had disappeared from the airer—not that she could have repaired it, anyway. So Aimée lifted her dark-grey morning gown from where she had packed it at the top of the trunk. She shook it out and hung it up while she had a quick wash. She had bought it because it made her look sober and respectable, like a very severe governess.

But that image, coincidentally, was exactly what Captain Corcoran appeared to be looking for in a wife. A sensible, respectable woman, upon whom he could rely.

She hid her face in the towel, rather than meet the accusation she feared seeing in her own eyes. She would not cheat the Captain, once she was his wife! She was not *exactly* cheating him now. He had not specified he wanted her to have an impeccable background. It was only her future conduct that he was interested in.

She whirled from the mirror, hooked her buttons up swiftly and patted her hair into place.

Captain Corcoran got to his feet when she returned to the same little parlour in which she had already spent so much time. He looked quite splendid in what she surmised was his dress uniform. It had the effect of making her feel at even more of a disadvantage than ever in her plain, drab little gown.

And very conscious that the power was all in his hands.

Feeling suddenly very nervous, she went to the chair in which she had been dozing earlier and sat down.

'I may as well tell you, right now,' she said, 'that I have almost made up my mind to accept your proposal.'

His face remained impassive as he took his own seat, across the hearth from hers.

'Almost?' he drawled, leaning back and crossing his legs. 'May I remind you that I require your decision tonight?'

'Do you think this is easy for me?' she flared. 'I know that you are used to simply ordering your crew about. That you have come to expect instant obedience. But have you no notion of how hard it will be for me to simply hand over complete control of my life to a man I barely know? And you are so very autocratic!'

'You seem to have no problem with voicing your objections, however,' he said coolly. 'From the very first moment you saw me, you have not hesitated to berate me for one crime or another.'

'Yes, but that was when I thought you were a coachman! And then…'

'A kidnapper,' he agreed. 'Yes, I know what you have thought of me.'

'But as my husband, you will expect me to obey you!' she said plaintively. 'Without question!'

'That, madam, is only what every man expects from his wife,' he replied coldly.

His heart was beating uncomfortably fast. She was teetering on the verge of making up her mind in his favour. He wished he could do something, say something to persuade her…but then she would know how very much this meant to him. He would seem weak. He would rather let her go than admit his susceptibility to her considerable charm was a weapon she could wield against him.

'Miss Peters, you have only two choices. Either take me as I am, or return to London.'

Aimée could have screamed with frustration. Why would he not just give her some kind of reassurance? Would one kind word be so hard for him to utter?

She was so afraid that she was on the verge of making the most colossal mistake of her life! Marriage was so final. A woman who made an error in her choice of husband would spend the rest of her life regretting it. She had only to remember the circumstances her own mother had been reduced to by marrying her father. She forced herself to keep looking him straight in the eye, though her heart was pounding hard.

But he saw her clasp her hands in her lap to hide the way they were trembling. His glare became so ferocious her tongue dried in her mouth.

He got to his feet, and came to stand right in front of her chair. He was so close that his boots brushed the tips of her stained slippers. His eye glittered strangely as he leant down and took her chin in one hand. It was all she could do not to shrink back into the cushions.

'Or is the truth really that you are afraid of becoming intimate with me? Is that it?'

As the warmth of his breath fanned her cheek it occurred to her that it was strange she had scarcely considered that aspect of marriage with him, for he had stressed that the whole point of remarrying was because it was now his duty to produce heirs.

She swallowed, and had to crane her neck to keep looking up into his face. He was so close to her that she could feel the heat emanating from his body. She was suddenly struck by a vision of lying in a bed next to this strong, hot-tempered, vital man. It made her cheeks flush. In fact, it felt as though her entire body flushed.

It was very far from being an unpleasant feeling.

'N-no,' she stammered. 'I am not afraid of you. Of that…'

She felt her cheeks grow hotter still.

'That is as well,' he said, and his thumb swept over her parted lips. 'Because one of the reasons I specifically advertised for a woman who was willing to become a governess is because I must have children. They will be yours…' he released her chin, but so slowly it felt like a caress '…and mine, if you marry me. Do not forget, also, that you will also become a wealthy woman. A titled woman. I have recently become the Earl of Bowdon. You will be my Countess,' he purred seductively.

Goodness! If one caress could make her feel like this, all warm and breathless and…girlish, what would it be like if he kissed her? Held her?

'Yes,' she whispered, her heart beating very fast. 'I think I shall marry you.' And then, slightly louder, almost feeling as though she should be requesting permission to come aboard, 'Yes, Captain. I will marry you.'

Something that looked like relief flickered across his face. 'Thank you,' he grated. Then, taking her by surprise, he leaned forwards and grasped her hands tightly between his own callused palms.

It had been the lure of a title that had weighted the scales in his favour, but he did not care. She had agreed to marry him, and that was what counted. With a sense of jubilation, he pulled her to her feet, and before she had time to take evasive action he kissed her full on the mouth.

Aimée had wondered what it would feel like if he should kiss her. And now, as he pressed his mouth hard against hers, just briefly, as though he was intent on stamping his mark on her, she knew. It was as though somebody had lit a barrowload of fireworks inside her.

'Let us go in to dine,' he said, apparently oblivious to the fact that his kiss had produced such an astonishing effect, 'and share the good news with the rest of my crew.'

The rest of his crew. She smiled at him dazedly. She had always suspected he would regard her as another crew member.

He took her hand, linked it through his arm and led her across the hall and into the dining room.

The others were all there, clearly waiting to hear the latest, although they were all trying, not very successfully, to look busy.

'She's agreed,' said Captain Corcoran.

There was a moment's silence, and then, to her slight embarrassment, and great delight, the entire crew gave her three rousing cheers. Mr Jago bustled off and came back with some champagne. After that, the meal became a full-blown celebration.

She felt a smile spread throughout her entire being. She would belong to a group of people in a way she had never experienced before. Billy, and Nelson, and Jenks, and the fat cook and Mr Jago…they would all be like a sort of family!

She had always envied those families she sometimes became acquainted with, who lived in houses handed down to them from their ancestors, who had regular incomes and recognised positions in society. Now she was going to know what that felt like!

She might become the kind of woman who inaugurated societies for the improvement of the local poor. The Captain seemed inclined towards charitable works.

And, oh, there were so many people out there in need of a helping hand!

As for herself, she might do something as simple, yet foreign to her experience, as making friends with whom she could sit gossiping over cups of tea in a drawing room. She would have shelves in that drawing room. And she could fill them with knick-knacks of no intrinsic worth, but which held, for her, some sentimental value. She had never been able to keep souvenirs of any of the places she had visited before. Had never owned more than could be crammed into one case should hasty flight from an irate landlord become necessary.

But now, thanks to Captain Corcoran, anything might be possible!

'We shall be married tomorrow afternoon,' the Captain informed her at the end of the meal, as he passed her a glass of port. 'Do you care for port? I should have asked.'

'Tomorrow?' she replied, shaking her head and pushing the untasted drink from her. She never drank anything so intoxicating. She had seen the results of inebriation far too often to fall for its dubious delights. A girl in her position had to keep her wits about her, not render herself vulnerable by fugging her senses with alcohol fumes. And now, when it might have been permissible to indulge in just one celebratory drink, she had not developed the taste for it.

'I have had a special licence in my possession since the day Jago described you to me,' he said, downing his own drink in one gulp and setting the empty glass down next to his plate. Though his fingers closed tightly round the stem as he said, 'And I have already informed the local vicar, the Reverend Dean, that my fiancée would be joining me before I left the area, so that we could be married quietly before meeting my grand new relations.'

She thought she detected a hint of sarcasm as he referred to his family. It sounded as though he was not overly fond of them, but the mention of them still brought her a *frisson* of unease. Mr Carpenter had shown her how reluctant most decent men would be to have a woman with a past like hers brought into their family. And if his relations were so very grand…

She just hoped he had not made a very grave mistake in choosing her without enquiring too particularly into the details of her past life.

Not that there was anything wrong with her pedigree. Her grandfather was the Earl of Caxton. Unfortunately, her mother had eloped with a man the Earl had held in such contempt that he had refused to ever acknowledge Aimée. When her mother had written to inform him of her birth, there had been no response. No granting of an allowance that the necessity of feeding an extra mouth might have wrung from a more forgiving man. If she had been a boy, her father had said time out of mind, things might have been very different. For at that time the Earl of Caxton had no direct male heir. Still did not, as far as she knew. Her aunt, her mother's older sister, the one who had dutifully married where she was instructed, had never managed to produce any sons that lived to adulthood.

'I do not want to waste any more time,' Captain Corcoran said, jerking her from her reverie. His gaze strayed from her face to what was visible of her form beneath her ill-fitting, high-necked gown. His fingers crept up the stem of the glass, absently stroking over the bowl in a way she found highly suggestive.

'The sooner we are wed,' he said, finally ending his leisurely perusal of her figure, 'the better.'

There was, in his face, an expression she usually found abhorrent. Men had looked at her in *that* particular way many times before—usually just before it became necessary to take evasive action from their groping hands and slobbering lips.

So it was a shock to find that instead of engendering revulsion, or even fear, the Captain's heated look was provoking an altogether different response. She could not help watching the way his fingers were caressing the wine glass, and imagining what those strong brown hands would feel like upon her body.

She tore her fascinated gaze from the subtle movements of his fingers and tried to look him in the face.

Oh, Lord! Now all that filled her mind—no, her entire being—was the remembrance of just how extraordinarily pleasant it had felt when his mouth briefly closed over hers in that kiss.

She swallowed, and raised her eyes to meet his gaze.

Something flashed between them. Something that made her stomach flip over and her heart trip into a staccato rhythm, and robbed her lungs of breath.

Suddenly the room seemed far too warm. She had never felt anything like it!

Completely flustered, she got to her feet, her napkin dropping unnoticed to the floor.

'Well, until then, you had better keep your hands to yourself! Just because I permitted you one kiss, as a…to seal our agreement, it does not mean…don't go thinking you can take liberties with me whenever you feel like it!'

Even to her own ears, she sounded like a shrew. But she could not help it.

'It is not decent!' she said, turning and striding with unbecoming haste towards the door.

She could feel his eyes boring into her back all the way across the room.

She pounded up the stairs, guiltily aware that she was not fleeing from the desire *he* had displayed towards *her*, but the way her own body was clamouring for indulgence. Even when she had reached the seclusion of her room, and shut the door behind her, the aftereffect of that one heated look was still throbbing through her veins.

She had always despised women who succumbed to the blandishments of men as weak-minded fools. But if what they felt was as powerful as this—well, no wonder so many of them fell pregnant outside wedlock.

'I am not suddenly become a wanton,' she muttered, pressing her hands to her overheated cheeks. 'He is going to be my husband!'

His caresses would not result in her shame and degradation—so why, exactly, was she suddenly so frightened?

Chapter Six

The next day dawned bright and fair. And, since sleep had eluded her for most of the night, Aimée knew exactly how bright. From her bed, she could see out of the window across the wide, rolling moors that surrounded The Lady's Bower. The speed with which the puffy white clouds scudded across the azure-blue sky promised the kind of summer day that she had grown to appreciate since coming to England. In years gone by, at this time of year, all she had been able to think of was finding some respite from the heat. Here and now, she felt as though she could really breathe. She got out of bed, flung up the sash and leaned out, with her hands braced on the window-sill, drinking in the cool, early morning air that was as invigorating as a dip in a mountain stream.

It was going to be a perfect day, she sighed. Her wedding day. The day all girls dreamed about, but none with such mixed feelings as she had done. For she knew what dangers lay in wait for unwary brides.

She did not know how long she stood there, just

admiring the ever-shifting patterns of light and shade that rippled across the moors, but she was still enraptured by the scene when there was a loud knock on the door and Nelson's muffled voice asking if he might bring in her washing water. She scuttled back to the bed, grabbed a shawl and, having wrapped it securely round herself, called out that he could.

Nelson came in, carrying two cans of steaming hot water, and behind rolled bow-legged Jenks with an enamelled hipbath and a pile of clean towels.

'We'll bring your breakfast up in half an hour,' said Nelson. Then frowned. 'If that gives you long enough?'

'Oh, yes,' she answered, blushing. Once she had stripped off, she would be excruciatingly aware she was the only female in a household of men. She was definitely not going to want to linger in that tub, naked, when there was no lock on the door!

'Do you have everything you need?' he asked. 'Do you need your gown pressing, or…?' He faltered, looking as uncomfortable as she was already feeling.

She shook her head. There was no way she was going to let any one of these men handle her gowns, or, worse still, her undergarments. Nobody, but nobody, must ever discover how much money she still had, stitched into panels all the way round her stays—though that money was better concealed than the coins that weighted down the hem of her petticoat. Not that these men looked as though they had any wish to handle her undergarments. The mere thought she might wish them to press one of her gowns was enough to make them blush and stutter and avoid meeting her eye!

Once they left, she hastily stripped off and stepped into the tub of steaming water. As she settled down, her spirits momentarily sank too. All that talk of clothing had reminded her that she did not have a proper wedding dress. Even her mother had managed to smuggle a dress, in which she looked like a picture, into her luggage when she ran away with her father, whereas *she* had ruined her one and only silk dress in that headlong flight through the woods.

She lifted her chin and began to soap herself thoroughly. She had no reason to feel sorry for herself. Her mother might have rushed to the altar, all wide-eyed and glowing at the prospect of marrying the man who seemed so exciting, in the silken gown she had kept a scrap of to her dying day, but the gloss had worn off once it became clear that the Earl of Caxton would not relent and release the money her father had expected would fall into his greedy hands.

At least the man she was marrying was nothing like her father! On the surface, Papa was always charming, urbane and witty. The Captain, she smiled to herself, was his very antithesis: rude, hot-tempered and autocratic. He had not used soft words, or made false promises of love, because he thought she had a fortune. Instead, he had very sternly warned her that love was to form no part of their bargain!

Anyway, she still had the dress she had thought to keep for Sunday best. It was not silk, but it fitted her. And she had splashed out on purchasing all sorts of matching accessories. A governess she had thought she was going to be, but on Sundays she had intended to be a rather smartly attired one! The high-necked, long-sleeved cotton gown had a lovely pattern printed on it, which reminded her of sprigs of cypress. She had treated herself to a brand new pair of gloves, in a toning shade of green, and a ridiculously expensive spencer jacket, purely because it had a green velvet collar. And some little nankeen halfboots that she had quite fallen in love with, because some previous owner had embroidered daisies along the side seams. She had imagined walking to church, those daisies appearing and disappearing as her skirts swished round her ankles, to the fascination of the young charges she would have in tow.

She reached for the spare can of water to rinse herself off, smiling at her flight of fancy. It had gone to her head, having enough money to buy whatever clothing she had wanted. After all the years of feeling the cloth to decide how much wear it had left in it, then sniffing it to discover if the odour of its previous owner was not too objectionable, it had been totally irresistible to just splash out on garments that had caught her eye.

She finished her bath swiftly, dried herself, put on the undergarments stuffed with money, and then pulled the sprigged cotton gown over her head. It buttoned down the front. That was the one restriction she had had to bear in mind when she was tempted into making reckless purchases. It would have been no use buying anything she could not fasten without the help of a maid.

Though, she mused as she went to the dressing table and began separating out her braids, she would have to employ one now. Especially if Captain Corcoran wished her to impress those grand relations of his.

She had undone the plaits that were frizzy from being rubbed all over the pillows during her restless night and had just set to methodically combing out the tangles when there was another knock at the door.

The half-hour allotted to her for her bath was up, and Nelson was back with her promised breakfast. With a smile, she rose from her stool and, flicking her still-unbound hair over her shoulders, went and opened the door herself.

Nelson hastily averted his eyes and put the tray on the table just inside the door, backing out as though he had inadvertently caught her without her clothes on. She was puzzled, but by then she had been awake for such a long time that she could not spare much time to wonder what was the matter with the man. There was a cup of steaming hot chocolate on that tray. Warm rolls fresh from the oven. Butter and honey and cheese. And a few sun-ripened strawberries. Tucking her hair behind her ears, she took a seat and paid the cook the compliment of devouring her breakfast while it was still at its very best. Only then did she return to the more mundane task of combing and braiding her hair, then pinning it up so that she could conceal it decorously beneath her bonnet.

For once, she tied the ribbons saucily beneath her left ear, rather than more soberly under her chin, before leaving her room.

She felt another small pang of self-pity when Mr. Jago told her that he would be accompanying her to the church, leading her up the aisle and giving her away, for that task ought more properly to have fallen to her father.

But then he had already, in his own fashion, given her away!

Her spurt of anger at his betrayal was tempered by the sight of Captain Corcoran's crew gathered in the church doorway, all grinning and craning their necks for a sight of her as she got down from the carriage. Jenks came forwards, and with a bow and a toothy grin thrust yet another bunch of flowers into her hands. This time it was not a random selection of hastily wrenched-up wild flowers, but a bouquet of roses and honey-suckle, bound together with one of those nautical knots she was sure were going to become a familiar part of her life in future.

And the ceremony got underway. She walked down the aisle to a groom resplendent in dress uniform, complete with ceremonial sword and gold lace, feeling suddenly very nervous.

Was she really entrusting her entire future to a man she had only just met? Was she mad?

By the time she reached his side, her heart was beating wildly. The vicar opened his prayer book and began to intone the words of the ceremony that would bind her to him for ever.

Love, honour and obey.

He did not want her to love him, and he would not love her. He expected her to honour and obey him, however, though he fully expected her to argue with him, if he became too autocratic.

She took a deep breath to steady herself before she repeated her vows. Before she knew it, he was her husband, and he was planting a rather chaste kiss on her cheek. Just that one brief contact with his skin sent a shaft of something that she recognised as desire shooting right through her body.

She darted a shy, hesitant glance at his profile as he took her arm, and led her from the church. And her spirits plunged when she could see no echo of the feelings that were making her so jittery. No, he looked his usual stern, impassive self.

When they returned to the house for the celebratory meal, she found that her appetite had vanished once more. She could only toy with the food set before her, although in her mind she could acknowledge that it all looked delicious. She tried to smile, to join in with the laughter and gaiety that the rest of the crew were displaying. But she felt somehow detached from it all, as though she did not know quite who she was, or how she ought to behave any more.

By the time she went upstairs to prepare herself for bed, she felt as though she had spent the entire day wrestling to control the varying emotions that had gripped her, at one point or another.

She was worn out with it!

And now she had to get washed and undressed, and prepare herself for her husband. Mechanically, she went through her nightly routine, keeping back a little of her washing water in the jug so that she could place her bouquet in it. She had kept it close from the moment the crew had given it to her. It was so beautiful, so fragrant, and so unexpected. Somehow, it symbolised hope for her future.

She took especial care to tuck her underwear that contained all her money under the mattress out of sight. Only then did she unbraid her hair, pick up her brush and sit down on the stool before the dressing table.

She was a little startled by the reflection that looked back at her from the mirror. Who was this woman, staring back at her with those dark, yearning eyes, her lips already parted in anticipation of her husband's kiss? She had gone to church that morning, looking and feeling like a governess, and now, here she sat, her hair spread out all over her shoulders, looking like...another person entirely. Not Aimée Peters, that was for certain!

But then she was no longer Miss Aimée Peters. She

had taken a new name today. That of Septimus Corcoran, Earl of Bowdon. So she was Lady Bowdon now. In a sense, Aimée Peters, with all her problems, no longer existed.

She sucked in a sharp breath. And exhaled on a sob, astonished to see tears begin to stream down her face. What had she got to cry about? She was safe now. And, best of all, hidden. Under a new name. A name nobody would connect with that humiliated girl, who had been sold to the highest bidder by her debt-ridden, drunken excuse for a father!

Another sob racked her whole body, and then another, and another. She could not hold herself in check. Sobbing helplessly, she went to her trunk and dropped to her knees to rummage for a handkerchief. And then she knelt there, holding it to her eyes while the sobs continued to rack her and the tears flowed like waters gushing from a breached dam.

'This is absurd!' she cried, getting to her feet. All the things she might have wept over, had she been that kind of a girl, were behind her now. 'Stop this, you idiot,' she chided herself as she walked up and down, up and down, alternately wrapping her arms round her waist and dabbing at her wet cheeks, as she vainly struggled to get herself back under control.

But, she gradually began to perceive, this was years and years of pent-up emotions finally finding release. She saw that her increasingly desperate circumstances had stretched her as tight as a bowstring. No wonder she had panicked the first night she had been here! She had been only one step from that state for weeks. Months. But now that she was safe, the past firmly put behind her, and she had the luxury of letting go, that was exactly what was happening.

In the midst of her tears, she hiccupped with laughter. Oh, Lord, but she was coming unwound with a vengeancc!

Captain Corcoran tightened the sash of his dressing gown, then opened his bedroom door. He had given her enough time, surely, even though she did not have a maid to help her prepare for bed?

He would knock before he went into her room, naturally. He did not want to embarrass her by walking in on her unawares. The poor girl was nervous enough about things as it was. But she *had* said she was willing to provide him with heirs. He had offered her the chance to leave and return to whatever life she'd had before she answered his advertisement. But she had not taken it.

So she was his wife now. And would be his wife in every sense of the word!

He had raised his hand to knock on her door when he heard her, pacing up and down, and sobbing as though her heart was breaking. He uncurled his clenched fist, and let it fall to his side. Hell, this was just what he had been afraid of.

How many times today had he noticed that she was having to steel herself to marry him?

She had kept her chin up, most of the time. But several little instances had alerted him to the fact that all was not well with her. The first thing to smite his conscience had been the way her face had lit up when his crew presented her with that bouquet. He saw that he had been remiss in not thinking of giving her flowers himself. It was one of those little courtesies a man should extend to his bride. These things mattered to women.

Then again, until that smile, he had not been aware

how sombre her expression usually was. And as she had stood there next to him, her features rapidly settling back into that sombre, and, yes, slightly wary expression that was the norm for her, he had become uncomfortably aware that this was not the kind of wedding most girls dreamed about. It was all very well telling himself that she must have given up any dreams of romance long ago, given that she had decided to work as a governess. That the way she cleared every plateful of food set before her proved he was rescuing her from circumstances that must have been extremely harsh. That he was, in fact, doing her a great favour by plucking her from obscurity and raising her to such an elevated position in society.

But the way he had gone about securing her compliance fell very far short of any kind of ideal.

The thing was, until he had set eyes on Miss Peters, his notional bride had only been a means to an end. When he had come into the title, and he had been made aware of his new responsibilities, it had felt very like getting a fresh set of orders from the Admiralty. Before embarking on any mission, it was a captain's duty to muster a full complement of crew. Getting hold of a wife, he had reasoned, need not be so very different to that. Hell, some of his peers accepted matches arranged by their families to women they did not care for one bit!

But just one sight of Miss Peters had knocked all his plans into a cocked hat. *Mine*, he had thought, before she had so much as uttered one word. And she had roused his protective instincts even before he had become legally responsible for her this afternoon. Yesterday, he had tended to her comfort while she slept, vowing no man should harm a hair on her head.

It tore him up inside to know that it was because of him she was weeping so bitterly now. She had screwed up every ounce of her courage to get this far. The prospect of getting three good meals a day had temporarily overcome any qualms she might have had about casting in her lot with a stranger. But now it had come to the moment when she would have to face the ordeal of having him in her bed—and she had broken down.

He strode back along the corridor, cursing quietly under his breath. He would rather face a broadside from a French frigate than go toe to toe with a weeping woman!

He had always hated Miranda's tears. By the time she had finished crying, she had always, somehow, managed to extract from him the very last thing he had wanted to give.

A proposal of marriage, for one thing. He had been going back to sea, and she had wept and clung to him, and said she could not bear to be parted from him. That her life would not be worth living…

The door bounced off the wall as he slammed into his room, strode across to the buffet and yanked the stopper from a decanter of brandy.

First of all, he reminded himself, sloshing a generous measure into two glasses, Miss Peters was not Miranda! Miranda, he had very soon learned, turned on the tears to get her own way. Miss Peters was weeping alone, behind closed doors.

And no wonder, he thought savagely, catching sight of his reflection as he stalked past the cheval glass on his way back to the bedroom door.

It would be far easier for her tonight if he was not such a gruesome-looking specimen. Though it would most likely be hard enough for her, no matter what he looked like. She had run off in a panic because she had mistakenly feared he meant to force her to become his mistress, as though she had some deep, abiding fear of intimacy.

He scowled as he stalked back along the landing, only to find his entire crew standing outside her door, listening to his wife of less than a day sobbing her heart out.

'Take yourselves off,' he growled. 'This is not your business.'

For a moment, he wondered if his crew were going to mutiny. They had trusted him completely in the engineering of this enterprise. Flung themselves into every aspect of the subterfuge necessary to get her here with an enthusiasm that had amazed him. Only now were they beginning to question his treatment of the woman.

Why should that surprise him? He was questioning it himself!

It was because of the way she was. If she had been hard faced, or petulant, she would have evoked no sympathy from any of them. But she was neither of those things. She was that rare creature, a woman who was as gracious as she was beautiful.

'I will take care of her,' he said more gently.

He vowed, there and then, not to bed her until she was more accustomed to him. It was too much, even he could see that, to expect a girl with as much natural modesty as her to suddenly open her legs just because he had put a ring on her finger.

Only once his men had dispersed did he take a deep breath, knock firmly on the door and shoulder it open.

She had been pacing the floor, but at the sight of him she checked mid-stride and turned to face him. Her whole body was quivering with distress. Her eyes were puffy, her nose red and her cheeks blotchy. In one hand she still clenched a sodden handkerchief. With the other she wiped away at tears that still coursed down her face. The sight should have revolted him, but he felt none of the disgust that Miranda's tears had always evoked. Instead, he just wanted to pull her into his arms and comfort her. But pulling her into his arms was not going to soothe her. It would only make a bad situation worse.

He would have reassured her, verbally, if only he were a man with the facility for soft words. But he was not.

'Here,' he said gruffly, thrusting one of the glasses towards her. 'Drink this.'

She shook her head. 'I don't partake of spirits—'

'It's medicinal,' he countered, pressing the glass into her hand. 'It will help, I promise you.' He tossed his own drink straight down. It went some way towards beating back the bile that was rising in his gorge.

What kind of man reduced a woman to this!

She did not think it would help at all, but he must have heard her crying, and had gone to the trouble of fetching the only remedy he could think of. So she followed his example, and gulped down the entire contents of the glass in one go.

And choked and gasped as it burned its way down her throat. How could men sell their souls for this revolting stuff?

But then she felt a warmth in her belly, which radiated outwards, bringing in its wake a kind of peaceful feeling.

'Oh, I see!' she said, regarding the empty glass with new appreciation. 'I am certainly calmer now, thank you,' she said, handing the glass back to Septimus.

Goodness, she had thought of him by his given name! She had first heard it in church today, but as yet, he had not given her permission to use it. She was amazed she had dared to even *think* of him in such a familiar way!

It was his kindness that encouraged her to be so bold. Not many men would have taken the trouble to bring her exactly what she needed, then obliged her to take it, in spite of what would have been her foolish objections. Tears welled in her eyes again, although now they were tears of gratitude as she looked at the man who today had given her both security, and a name she need no longer be ashamed of bearing.

As she looked at her stern-featured, yet innately decent husband, she felt an almost overwhelming urge to fall at his feet, take those rough, yet gentle hands in between her own and shower them with kisses.

It must be the brandy, she thought, appalled at the prospect of behaving so shamelessly with any man, no matter what he had done. Bewildered, she raised her hand to her brow. So she did not see Septimus flinch.

The brandy had stopped her crying, but she was still making agitated little movements with her hands, as though resisting the urge to push him away. And nobody could have missed that horrified look that had flitted across her face—no doubt brought about by the fact that it was their wedding night, and they were alone in her bedchamber, dressed only in their night attire.

'If I leave you alone now, will you promise you won't cry any more?' he said.

'N-no, I won't cry any more, but...'

'Then I will see you early in the morning,' he said, making for the door. 'I want you packed and ready to leave at first light.'

He had left and pulled the door closed behind him before Aimée could so much as blink. And then she just stood there, staring at the door, her mind in a whirl. Never mind leaving her alone on her wedding night— what was all this about packing and leaving at first light? To go where? She had thought they were going to live here, in Yorkshire.

She clenched her fists, as the feelings of relief and gratitude ebbed away like grain from a ripped sack.

Thank heavens she had not fallen to her knees and kissed his hands! He had made her think she was going to be safe and now it turned out he was going to take her heaven knew where!

Oh, Lord, what had she done? Begun to trust a man, that was what, she reflected bitterly. She began to pace again, but this time it was anger that drove her to restless action. Why had she not made him tell her what his plans were before she took her vows? He *had* said something about leaving the area, and meeting his grand new relations, now she came to think of it. What if he intended to travel to London? The whole point of marrying him had been tied up with living safely in obscurity in the north of England.

Oh, bother her vows. If he was going to London, then she was jolly well not going with him!

She pulled herself up short, shocked at herself for so much as contemplating such a desperate course of action. She *had* made vows, even if she had done so in a haze of misguided hope. And she could not just break vows made before God!

Not, at any rate, without first having determined whether he really was going to put her in harm's way. Had he not told her he fully expected her to question him, if she thought he was being too autocratic?

Firming her lips, she opened her door and marched out. And stopped dead. Bother! She had no idea which of the many doors on the landing led into Septimus's room.

But then she saw a flicker of light emanating from the hall; when she leaned over the banister rail, she saw Septimus enter his study and close the door behind him.

She followed him down the stairs, bitterly regretting not pausing to put on some slippers first.

She knocked on the door and slipped inside quickly, before her courage failed her. It almost did fail her when she saw her husband of less than a day, the man she already had half a mind to flee from, sitting at his chair, a decanter and a glass and his eyepatch on the desk before him. His hair was furrowed too, as though he had been repeatedly combing it with his fingers.

She was not sure how she managed to demand, 'What are you doing down here?' She eyed his half empty brandy glass askance. 'And what do you mean by telling me we are leaving The Lady's Bower tomorrow? I thought we were going to live here!'

She wrapped her arms round her waist as Septimus glared at her in silence for a few seconds before reaching for his eyepatch and drawing it on over his head. She wished she had wrapped a shawl round her shoulders before coming down here in hot pursuit of some answers. It was a distinct disadvantage, standing there barefoot and shivering in her nightgown. Oh, how she envied her husband his magnificent brocaded dressing gown. There was no fire in the grate. And the night was cold, even though the day had been so fine.

'Impulsive little thing, are you not?' he said. 'Always dashing off without adequate clothing.' But he was not going to suggest she leave and get a wrap and some kind of footwear. She was far less wary of him now they were not in a bedroom. In fact, by the looks of her, he would say she was spoiling for a fight. He got up, went to the hearth and reached for the tinderbox, knelt and struck a spark to the kindling. 'You must be absolutely frozen. Come over here,' he said, glancing at her over his shoulder. 'It won't take long for the fire to get going.'

'Do you intend to give me some answers?' she said crossly.

Answering whatever questions she had seemed as good a place to start with her as any. He had been racking his brains to think of some way he could set her at ease. But now she had come to him. Oh, not for any reason he could have wished, but it was better than nothing.

When he nodded, she stalked across the room and knelt down on the hearthrug next to him, her back rigid, her chin lifted at a mutinous angle.

'How is your ankle, by the way? You did not seem to be limping today.'

'My ankle is much better, thank you,' she said politely. Though she could not believe they were having such a mundane conversation, while she was barely decent! And mentioning her ankle made her think of the sure way his hands had glided over her skin. Her feet felt so very naked that she was obliged to tuck them under the hem of her nightgown, to hide them from his view.

'I am glad to hear it,' he said, reaching for the tongs and placing more coals on top of the kindling. 'So, what was it you wanted to ask me?'

'Why are we leaving here?'

'I only rent this place,' he said, hanging the tongs back on their hook, marvelling at the plaintive note in her voice. 'It served my purpose while I was single, but now that I am married, I need to return to Bowdon Manor and take up my duties.'

'B-Bowdon Manor?' He was the Earl of Bowdon. 'Is that your principal seat?'

So, she was worried about facing yet another dramatic change in her life. He supposed he could understand that. Perhaps it would help if he explained that the change would be for the better.

'Yes, it is. Though it is only one of many properties I now own. Should you like to see a picture of it?'

Not really. She just wanted to know how far it was from London. But he had already got up, gone to his desk and opened a drawer.

'Here it is,' he said, extracting a sheet of paper, and returning to the fireplace. He knelt down beside her, laying the picture on the hearthrug before her. 'My grandfather's brother commissioned a painting of his grand folly. This is one of the preliminary sketches. What do you think of it?'

She looked down at the pen-and-ink drawing of a massive mansion. It was rectangular, and built of stone, and looked vaguely Italian with its rotunda and many-pillared frontage.

'F-folly?' she parroted. It was a wonder he could carry on any kind of conversation when they were kneeling so close together that she could feel the heat from his body reaching hers through the flimsy material of their respective nightwear.

Contempt flickered across his face. 'The building of this elaborate mansion—' he flicked the edge of the page with one fingernail '—almost bankrupted my grandfather's older brother. And then his only surviving son, my father's cousin, made matters even worse by living a lifestyle compounding profligacy with ineptitude.'

She frowned. He had told her he was wealthy…but they were straying from the point.

'Wh-whereabouts is it, exactly?' she asked, after perusing the picture for long enough to make it seem likely she was truly interested in it for its own sake. 'Do you have a map on which you could show me?'

With a grunt, he got to his feet, went back to the desk and returned with a rolled-up chart.

'You will have to hold down the edges,' he said, taking one of her hands and placing it on a corner while he unrolled it. He held the other top corner flat with one hand, placing his knee on the bottom, leaving his right arm free.

'We are here, now,' he said, indicating a spot some miles to the east of York. 'And your new home will be here.'

His finger traced a route that did indeed go some way south of their present location. But to her immense relief, mostly it went to the west. She would not have to forget her vows and strike out on her own again!

Not immediately, she reflected, chewing on her lower lip. And perhaps, by the time he decided they ought to go to London, for the next session of Parliament, she would be able to persuade him that she loved country life so much that she simply could not bear the thought of going to town. He had spoken of making her mistress over all his properties, she recalled from their first dinner together. And the upper classes had property all over the place. Her mother had told her how, as a child, she travelled from one house to another, according to the social calendar. She could become so involved with overseeing all his holdings, there might always be an excuse for avoiding the capital.

'The nearest town is Burslem,' he said, tapping his forefinger on a small dark patch, which represented an urban area, 'which was a smallish place, until the ingenuity and industry of Josiah Wedgwood, and the coming of the canal, brought prosperity to the region.'

'Is it,' she asked with some trepidation, 'a fashionable sort of place?' Her father had told her once that if he had no luck in London, there were other fashionable watering holes in various parts of the country to which they could remove. He had mentioned Bath and Brighton, but she could not recall ever having heard him mention Burslem.

She had stopped shivering now. The coals had caught, and were giving off a steady stream of warmth, but she thought most of the reason for her physical state was due to the proximity of her husband's body. It made her feel quite shy, to be kneeling on the hearthrug, poring over a map by firelight. She glanced up at him, wondering if he was at all affected by the intimacy of the situation.

'Not in the least,' he retorted quite sharply.

She flinched, before realising that he was not answering her unspoken question at all. Though by the sternness of his features and the sharpness of his tone, he might as well have been.

'Much to the resentment of my newly acquired family. They decry the way enterprising men who have come from nothing figure so largely in the society of the area. They think themselves far above such fellows and hold themselves aloof. Breeding, to them, is of more worth than intelligence and industry,' he finished acidly.

She could hear a whole wealth of meaning behind

the bitterness to his words, but she would deal with that later. For now, it was enough to know that not only was this Burslem place nowhere near London, but also that it was not one of those places where she would be constantly worrying she might come face to face with any of the men who had connived at her ruin.

With a sigh of relief, she knelt back, inadvertently letting go of her corner of the map. It sprang shut on his fingers.

'Oh, I beg your pardon,' she said, bending forwards to unroll it again. For a moment, their fingers tangled as they sought to control the springy piece of parchment. Then he caught her hand and stayed it, letting the map furl itself into a roll. He could feel her trembling. She was still afraid of him. And no wonder.

'It does not matter,' he said, taking the risk of raising her hand to his mouth, and brushing his lips across it swiftly. 'We have finished with the map.'

'Oh?' For a moment or two, her gaze was trapped by his. His breath fanned the back of her hand. The fire crackled in the grate. She felt as though the whole room was holding its breath.

His blood pounded through his veins. All he would have to do was sweep her down on to the rug, lift the hem of her nightgown and he could have her. Right here, right now. But the way she was looking at him, wide-eyed with confusion, made her seem so very young. And vulnerable. He had sworn he would not let anyone do her any harm. And that included himself.

He dropped his gaze and let go of her hand. She had not seemed too disappointed to learn that their new home was not going to be in a more fashionable location. But the fact that she had asked at all was telling.

He had no intention of gadding off to London until he had got his estates in better order. But there was no reason why he could not give her a bit of a treat to tide her over.

'We will make a stay of a few days in Harrogate,' he said gruffly, picking up the map to give his hands something to do, 'and fit you up with a new wardrobe.'

'Oh, no…' she began. Her father *had* mentioned Harrogate in some respect. She frowned, trying to remember what it was he had said.

'Oh, yes,' he said, getting to his feet and tossing the map on to the litter of papers scattered across the surface of his desk. 'You will not want to meet the ladies currently in occupation without being properly armed with the latest fashions.'

Just then she finally recalled what her father had said. That the place might be worth considering, but only as a last resort. Only elderly invalids went there, people who could not afford the more fashionable places, such as Bath. The pickings would be slim.

She relaxed. And then admitted, 'In truth, I would not want your family to see me only in the garb which I deemed suitable for the life of a governess.'

She did not want to let him down, she realised with a sense of shock. He had taken a gamble, marrying her on such short acquaintance. The least she could do was look the part.

'You will be more than a match for them, Aimée,' he said, with a smile that made him look devilishly piratical. 'I have every confidence that you will make a very able lieutenant in this enterprise.'

His words sent a shiver of foreboding skating down her spine. He had promised her that he was not planning anything illegal, or immoral. But, judging by the sinister smile that was playing round his lips, and the terminology he had just used, he was planning *something*.

She picked up the drawing of Bowdon Manor, scrambled to her feet and followed him across the room until she stood before his desk.

'What enterprise?'

Damn him, if he had double-crossed her, vows or no vows, she would rather strike out on her own again!

Chapter Seven

He took the picture from her hands and stared at it moodily for so long that she began to wonder if he was ever going to tell her anything.

But at length he sighed, tossed the paper into a drawer and said, 'The enterprise in question…well, in a nutshell, it is becoming the Earl of Bowdon.'

Aimée felt the tension drain from her. She was so quick to suspect him, but every time it turned out that he had a perfectly good reason for acting as he did. She wrapped her arms round her waist, rubbing at her arms abstractedly. He had told her he needed a wife to fulfil his new role as Earl of Bowdon. But, given the way he had recruited her, like a new member of his crew, was it any wonder he referred to her as his lieutenant?

'I told you, did I not, that my new family have a very inflated opinion of themselves? It was quite a shock to them to discover a rough tar was the next in line for the title. Almost as much of a shock as it was to me.'

'A shock to you? What do you mean?'

'It is hard,' he said, strolling round the table and

returning to the hearth, 'to know quite where to start. The tangle goes right back to my childhood, and beyond.'

He beckoned to her. 'You had better make yourself comfortable. This is going to be a long story.'

She joined him on the hearthrug, curling her legs up so that her feet were tucked up under the hem of her nightgown.

'I grew up in obscurity,' he said, 'in a pleasant little town where my father was the doctor. My mother was the daughter of a quite prosperous tradesman. I always expected to work for my living at some trade. For various reasons, my parents decided to send me to sea as soon as they could find a ship to take me on.'

He wondered how she would react if he were to stroke her hair. It looked so soft, flowing round her shoulders, reflecting the colours of the flames as they leapt up the chimney. But if she recoiled, then all the ground he had so far gained would be lost. Better to just talk to her. Let her know she had nothing to fear from him. Let her grow accustomed to her new status as his wife.

'I assumed,' he said, 'that I would stay in the navy for the rest of my life. I showed some aptitude, which meant my promotions came with pleasing regularity. And, of course, with the war raging so fiercely, there were perhaps more opportunities than in peacetime. Do you know much about prize money?'

'No,' she admitted, stifling a yawn. The day's events must be catching up with her. Or perhaps it was the brandy. It was the only thing that could account for her peculiar urge to tell him she was sorry for misjudging him again, snuggle up against him and lay her head on his shoulder while he told her all about his childhood.

She did not think Septimus was the kind of man one snuggled up to!

'When an enemy ship is captured,' he was saying, 'a financial reward is given to the captain and crew, the captain taking the lion's share. Though it can augment a junior officer's income considerably, too, should he be fortunate enough to serve under an able captain, and be stationed where there is likely to be plenty of action. Which was the case for me. Later, when I got my own command, I was lucky enough to secure one or two prizes large enough to make me quite a rich man. Made a bit of a name for myself.'

There, she reflected, she had been correct. Her husband was not the kind of man to cuddle in front of a fire. Even as a young officer, his superiors had seen that he was the very man to station wherever the action was likely to be the hottest. By the sound of it, he'd spent the majority of his life roaring from one battle to another, and killing anyone who got in his way. She eyed his stern profile assessingly. There was nothing soft or yielding about him at all.

'I no longer had to rely so heavily on my pay, just to survive. I continued to go to sea, though, because I knew that able captains were still needed to scupper that upstart Corsican's ambitions. And also, because there was nothing in particular to keep me ashore. Not once my wife…died.'

It was ironic, he mused, that she had run off with a wealthy man only just before all that prize money started coming in. Would she have stayed with him, had she known it was within her grasp? Or would his injuries have still proved too much for her to stomach?

'So what changed?' she prompted him, after he had been brooding in silence for quite some time. There was nothing to stop him pursuing his career at sea, even if he had inherited such a grand title. It would probably just hasten his rise to the rank of Admiral.

'Oh, I received a letter,' he frowned, as though brought back to the present with a jolt. 'It informed me, in that sort of incomparable legal jargon that is particularly hard to grasp in one reading, that I had become the Earl of Bowdon. A title of which I had never heard.'

All of a sudden, she felt wide awake again.

'How is that…I mean, you must have known…?'

He shook his head. 'At first, I really believed it to be some kind of elaborate hoax, though who would have set such a thing up I was at a loss to comprehend. But eventually, investigations proved to my satisfaction that I was, indeed, descended from a noble line. My father, who was dead by then, had never spoken much about his family, except to mention there had been some unpleasantness that had resulted in a breach. It turned out that he was the younger son of a son who had been cut off from the main branch for marrying beneath him.'

Oh! thought Aimée. What a coincidence! She was the result of such an unequal liaison, though it had been her mother's family who had cut her out of their lives.

'I had known nothing of my titled relations, nor they of me, until the lawyers winkled me out of their genea-logical charts. On my next spell of leave, I went to meet them, thinking…' He shook his head.

'The family did *not* welcome me with open arms,' he said with a grimace. 'My grandfather might have married beneath him, but my own father made an even worse match. A tradesman's daughter! And as for my own wife—a wharf rat's daughter, a woman who thought marrying a junior naval officer was a step *up*—well, there was absolutely no way she would be fit to become the next Countess.'

'I thought she had died?' Aimée was beginning to wonder if the brandy was still fogging her mind. 'And was she really the daughter of a wharf rat?'

'No, of course she was not the daughter of a wharf rat. That was just the way the Dowager Countess chose to refer to her. And, though Miranda *was* dead by then, I was so angry already, after the way they had denigrated my mother and my grandmother, both of whom I was extremely fond, that I saw no reason to stoop to explain myself to that—' He bit off whatever he had been going to say.

The fog cleared. Aimée could easily imagine how angry he must have been. She had seen him lose his temper with far less provocation.

'Sadly for the family, they have no choice but to acknowledge me. I am the rightful heir. You see,' he said with a wry twist to his mouth, 'whilst my grandfather produced a healthy son, who in his turn fathered me, the more selectively bred, proper family members managed only to rear girls to adulthood. The last Earl's widow assumed that a young nephew of a cousin of hers would inherit. She had her own daughter all lined up to marry him and replace her as mistress of Bowdon Manor. She could barely manage to contain her fury on learning that my claim took precedence. Especially when I did not rush to take up my place at Bowdon Manor, but continued with my naval duties until such time as it was convenient for me to pay them a visit. Had I gone there, cap in hand, suitably grateful for the immense honour of being allowed back into the bosom of such an elevated family, things might have gone differently, I suppose.

'But the way they received me...' He shook his head.

He did not need to say any more. He had been grossly insulted. And even on such short acquaintance, she could see that his pride would have made it absolutely impossible for him to attempt to placate his newly discovered relatives.

'Matters went from bad to worse once I began to look about my new estates. I told you, did I not, that my predecessor was a spendthrift? Well, by the time I arrived on the scene, the Dowager Countess and her daughter were in severe difficulties. And the Dowager chose to lay the blame at my door, for not rushing straight there and taking up the administrative reins the moment her husband died. I admit,' he said grudgingly, 'that my long absence compounded their misfortunes, because the steward used the absence of a firm hand at the tiller to do as little as possible.

'So, there you have it,' he said, turning to her with a wry smile. 'My family despise me for my blunt manners and lowly origins, whilst I, in my turn, have been shocked at the neglect and maladministration they had permitted to go on, right under their noses. Some of my tenants are living in conditions not fit for swine!'

'Oh dear,' said Aimée faintly. He was a man who took his duties very seriously. Not just to his work, but also to his subordinates. And Jenks had said that even though he was a pressed man, he soon found life on board tolerable, because he was serving under 'Cap'n Corky'. He would not sympathise with anyone who turned a blind eye to the sufferings of their dependants, to say the least.

'But when I remonstrated with them, they tried to tell

me I had no right to criticise them, that the estate coffers were not deep enough to make any of the improvements I insisted needed to be set in train at once.' He smiled again in that rather sinister way, which made her think his humour did not stem from a very pleasant source. 'It was amazing how much less unsuitable to hold the position I became, once they discovered I was not only willing, but more than able, to dig into my own pockets. And about the same time they discovered exactly how deep my pockets are, the Dowager Countess of Bowdon began to ask a lot of searching questions about my wife. And then subtly, and sometimes not so subtly, throwing her daughter into my path.'

Aimée frowned. 'Do you think she discovered your wife had died?'

'It crossed my mind,' he admitted, 'that she might have put some kind of investigators on her trail, when she did not put in an appearance in person. Though it would not have been easy to uncover the facts. Miranda…was not living under her married name when she died.'

His mind flew back to that uncomfortable scene when her wretched father had come to him and explained she had thought it for the best. That she had not wanted to cause him more embarrassment than necessary.

Embarrassment? It was *not* embarrassment he had felt when she upped and left him for the lover who had sworn he could keep her in the lap of luxury.

'And there had been an epidemic in that town,' he forced himself to go on. 'The record-keeping would have been patchy, at best, I would think. Anyway, it seemed quite clear that should the Dowager discover the truth, nothing would stop her from going into full matchmaking mode.'

'Do you really think so?' She could not imagine anyone daring to attempt to manipulate this autocratic man.

'Oh, yes. She was already thrusting her poor daughter at me, as I have told you. In a sly sort of way. Leaving us alone together, that sort of thing.'

Aimée frowned. 'What did she hope to achieve by that?'

'Oh, I think she thought Lady Fenella might manage to smooth down some of my rough edges. Teach me how to go on. And at the very least, the next generation would stem from what she considered a proper blood line.'

'That's…outrageous! That is…if she really meant…'

'…to somehow have her own daughter set up as mistress in her place, by hook or by crook.' He made a disparaging noise in the back of his throat. 'Yes, I thought so too. Anyway, before she found out that I had no wife, and that I was actually free to marry that jellyfish of a daughter of hers, I set matters in train to equip myself with the kind of wife I would not object to having at my side.' He looked at her with such a proprietorial air she suddenly found it hard to breathe.

'An intelligent, pretty woman,' he said softly, 'with enough backbone to cope with that dreadful woman.'

She had thought having backbone was a requisite to dealing with *him*. Aimée felt a shiver run down her spine. What on earth must this Dowager be like?

'So you see, do you not, why I was reluctant to advertise openly for a wife, apart from bringing all the worst type of women crawling out of the woodwork? If poor Lady Fenella had heard that, rather than marry her, I had gone out and advertised for another female, she would have been devastated.'

A stab of something that felt remarkably like jealousy pierced Aimée to the core. He had seen nothing wrong with deceiving, bullying and coercing *her* into compliance. But in the acquisition of his convenient wife, he had done what he could to spare this Lady Fenella's blushes.

She lowered her head, twisting the material of her nightgown between agitated fingers.

He was not a cruel man. He had not set out to hurt her.

But, oh, how she wished *she* was the woman whose feelings he took into account—instead of being just a means to an end.

'Is something amiss?' he asked her.

She shook her head. 'Thank you for telling me all this,' she said stiffly. 'But I think I had better go back to bed now.'

She got to her feet and practically ran to the door. Damn! Things had been going so well. He did not know what he had said or done to make her jump like a scalded cat and run back to the sanctuary of her room.

But perhaps it was just as well. If she had stayed for much longer, he might not have been able to keep his hands off her. It was hard to forget this was his wedding night. And that, by rights, he should be in her bed by now. In her arms.

In her.

Muttering an oath, he got up, went to his desk and reached for the brandy. At least there was no embargo on that.

Aimée pushed herself up the stairs slowly, the slow throb of pain in her ankle pulsing in time with the dull ache in her heart.

Septimus regarded her only as a means to an end. She had always known that. And did she not regard him in the same light?

Well, she had to begin with. But for some reason, and, against all the odds, he was beginning to inspire a great deal of admiration in her breast. As well as rousing all sorts of feelings that, were she not married to him, she would think entirely inappropriate.

The moment she reached her room she got into bed and pulled the quilt up to her ears.

Just a means to an end, she sighed, going over the things he had told her. And the end he had in sight was to *be* the Earl of Bowdon. To the best of his not inconsiderable ability. His aims were noble, she was sure of that, even if she could not quite understand his methods yet.

She chewed on her lower lip. Only a couple of nights ago, she had lain here, wondering what her mother would have done in similar circumstances. And she knew that Lady Aurora would have reminded her, gently, that she was a Vickery. And that a Vickery always rose to the occasion. It made no difference how her husband viewed her. She owed it to herself to do her very best.

As soon as she had made that decision, she felt much better. And then it occurred to her that though Septimus might not yet be aware of it, he could not have lit on a more suitable bride for his purposes. In his advertisement, he had stipulated he wanted a woman of good birth and education. Well, her antecedents were every bit as good as his. And her mother, Lady Aurora, had taught her everything she herself had gleaned from the most exacting of governesses, as well as from mixing routinely in the most exalted company. Aimée knew all about the niceties of seating people at dinner parties according to their station in life, and the correct depth to curtsy to a bishop or a duke…

And she had the requisite backbone Septimus had demanded.

There was absolutely no reason why they could not make this marriage work. She already admired him greatly, as well as finding him attractive. And while he had been telling her about his childhood, she had felt as though they shared a common bond. They had both grown up in straitened circumstances, in spite of coming from noble parentage. She could even understand why he had employed a little subterfuge in getting her to The Lady's Bower.

Though she hoped that Septimus did not want her to pretend to be his first wife. He had not been very clear about what he wanted his new family to believe about that. Not that she would mind telling a *few* untruths, if the occasion warranted. She was well used to being economical with the truth. How would she have evaded her father's creditors, or hung on to her virtue for so long, without employing the occasional white lie? Sometimes, the end really did justify the means. Only look at the extreme lengths she had gone to, in order to preserve her virtue! She had stolen Lord Matthison's money and consorted with brothel-keepers and forgers in her determination to escape.

But telling an outright lie, or posing as somebody else, was another matter entirely.

Surely, once she managed to tell him about her background, he would see that it would be far better to let everyone know the truth. She chewed at her lower lip.

How did one drop that kind of thing into the conversation? Telling him about her grandfather would sound as though she was boasting, and as for admitting to her sordid descent into the fringes of the criminal underworld…

She shivered and pulled the quilt up higher. No, she was not ready to reveal anything of her past yet. Besides, he did not seem to be interested in it.

Much better to win his respect by showing him what she was made of. By being exactly what he wanted her to be. An able lieutenant at his side as he battled the doughty Dowager who reigned at Bowdon Manor.

She awoke early next morning to the sound of Nelson tapping firmly on her bedroom door. She blinked and sat up, pushing her plaits over her shoulder.

'Come in!' she called, hitching her blankets up to a more decorous level as the burly man shouldered open the door and brought in her breakfast tray.

She had lain awake for some time the night before, wondering if her new husband meant to start trying to produce an heir straight away.

But he had not come to her room.

It was a little lowering to think he had preferred a lonely vigil with a brandy bottle than her company on their wedding night, but then, this was not exactly a normal marriage, was it? He had no strong feelings towards her. How could he? They were virtually strangers.

She breakfasted, washed and dressed with an efficiency born of years of practice. And by the time Nelson returned, to ask how long it would take her to be ready to set out, she was already packed and buckling the straps on her trunk.

* * *

Well before nightfall, she was unpacking that same trunk in a comfortable inn in Harrogate.

In a separate room from her husband's.

Aimée knew she was not unattractive to the male of the species. She had been fending off would-be seducers since the day of her mother's funeral. So it was rather ironic to find that the one man she would willingly have taken to her bed seemed to be in no hurry to share it!

In other ways, though, over the next few days, he played the part of doting groom to the hilt. He spent hours uncomplainingly escorting her to the various outfitters Mr Jago had already ascertained were skilled enough to provide a wardrobe suited to her new station in life. He positively encouraged her to choose the most expensive materials and have them made up in the showiest styles. It might have gone to her head, had she not noticed that, when the new outfits began to arrive and she went to show him what they looked like on her, he barely raised his head from the papers that were always strewn across his desk.

'Capital,' he would say, or 'Just the ticket'. And once, impatiently, 'Yes, yes, every bit the Countess. Well done.'

After that, she had returned to her room feeling deflated. She had begun to think he enjoyed treating her to the new clothes. How could she have lost sight of the fact that he was just dressing her to look the part he wanted her to play?

And then, after they had been in town for the better part of a week, he declared she had done quite enough shopping and it was high time they got under way.

'There are urgent matters awaiting my attention at Bowdon Manor,' he snapped.

Well, she knew that! Was that not the whole point of marrying her, so that he could return, and begin to unravel the mess his predecessor had left behind?

She stalked off to her room and packed, seething with resentment. He had spoken to her as though she had *wanted* to buy so much stuff. As though she was deliberately lingering when he was impatient to be elsewhere. Men! She huffed, slamming the lid of one of her trunks shut. He was the one who had insisted she buy new clothes! But was that not typical? The only consistent thing about men was their inconsistency!

She dropped to her knees to buckle the straps. Married one week, and already he was shifting the blame for anything that went wrong on to her shoulders. She jerked the strap tight, admitting to herself that she would not be feeling so aggrieved if he had shown a little interest in her. If he had, even once, attempted to kiss her. In fact, she was beginning to wonder if she might have imagined the heated look he had given her the night she had agreed to marry him. *She* had felt a *frisson* of something, that was certain. But now it looked as though the attraction was all on her side.

He had not minced his words the night he had carried her back from the woods, she recalled on a shaft of pain. He had told her in no uncertain terms that she was too thin, bedraggled and plain to rouse any lust in him.

He had gone ahead and married her, because she had gone to him and more or less begged him to change his mind.

But he *had* said he wanted children. Had been most insistent on that point.

* * *

'Or have you changed your mind?' she blurted that night after sitting through another supper, in another inn, eaten in virtual silence.

He looked up at her with a frown. 'Changed my mind about what?'

'About the nature of our marriage.' She had not meant to say anything. She had meant to try to just fit in with whatever he wanted. But they would be reaching Bowdon Manor the next day, and she was no nearer understanding what might be expected of her once they got there than she had been on her wedding day. How was she to fit in with what he wanted, when she did not know what it was?

'Is this to be a marriage in name only, after all?'

He went very still. 'Is that what you wish?'

'No, oh, no!'

How could he think that? Had she somehow made him think she would not welcome his advances? But she had told him to his face that she was quite willing to provide him with heirs.

Yes, a little voice whispered in the back of her mind, you may have *said* that, but actions speak louder than words. Perhaps he cannot forget that you ran out into the woods, flinched from his touch when he had you on that bed, actually cringed in terror at one point…

Oh, no! How could she convince him that far from being afraid of his touch, she was growing impatient for it?

She could think of only one way.

Nervously, she stood up. Naturally, Septimus got to his feet as well.

She smiled at him as she went round the table. Looked up at him coyly, through her eyelashes, the way she had observed women doing to signal readiness to the male of their choosing.

His response was not very encouraging—he looked puzzled.

She must not be getting this…flirting, quite right! Well, she had never done anything but keep men at bay until now. She was bound to not be very good at it. She would just have to act more boldly.

'Septimus,' she said, looping her arms round his neck. 'You do not need to worry that I am afraid of you any more. You have been so very kind to me this week,' she said and, rather more daringly, reached up and pressed a kiss against his cheek.

He made a strange noise in the back of his throat, and then, at last, he turned his head so that his lips met hers.

Aimée gasped when he grabbed her and hauled her up hard against his body. Every point at which they made contact felt warm and tingly. Her soft breasts, pressed against his firm chest, her quivering thighs against the solidity of his. Oh, this felt good! She could not believe how good, for men had caught and held her like this once or twice before and pressed their slobbering mouths against hers, filling her with revulsion, and the overwhelming urge to escape.

Septimus did not slobber. His mouth was firm yet insistent, as he expertly prised her lips apart. Her knees buckled when he plunged his tongue between her parted lips and began to explore the inside of her mouth. And far from wanting to escape, her instinctive reaction was to cling to him. Tightly.

His hands traced the curve of her spine, leaving a trail of warm…yearning in their wake. When they came to rest against the upper curve of her bottom, a wave of sensation so strong surged through her that her entire body shuddered.

And suddenly, with an oath, he thrust her roughly away.

'Enough of this!' he growled, stalking to the door and yanking it open.

Aimée reeled, one hand pressed to lips that still tingled with the power of his kiss, staring at him with shocked eyes.

'Oh, but—'

'Do not say another word, madam!' he snarled, holding up his hand as though warding off a blow. 'It will not be like this between us!'

Septimus strode through the door, slamming it shut behind him. She had fluttered her eyelashes at him, puckered up her lips, and he had been helpless to resist. He had been torn between falling to his knees in gratitude or ripping off her clothes and falling on her! The tide of lust that had swept through him the minute he had felt her lips part under his had been so strong, so primal, that, for a few seconds, his mind had ceased to function altogether.

He entered his bedroom, went across to a side table and, with shaking hands, wrenched the stopper off a decanter of brandy. The worst of it was, he suspected this show of interest was a direct result of his generosity towards her this week. And, dammit, he'd suffered through one marriage where his wife only granted her favours in return for gifts! But at least the horrible suspicion that she was behaving like Miranda dealt with his painful arousal.

Could a husband not just be generous because he wanted to make his wife smile? Did it all have to be reduced to a sordid commercial transaction between them? He had not thought Aimée had the soul of a whore!

And what had there been in his behaviour to make her think he was the kind of man who would expect that of her? Going shopping had just been a way of spending time with her. So that they could get to know each other.

So that, when *he* decided the time was right...

He downed his drink in one go.

The trouble was, it would be the right time for him *all* the time. The change in her, when she had come tripping into his makeshift study, in one of the gowns she had chosen! Well, it was so startling that it was all he could do not to gape at her with his tongue hanging out. He had no notion how she had done it, but somehow the clothing she had picked out had accentuated her beauty. She looked so delicious that he had wanted to leap across the desk and ravish her on the spot.

And she was far too innocent to indulge in that kind of behaviour, in broad daylight. Though with each day that passed, it was growing increasingly difficult to maintain the self-control on which he prided himself.

It was feeling her shudder when he had ground his throbbing erection against her belly that had brought him back to his senses. He had been on the verge of confirming her very worst assumptions. Getting his money's worth out of her, right across the dining table, whilst she was having to steel herself to go through with it. Just as she'd had to steel herself to go through with the wedding.

And afterwards, no doubt, when she'd come to her senses, she would have broken down and wept again. Just as she had on their wedding night.

* * *

Septimus had calmed down considerably by the morning. He knew he would have to go and apologise for shouting at her. He should not have repudiated her misguided attempt—to reward him, he supposed— quite so roughly. He had upset her, storming out like that, when all she had been guilty of was trying to make the best of a circumstance he had imposed on her.

Aimée was a plucky little thing. And she meant well. Yes, he was sure she had no intention of insulting him by offering her body in return for what she must have seen as his generosity.

He would apologise for pawing at her like some ravening beast while he was at it, and make it quite clear she had no need to do anything she found unpal- atable. Explain that he would wait until she was more accustomed to him. His proposal had come as a shock to her; she'd had serious misgivings about taking the plunge, and, once she had said yes, he had rushed her to the altar before she had a chance to change her mind again. He was not going to rush her into anything else. Particularly not once he had recognised how highly she prized her virtue. Dammit, she had run out into the night in just the clothes she stood up in, because she had mistaken his clumsily-worded proposal for the worst kind of proposition!

He only hoped, once he had made it all clear, they could make a fresh start.

He knocked on the door of her room, twitching his neckcloth into place. He did not think he had felt so unsure of himself since he had been a young midship- man, sent to meet the captain of his very first ship.

She came and opened the door herself, her cheeks colouring when she saw who it was. He supposed that was only to be expected, after the way he had left things the night before. Before he could say a word, she had turned away from him and returned to the packing of her trunk, which his arrival had interrupted.

No tears and sulks and moping about in bed for his Aimée! He had noted before that she was always up and busy quite early, and was always efficient with her packing. He liked that about her. Some women, he had heard tell, made a great production about moving to a new place, but not her.

'I need to apologise,' he began, then found something lodged in his throat as she bent to retrieve something from the bed. The silk of her gown had draped provocatively over her delectable rear end, making speech quite impossible for a moment or two.

Eventually he managed to look away and focus on the jumbled pile of belongings that lay on the bed, to distract himself from the base urges that were surging through him. And form the words, 'I should not have spoken to you so roughly last night.'

She straightened up, and turned to look at him in surprise, at the very same moment he noticed a book that she must have borrowed from the library at The Lady's Bower.

'You do not mean to pack this, I hope?' he said, going to pick it up.

'Well, yes, I do.'

'I am sorry, Aimée, but you cannot keep it. I told you that the place is only leased, did I not?' He felt a surge of irritation that he had to deal with this minor issue, when there was a much more crucial matter he wanted to deal with. 'I suppose I should have explained that many of the items there belong to the owners, not myself, including nearly all the books in the library. I am afraid we shall have to return it.'

'Yes, of course,' she said, 'but I may keep it for a day or so, may I not, and send it back when, um…'

'It does not do to put off little tasks like this. Once put aside, they easily get forgotten. And I would not abuse my tenancy by depleting the library of books that may very well have some sentimental value to the owners.'

He actually had his hand on the book when she darted forwards and tried to snatch it up. Between the pair of them, somehow, the book slithered from both their grasps, and landed with a thud on the floor.

'What the…?'

From between the yellowed pages, half-a-dozen flowers fluttered to the bare boards of the inn floor.

She dropped to her knees, gathering them up with her head bent, though he could see the dull flush on her cheeks.

'I only took the book so that I could press some flowers between its pages,' she muttered. 'Here,' she said, standing up, and thrusting the book into his hands, before dropping to her knees again to gather up the sorry-looking specimens of flora.

'Who has been giving you flowers?'

'Your crew!' she said tartly. 'Don't you remember?' Her eyes flashed angrily. 'Nobody has ever given me flowers before, and it was such a lovely gesture that I wanted to preserve the moment…'

She blinked, got up and spun away from him, but not before he caught the sheen of tears in her eyes.

'It was quite ridiculous of me…' she paused to swipe away something from her face '…to indulge in such sentimental nonsense when this is just a b-business arrangement. You have made it perfectly clear that I am nothing more than a means to an end…and that is perfectly f-fine…'

'Aimée,' he groaned, taking her by the shoulders and turning her towards himself. 'Don't cry…'

He could not believe how badly this had all gone wrong. He had come in here to make a fresh start and ended up making her cry.

'I am not crying,' she retorted, pulling herself out of his embrace. Indeed, she was not. The sparkle in her eyes now was one of anger.

'Keep your stupid book,' she said, flinging up her chin. 'And your stupid flowers, too.' He found a soggy mass being pressed into his hands. 'Better be rid of them now, than…' She spun away again, her breathing ragged as she tried to master herself.

He beat a hasty retreat. Words would do her no good. Besides, he was clearly completely useless at apologising.

He went to his own room and cast the book on his desk. Then spread out the mangled relics of her wedding bouquet thoughtfully. Who would have guessed, after the way he had treated her, that she would have *wanted* a keepsake of their wedding day?

But she clearly did.

A smile spread from deep within him, making his whole being feel unaccountably weightless. He had found a way to reach her.

It was some time before he was ready to return to her room, but he felt that, all things considered, he had not made a bad fist of making some form of reparation for the hurt he had inadvertently caused her. She was sitting on the bed when he went in, her hands clasped in her lap, her expression as closed as her trunks. He eyed the neatly bound cords, and hoped she had not as efficiently shut him out.

'Is it time to leave yet?' she said coldly.

'Not quite,' he said, closing the door behind him. 'I have something for you.'

She eyed the book he held out towards her with suspicion.

'What is that?'

'The *History of the Present War with Spain and Portugal*.'

Not surprisingly, she looked baffled.

'It was the only book I had to hand. I suppose most men would have had something more suitable, like a book of verse, but, Aimée, you have not married a sentimental man. Look,' he said, flicking it open to one of the pages where he had carefully set one of her discarded flowers. 'I do not know much about pressing flowers. But you are welcome to use this volume, if it serves the purpose.'

'Oh,' she said, some of the frostiness melting from her face as she took it from his outstretched hands.

'And since you mentioned that nobody had ever given you flowers, I should like you to accept this, too.'

He held out a dog rose he had plucked from the plant that rambled over the inn's back porch. It was a poor specimen compared with the full-blown blooms his crew had purloined from Sir Thomas's well-stocked ornamental borders. And the puzzled expression on her face as she examined the puny little flower suddenly made him feel like an utter fool. What kind of woman would be pleased with what was little more than a weed, wrenched from the garden of a public inn? He should have sent out for an elegant little posy, made up with skill by some florist…

But then, to his amazement, her features softened, and she reached out to take the rather ragged little flower from his hand.

'Thank you,' she murmured, slipping the rose at random between the pages of Theophilus Camden's opus.

'And another thing…' He cleared his throat. 'I do *not* want our marriage to be in name only. I thought I had made it clear that as head of this family, part of my duty is to produce heirs. Which I very much want to do.' Damn, this was not coming out right! 'With you. I want…'

She frowned in evident bewilderment. 'But you have never attempted to…that is, you do not seem to find me very attractive. When I tried to show you that I wanted…' Her cheeks went bright red.

He sat down on the bed next to her, took her hand and kissed it fervently. 'You are very brave to try to inure yourself to me, Aimée, but remember, I heard how you wept on our wedding night. I am not a brute who would demand my rights while you are still trying to accustom yourself to being married…'

Oh! So *this* was why he had been so restrained with her since they had got married. This was why he had turned into a polite stranger, a man who was so very far removed from the blunt, autocratic man she had first encountered. He was trying to give her time to get used to him!

And no wonder she had not recognised his behaviour for what it was. She had never witnessed any man acting so selflessly in her entire life. Nobody had ever put her feelings before their own. Not even so mistakenly.

'Septimus! It was not that, I was not upset!'

'Do not lie to me, Aimée,' he said sternly. 'I heard you crying…'

'Oh, yes, I was crying. But what I meant was that it was not because I was upset.' She grasped both his hands hard, and looked up at him earnestly. 'You have no idea…the way I have had to live…' She checked herself. Now was not the time to tell him about any of that.

'S-suddenly it was all over. I was safe. I had been so scared, for such a long time. And it did not really hit me until I looked at the ring on my finger that I really was married. I was not on my own any more. I did not have to hold myself together any more…and I let go, and it all came out. All the years of anxiety, and making do, and dodging and hiding…'

He reached out and ran one finger along the curve of her cheek. 'So why did you look so appalled when I came in and gave you that brandy? You were like a cat on hot bricks…'

'Oh, dear.' She gulped. 'I see I am going to have to confess…' Her cheeks turned pink, but she kept on looking him straight in the face as she explained, 'I am not used to brandy. I was shocked at the effect it had on me. You see, I…' she gulped '…I experienced the most humiliating urge to fall at your feet and kiss them. Because, thanks to you, I am respectable. Beyond the reach of—' She shut her mouth abruptly and averted her eyes.

'It is not my feet I should like you to kiss,' he murmured.

'No, I know,' she said mournfully. 'You do not want me to kiss you at all…'

'The hell I don't!'

'But when I tried to, you pushed me away!'

It was his turn to look uncomfortable. 'I thought you were trying to repay me for the things I had bought you. I thought you were forcing yourself to go through with a task you found repulsive...'

'No! Oh, no! I just wanted...' Her voice trailed away.

'Did you? Truly?'

She nodded shyly.

His brows knit in a ferocious scowl. 'Do you mean to tell me we have been at cross-purposes all this time?'

She reached up her hand to smooth away the scowl. 'Well, now that we have that sorted out, perhaps we need not waste any more time,' she suggested timidly.

'Oh, God, yes,' he growled and took her in his arms.

He felt no need to hold anything back this time. Not now that he knew she was not unwilling. Had been willing, since their wedding night. And, as he kissed her, caressed her, it did not escape his notice that she was, albeit inexpertly, kissing him back. Touching him all over with inquisitive little hands. This did not feel like gratitude for the things he had bought her, a mechanical performance designed to pleasure him. She was with him every step of the way!

Before very long he was no longer thinking anything. He was just holding and squeezing, unbuttoning and panting, and giving little groans as skin found skin, and somehow they were lying full length on the bed, with him half on top of her, their clothing disarrayed and their legs intertwined.

Then somebody knocked on the door.

'You ready to leave, miss?' came Nelson's voice.

'Dammit!' Septimus raised his head and glared at the door. 'Not yet!' he bellowed. Aimée had tensed, so he cupped her cheek with the palm of his hand and said gently, 'No, my sweet, do not think I am about to hastily consummate our marriage now, with my men waiting outside to load your luggage into the coach!'

She looked crestfallen for a second, but then he saw the practical side of her nature reassert itself. She sat up, straightened her skirts and patted her hair back into place.

He got to his feet and pulled her into his arms for one more lingering kiss, not stopping until she was limp and quivering.

'Tonight,' he growled, 'I promise you, nothing and nobody will stop me. I shall not rest until I have made you my wife…' he kissed her again '…completely.'

Chapter Eight

Oh, Aimée wished he had not said that! Not that she was not glad they were going to consummate their marriage. But now all she could think about was what the coming night would bring!

It was extremely hard to sit beside him in the close confines of the hired post chaise and four all day and behave demurely. She could not stop darting surreptitious glances at him. The fact that they were both fully clothed was absolutely no impediment to the explicit nature of her thoughts. She had a pretty good idea what the body beneath was like. She had guessed he must be in splendid form, after the ease with which he had picked her up and carried her in his oak-like embrace all the way from the woods. And then, this morning, her hands had explored the breadth of those shoulders, felt the firm tone of his back and his stomach. Yes, she sighed, she knew *exactly* how hard were the muscles concealed beneath those coat sleeves.

But though he was so strong, he had the capacity to be very gentle, too. When he had bandaged her ankle, he had not been in the least bit rough. She sighed dreamily. She was absolutely certain he would put all that leashed strength to very good purpose tonight!

She knew she ought to have taken more note of the grounds as their carriage approached the house. But when he had turned to her and said something about gravel driveways, she was far more interested in watching the way his lips moved than attending to his words. His kisses had been so exciting!

And when he leaned past her, to open the door, and she caught the scent of his skin, it shot her straight back to those few glorious moments when they had been lying, all tangled together, in a writhing mass of mutual passion on top of that hotel bed.

But then they were standing in a lofty marble-pillared hallway, with liveried staff lined up on each side and finally something her husband said jolted her back to the here and now.

'Ah! Lady Fenella! How good of you to come and make my wife welcome.'

A short, square-faced girl in yellow satin was standing at the head of the stairs, her round eyes sliding across Septimus's features with evident discomfort before coming to rest upon Aimée. She smiled hesitantly and began to glide gracefully down the stairs.

Though she felt half-inclined to dislike her after what Septimus had told her about her mother's plans in her regard, Aimée smiled back politely.

Lady Fenella held out both her hands, and said, 'You must be so thirsty after your journey. Mama and I are just having tea in the gold sitting room. Won't you come and join us?'

'Shall we?' Aimée asked, glancing up at her husband.

He gave a curt nod.

'Tea would be most welcome, Lady Fenella,' he said, causing the girl to visibly sag with relief.

As they followed her up the stairs, Aimée thought she could see why the crew had rather unkindly named her Frog Face. The rather plump young woman was not ugly, she would not go so far as to say that. But she had scarcely any chin, her mouth was on the wide side, and her muddy-coloured eyes were somewhat protuberant.

And nobody with that skin tone, she decided cattily, should ever wear that particular shade of yellow!

It did blend in rather well with the décor of the room she led them to, though. The gold sitting room was done out in greens and yellows that must have looked spectacular when new, but now the silk wall hangings were faded to a muted mustard colour. The curtains were of no discernible shade whatsoever. And she could not decide whether there had once been patterns on the upholstery that had now faded, or whether they had been plain and become stained with use. In any case, wherever Lady Fenella stood, she was camouflaged so well that if she made no sudden movements, she was in danger of disappearing altogether.

'M-Mama, they are here. That is…' Lady Fenella floundered to a halt under the withering glare of the woman sitting on a sagging sofa that was made comfortable, if Aimée was any judge, only by the massive assortment of cushions piled upon it.

She was, very clearly, Lady Fenella's mother—the facial features were so markedly similar. Except that the passage of time had made everything slide and pucker until it was not a frog she resembled, but a rather irritable pug dog.

'I can see they are here!' she snapped. Then, having

run her eyes contemptuously over Aimée, she turned to Septimus and said, 'So *this* is your wife?'

'Yes. My bride. Lady Bowdon.'

The fat little woman on the sofa seemed to swell to twice her size with indignation. But then the way Septimus had placed such emphasis on Aimée's new title had seemed deliberately antagonistic.

'I do hope…' Lady Fenella interjected, turning towards Aimée with an air of desperation, 'you will be happy with the arrangements we have made for your stay here, my lady.'

'Of course she will be!' snapped the Dowager Countess. 'She has the suite that belongs to the lady of the house. The very suite I myself occupied when I came here as a bride!'

Aimée reflected that the tradition of placing the new bride in the suite occupied by the lady who had formerly held the position of Countess of Bowdon was not a very good one.

Nor had she demanded it be observed. So there was no need for the woman to glare at her as though she had ousted her from her position. Or was it that she was daring her to have the effrontery not to like the rooms?

Mentally, she shrugged, facing the Dowager's glare with her head held high, her hands unconsciously curling into fists at her side.

This woman hated her. Hated the mere thought of her. And there was nothing she would ever be able to do to win her round.

All she could do was stand her ground.

'Fenella!' the Dowager finally barked, when, at long last, it became obvious to all she was not going to intimidate Aimée. 'Take this person off to her rooms. I need to have a few words with his lordship.'

'Yes, Mama,' replied the girl, looking distinctly harried. She scuttled over to the door, from where she shot Aimée a beseeching look.

Aimée had been somewhat baffled when Septimus had told her that the Dowager was pushing her daughter at him. She had said nothing at the time, but she could hardly believe that any gently reared girl with an ounce of self-esteem would fall in with such a plan. But now it flashed into her mind that at one point Septimus had referred to her as a jellyfish. And she could see why. This girl lacked any sort of backbone. Not only did she meekly obey whatever her mother told her, but she somehow gave the impression that she would be quite happy to float along with whatever anyone with a stronger will decided for her, in just the same way as those almost invisible creatures drifted along on the surface of the waves wherever the strongest current carried them.

Though she felt truly sorry for the girl, she turned to Septimus and asked him, 'Do *you* wish me to leave you to discuss your business?'

Septimus merely gave her a brief smile and a nod.

She made her curtsy to the seething Dowager and made her way across the room to where Lady Fenella stood quivering in the open door.

'I am so sorry about Mama,' Lady Fenella breathed as soon as they were safely outside in the corridor. 'She is not in the best of moods today. I am sure she did not mean to be so rude.'

Aimée was equally as sure that she had, but kept that opinion to herself. 'Perhaps we can have some tea sent up? Which I am sure I shall enjoy all the more in peace and quiet.'

Lady Fenella had been leading Aimée along the corridor, but at this, she whirled round and said earnestly, 'Oh, yes, indeed! I do so dislike it when Mama and his lordship have one of their discussions. They say such unpleasant things to each other and become so heated. Sometimes, they even shout!' She wrapped her arms about herself. 'I do so hate it when people shout,' she said miserably. 'It gives me the headache.'

Aimée attempted a sympathetic smile.

'And his lordship has such a very loud voice, *all* the time,' said Lady Fenella, unwinding her arms and setting out along the corridor again. 'Even when he does not mean to, he frequently makes me jump out of my skin. I dare say it comes from spending all those years at sea, bellowing orders at rough sailors…' She shuddered.

Really, thought Aimée irritably, the Dowager must be all about in her head to think a poor little dab of a girl like this could smooth off her husband's rough edges! Or, indeed, make any impression on him whatever.

'Oh, dear! I do beg your pardon. I should not be saying such things to *you*. Please say I have not offended you!'

'Not in the least,' she said coolly. 'I admire my husband very much. He was an excellent example to his men of the kind of gallantry that has made our navy so very successful.'

'Oh, yes!' Lady Fenella clasped her hands together at her breast. 'It was so very brave of him, to return to his duties after suffering such a terrible injury. To think of those dreadful Frenchmen firing their cannon at his ship like that, and t-t-tearing out his eye!'

Aimée refrained from pointing out that British seamen fired their own cannon straight back, and to rather more effect, given that England now ruled the waves.

Lady Fenella came to an abrupt halt outside a door and grabbed hold of the handle. 'Every time I look at his face, and imagine how much it must have hurt him, my stomach turns right over. D-did you nurse him?'

'No,' said Aimée, choosing her next words very carefully. Though she did not want to tell outright lies, Septimus had indicated he did not really want this girl to know the exact circumstances of their marriage.

'Sadly, that task fell to another,' she said, then ruthlessly changed the subject before Lady Fenella had a chance of discovering that she had not even the vaguest of notions during which action he had sustained the devastating injury. 'Is this my room?' She indicated the doorknob to which Lady Fenella was still clinging.

'Oh! Yes!' She flung open the door, and led the way into a room that was shrouded in gloom. 'Oh, dear, the maid should really have come in and drawn the curtains this morning.'

As she fluttered across to the bell pull by the fireplace, Aimée strode across to the window and yanked the curtains open herself.

'I am so sorry,' gulped Lady Fenella as a cloud of dust burst from the yards of faded velvet. 'We had so little time to prepare. N-no idea of the day you would arrive…'

Aimée turned to her, brows raised. 'But his lordship must have informed you, last time he visited, that he intended to bring his bride here. Surely that was the signal to begin making preparations?'

Lady Fenella looked ready to sink through the rather motheaten hearthrug on which she stood. 'I do not expect you to understand, but the thing is, Mama got

it into her head that you would not come. I do not
know why!'

Aimée thought she did. Septimus had told her that
the Dowager might have begun nosing about into his
first wife's background. Had the woman discovered he
was a widower, after all? If so, she would have thought
he was bluffing when he told her he was bringing his
bride with him this time.

Oh, dear! No wonder she had looked so furious when
Aimée had walked into the faded glory of her sitting
room on his arm.

'Never mind,' she said, flinging up the sash to let in
some fresh air. 'I will not be needing to use the room
straight away.'

When Lady Fenella frowned her confusion, Aimée
added, 'I shall be sharing his lordship's bed, you see.'

Lady Fenella blushed crimson.

Aimée hid her amusement by going over to the wardrobe, opening the door and peering inside. The floor
was littered with dead moths.

'I will need somewhere to store my clothes, though.'

'O-of course!'

Right on cue, there came a knock on the door and
Nelson strode in with one of her trunks balanced on
his shoulder.

'Thank heavens,' said Aimée. 'I am supposed to be
using these rooms, but they are in a dreadful condition. Do you think you can get a fire lit, so that at least
the place may air out a little? And find somebody to
clean out the cupboards? And the drawers,' she added.
'I suspect they may be harbouring all kinds of creepy
crawlies.' She was loathe to offer her beautiful, brand
new clothes up to all those hungry little jaws.

He nodded. 'I'll see to it. Me and the lads will have the place spick and span in no time.'

It was only once he had left that she noticed Lady Fenella had shrunk into a corner and was staring at her wide-eyed with admiration.

'H-how can you bring yourself to give orders to that great hulk of a man?'

'Because he is Captain…that is to say, his lordship's servant, of course.'

'Y-yes, but would it not be more…appropriate for you to have a maid to look after you? To do your hair? And dress you? And launder your things?'

'It has occurred to me more than once, just lately, that now I am married to an Earl, I should engage somebody. Although I have never employed anyone before…'

'What, never?'

'No.' She laughed. 'I have never had so many clothes that I needed somebody to launder them for me… Perhaps…could you recommend somebody who would know what to do for me?'

'M-me?' Lady Fenella's plump white hand fluttered to her throat.

'Well, you have lived here all your life, have you not? And you know all the staff, and what their capabilities are.'

She saw the remark sink into Lady Fenella's brain and work a transformation on her entire demeanour.

'Yes,' she said, 'I *could* help you. And I shall!'

For a moment she looked so triumphant, Aimée would not have been surprised had she added, 'So there!'

A maid arrived then with the tea tray, which Lady Fenella directed her to place on a low table before a faded sofa. Then she sat down and kept up a stream of chatter while Aimée steadily cleared her plate.

As Aimée had already guessed, she had spent all her life at the Manor, excepting for the two occasions she had visited London for the Season. It was easy to nudge the conversation away from her own past and back to Lady Fenella's extremely restricted existence, whenever she ventured into dangerous territory. It was as though she had never had anybody willing to sit and listen to her before.

'Oh, how I have rattled on,' she exclaimed as the clock on the mantel struck four. 'I must go and change for dinner. It would never do to be late!' She leapt to her feet. 'But I have enjoyed meeting you so much.' To Aimée's surprise, Lady Fenella bent down and kissed her cheek. 'I just know we are going to be great friends!' she said and practically skipped out of the room.

Aimée slumped back into the cushions and blew out a gust of breath. The way Lady Fenella had declared they would be friends was the kind of thing a little girl would say, not a grown woman!

Though Aimée was not so sure anything would come of that. She had the feeling the Dowager would disapprove of her daughter fraternising with the enemy, so to speak.

She pushed herself to her feet and went to prepare for dinner. Not that she cared for herself, but somehow she knew that Lady Fenella would bear the brunt of the Dowager's displeasure, should she be late. She smiled at herself. How easy it was to slip into the role of protector when it came to Lady Fenella. She supposed this must have been how Septimus had felt about her on his last visit. She could now see exactly why Septimus had not wanted to insult her by going straight out and openly advertising for a wife. The poor girl had quite enough to contend with.

She had no difficulty getting changed without the assistance of a maid. In spite of the Harrogate modiste's protests, she had had the fastenings of all her gowns situated so that she could manage them herself.

A butler came to escort her down to the gilded saloon where, he informed her in a not unfriendly manner, the family was in the habit of gathering before dinner. She supposed she ought not to have been surprised to find only the Dowager and Lady Fenella there. It might be their habit to sit there before dinner, but she could not see Septimus bowing to anyone else's conventions, not unless it suited him.

'Come, girl, and sit by me!' said the Dowager from her sofa. 'And tell me all about yourself. I must admit, I was pleasantly surprised when I heard you speak earlier. I had thought your voice would be quite coarse. Have you had elocution lessons, perchance?'

Aimée smiled serenely as she sashayed across the room. The Dowager must have deliberately separated her from her husband, assuming that without him there to protect her, she would be able to prise her open like an oyster. From the remark about her diction, it sounded as though Septimus had not yet informed the Dowager she was his second wife. She glanced at Lady Fenella, bearing in mind Septimus's wish that she not be put to the blush.

'Oh, no more than any young lady,' she replied.

Thank heaven for her mother's rigorous training, which enabled her to maintain her poise no matter what the provocation. And, ironically, her father's own example. The trick, he had taught her at a very young age, when in a ticklish situation, was to avoid answering any questions directly. Imply much. Confirm nothing.

And, when all else failed, turn the conversation back upon the interrogator.

This last worked like a charm. The Dowager was the kind of self-absorbed woman who naturally assumed everyone else would find her fascinating.

By the time Septimus arrived, she had learned a little about the Dowager's girlhood in Sussex, a good deal about the brilliance of her Season, and far more than she had wished to hear about the foibles and failings of her late husband.

The Dowager had not even managed to discover her maiden name!

The verbal duel would have continued throughout dinner, had Aimée been capable of keeping up her end.

But the moment Septimus had entered the room, everyone else faded to the periphery of her consciousness, for the look he sent her way was so smouldering, it was all she could do not to suggest they skip dinner and go straight up to bed.

The Dowager had to content herself with maintaining a flow of small talk while the servants efficiently served an excellent meal. Aimée paid scant attention to it. Septimus was sitting directly opposite her, and all she had to do was raise her eyes from her plate to be able to drink her fill of him.

He was so...manly, she sighed. Vibrant, and vital and virile. She could just picture him, striding about the quarterdeck, bellowing commands to the myriad minions who rushed to obey him. Standing firm under a hail of cannon fire as the deck splintered all around him. She noted that Lady Fenella avoided looking directly at him and recalled her saying that the sight of his ruined face made her stomach turn over.

It did not have that effect on *her* at all! On the contrary, the visible proof that he had fought and bled for his country made her go all weak-kneed with admiration for his bravery. And made her totally aware of how very masculine he was.

There was, suddenly, such a deep silence that it woke her from her daydream.

By the way everyone at table was looking at her she gathered somebody must have addressed a remark directly to her.

Septimus came to her rescue. 'My wife is tired,' he said. 'We have been travelling hard for several days now.'

'And where, exactly, have you travelled from?' the Dowager asked.

The woman never gave up! Aimée quickly hid a smile behind her gloved hand, under the pretext of stifling a yawn.

'Oh, please do forgive me, my lady,' she said. 'These last few days have indeed been exhausting.'

Her husband got to his feet. 'I apologise for breaking with tradition, but I really think my wife should go to bed, rather than sit about drinking tea until all hours.'

Bed. The mere mention of the word made her whole body suffuse with heat. Getting to her feet, she said, her voice unusually husky, 'Yes, please do excuse me, Lady Bowdon, Lady Fenella.'

'Outrageous behaviour,' she heard the Dowager mutter as they drifted from the room, arm in arm. 'Staring at each other as though they could eat each other up! Not the behaviour of a well-bred lady. Not the thing at all! And you say she admitted she has never had a maid?'

Aha, so that was it! The Dowager would make use of Lady Fenella's wish to befriend her by making her repeat everything she learned.

She would have to watch what she said to the girl.

'We should have agreed on the story we were going to tell them,' Aimée said as Septimus shut his bedroom door behind them.

She had not seen him between entering Bowdon Manor and the dinner hour. It was clear that he would have many demands upon his time, so she needed to make the most of this opportunity to get some things straight.

'Story?' he grated, tugging impatiently at his neck-cloth.

'Yes, it only occurred to me once I was alone with the Dowager that you had not told me what you wished me to tell them.'

'Why should you tell them anything?' He had no wish to discuss his pestilential family right now. And how could she be thinking of anything but getting into bed? He scowled as he tossed his neckcloth aside.

'Do not frown at me so. I am trying my best to be the kind of wife you want!'

'The kind of wife I want right now,' he growled, 'is one who will stop talking and get her clothes off!'

Aimée gasped and turned bright red.

Septimus turned from her, cursing under his breath.

He should not have been so blunt. She was still a virgin, and, moreover, one with more than her fair share of modesty. He needed to be gentle with her. Lead her by the hand, step by step.

'Forgive me,' he said, raking his fingers through his hair in exasperation with himself. 'But I have been waiting for this moment since this morning, in the inn.'

'So…so have I,' she replied in a voice so husky it made him more aroused than ever.

He heaved a sigh of relief. She was shy, yes, but she *had* responded to him with enthusiasm this morning. And he was not some callow boy who did not know his way around a woman's body. He had the experience to make this first time good for her.

'You may have heard that it can be painful for a woman, the first time,' he said, turning round.

Whatever he might have said next stuck in his throat as he saw Aimée dutifully fumbling open the buttons of her gown.

'You won't hurt me,' she said, shrugging out of the bodice, then shimmying off her skirt.

'You are so beautiful,' he said, when a look of uncertainty flickered across her face. Miranda had always demanded he pay her extravagant compliments before she would let him take her to bed. But there was no need to be insincere with Aimée. She was so beautiful it damn near took his breath away.

'I thought so the very first moment I saw you, all wet and windswept where you stood in the road.'

But now his breath was growing ragged as he took in the curve of her shoulder where the silk had slipped free of her skin. The line of her collarbone was exposed, but lace-edged undergarments still concealed all but the upper swell of her full, creamy breasts.

'N-not like a drowned rat?'

He shook his head. 'I was angry when I said that. I did not mean it. Here,' he said, because her supply of bravado seemed to have run dry, 'let me remove that for you.' Or was it just that his hands were itching to close around those tantalising mounds of flesh?

'No!' she gasped, stepping back smartly. 'Y-you asked me to undress for you. L-let me do this myself. I w-want to please you!' she finished, with an air of desperation.

'You do please me,' he said, a slow smile spreading across his face as he backed his way to a chair and sat down without taking his eye off her. Who would have thought she would have taken up his challenge like this? She was an amazing woman.

Aimée smiled at him nervously. She had averted one disaster, only to plunge herself into utter embarrassment. Had he begun to undo her stays, he might have felt the telltale bulges where she had sewn all the money she had got from Lord Matthison. And that would have made him ask questions she could not face answering now, if ever! No, she *never* wanted this upright, honourable man to find out about the shameful details of that nightmarish time in London. He was beginning to like her. Really like her! And she wanted nothing to tarnish the image he seemed to be forming of her. Not yet.

Which meant that now she was committed to stripping for him!

She fixed on her brightest smile, fluttering her fingers about the tapes that held her stays closed, hoping to distract his gaze from going anywhere but where it was safe for him to look.

Swiftly she bared her breasts, sighing with relief when he kept his eye riveted there, and not on the undergarments which she slid off swiftly and kicked under the bed. But she could only withstand the heat of that look for a second or two before shyness had her darting to the bed and diving under the covers.

Septimus got to his feet, crossed to the bed and began to unbutton his waistcoat. 'You do not need to do anything that makes you uncomfortable,' he said gently. 'I never intended to make you strip for me, not this first time…' but then a wicked grin curved his mouth '…though I cannot deny I enjoyed witnessing that brief display of daring.'

She smiled back at him shyly, and settled down more comfortably into the pillows as he swiftly removed his own clothes.

Lord, but he was well formed! There was nothing disappointing about finally seeing what her mind had been imagining all day. His shoulders were satisfyingly broad and his arms delightfully well muscled. His stomach was taut and firm, and his… She blushed, glancing away at the bed hangings as he removed his last item of clothing. She ought not to want to stare at *that*. It surely was not the behaviour of a lady!

But, she gasped, as Septimus threw back the covers and climbed in beside her, her husband was no gentleman. She did not know quite what she had expected, but it was not that he should immediately place his hand between her legs and begin to stroke her most secret parts.

Fortunately, he kissed her at the same time, so that the caress was not quite so shocking as it might have been. In fact, after only a very little while, she decided he must be the most knowing man she had ever met. All day, she had been feeling achy, and sort of full, down there. And the way he stroked and caressed her was so exactly what she needed, somehow managing to be both soothing and stimulating at the same time, that she very soon forgot any awkwardness and just gave herself up to sensation.

Lord, but she was good for him! To feel the essence of her, slippery on his fingers from the very moment he got in beside her, before he had even started to stimulate her! He had shocked her, at first, by touching her down there. But her excitement had steadily increased until, when he probed right into her wetness with his fingers, she had lifted herself off the bed and pressed her open mouth to his throat. He pushed her back into the pillows and sought her mouth with his own.

This was the greatest compliment she could have paid him: to be unable to hide how very much she wanted him, enough to cast aside her modesty and perform that jerky little striptease. Had it excited her, as it had excited him?

Or had she, like him, been thinking about this moment, all day long?

He raised himself a little and watched her in fascination as she panted and writhed beneath him, her eyes half-closed, her little hands fluttering inquisitively all over his body. She was really, really enjoying exploring him, which was immensely flattering.

He simply had to kiss her neck. The line of her collarbone. And then the fullness of one breast. Each kiss had its effect, but when he closed his mouth around one pouting nipple, her entire body arched off the bed. He nipped at her with his teeth and she cried out. Though not in pain.

Her response was elemental, like the tides. Modesty was on the ebb, as wave after wave of passion surged through her. He did not think she had any idea that she was spreading her legs for him now, tilting her hips up invitingly.

A low moan reverberated through her throat. He kissed it again.

Her eyes were shut fast, now, her head thrashing back and forth.

And she began to pulse about his finger.

If ever there was an optimum time to take her, it was now, while she was riding the crest of her own wave.

He mounted her and swiftly thrust into her. She gasped when he breached her barrier, but the full flood of her desire bore her over and through the pain. And as he kept on thrusting, her cry became one of ecstasy.

'Oh! Oh! Oh,' she cried, watching him wide-eyed with wonder as he shuddered to his own release. She clung tightly to him as they coasted down the other side. When he collapsed on top of her, spent and sated, he realised he was clinging to her just as tightly.

'Oh, Septimus,' she murmured, after a moment or two, when she had got her breath back. She ran her hands up and down his back, along his arms, hugged him, kissed his cheek, while he lay, panting, his face buried in her glorious hair.

He hugged her back, lifting his head to kiss her, his passion rousing all over again. Taking Aimée to bed had been like the fulfilment of dreams of love he had never even been aware he'd had.

Love? Why was he thinking in terms of love? On a jolt of panic, he broke the kiss and gently but firmly unclasped her arms. This had been sex, that was all. Fantastic sex, all the more enjoyable because he had been anticipating it for days. But he must not imbue the act with too much significance—or she could enslave him.

He rolled off her and she turned on to her side, draping one arm over his waist, and kissing his chest as she snuggled into his body. And his momentary panic abated at this affectionate gesture. She was not playing some game with him, the way Miranda had done. Miranda, who had used words of love like weapons to bludgeon him into submission. He dropped a kiss on her sweat-damp brow. His prim little bride was nowhere near experienced enough to wield her sexual power as a weapon.

Not yet.

He frowned, tucking the sheets up round her as he noted a wave of gooseflesh sweep down her arm. She opened one eye, smiled up at him sleepily, heaved a contented sigh and was fast asleep within seconds.

He suddenly felt old and jaded. He knew from bitter experience that sex was not love. You could pretty near detest someone, and still enjoy an energetic romp in bed with them.

How he hoped Aimée would never have to learn *that* particular truth.

Chapter Nine

He woke during the night, surprised for a moment to find a woman curled up against his side. He had rarely spent the whole night in bed with a woman before. For the majority of the time he'd been married to Miranda, he had been away at sea.

He rose up on one elbow, and looked down at Aimée. She was bare to the waist, the sheet clinging to the curve of her hip and hinting at the outlines of her long, slender legs. Silvered by the moonlight that filtered in through the slits in the shutters, her hair streaming across his pillows like that, she looked like a mermaid again, just like that time he had carried her in from the rain.

He lifted a strand of hair to his face, and breathed in deeply, half-expecting to smell the tang of the sea.

She stirred, half-opened her eyes and he froze, wondering how she would react to the sight of him, looming over her like some grotesque gargoyle in the dark, a great hank of her hair in his hand.

She smiled sleepily, her eyes straying to the arm on

which he was propped up. She lifted her hand and ran her fingers over the muscles, not hesitantly, inquisitively as she had done before, but with a proprietorial air.

And then she sighed, shut her eyes and lay back, extending her arms above her head. As if in invitation.

He kicked the sheet away, and, while she lay supine, gazed hungrily at the delectable sight of her, naked and completely relaxed.

And just like that, he was so hard and hungry for her, he knew that sleep would be impossible until he'd had her again.

Gently, he nudged her legs apart and dipped one finger inside her.

'Mmhh,' she sighed, and circled her hips lazily.

He decided to take it slowly this time. She was half-asleep and still new at this, and he did not want to hurt her. So he kissed her. All over. Touched her. Learned her curves, her dips and hollows. The satin smoothness of her skin. The luxuriant softness of her hair.

Watching her languorous responses was a pleasure in itself, for he could tell she was enjoying it as much as he was. For its own sake.

She was not doing this as a favour to him, or to reward him for good behaviour, as Miranda would have done.

'Aimée,' he whispered, his heart swelling with an emotion that was totally foreign to him.

Her eyes flew open as he mounted her. She reached up and caressed his cheek as he entered her. Wrapped her arms round his shoulders when he began to move inside her. This time, it was not so new and strange to her, and before long she closed her eyes and let her head loll back, relaxing into the rhythm he set up.

He had never taken a woman at such a leisurely

pace. Never been with a woman who seemed to wish to savour every nuance of his lovemaking like this. There had always been a slight edge of desperation to his encounters with Miranda. And since then, he had not been emotionally engaged in his occasional couplings at all. It had been a purely physical release, swiftly accomplished, with women whose faces he could not now even remember.

It was all so different with Aimée. He wanted it to last for ever.

Eventually though, her breathing came faster, each inhalation a gasp, each exhalation a moan of pleasure. She was almost there.

And the knowledge that he had done this to her filled him with such fierce triumph that he could no longer restrain himself. With a few deep, rapid thrusts, he sent a single orgasm pulsing through them both.

For a few seconds it was as though they were truly one flesh, merged and mingled together so completely that he wondered they did not melt into the sheets together like the stumps of two wax candles kindled on one plate.

It felt wrong to withdraw when his heartbeat had slowed back to something approaching normal. To become two separate beings again, after achieving such a complete state of union.

But he must be crushing her. He had collapsed, limp and spent on top of her, and she was bearing his entire weight. Contrite, he withdrew and gazed down at her anxiously.

Aimée just sighed and rolled on to her side, looping her arm about his waist, and snuggling her head to his chest as though even in her sleep, she was as reluctant as he to know so much as half an inch between their bodies.

He hugged her to him hard, burying his face in the soft fragrance of her hair. Did he really need to guard his heart against Aimée? So far, she seemed to be exhibiting the same kind of loyalty towards him that he expected from his men.

When she was breathing deeply and evenly, he eased her from his side, sat up and reached for the blankets they had kicked into a ball at the foot of the bed. Tenderly drawing them up over her, he kissed her once more, and, having brushed a stray strand of hair from her face, settled down beside her.

His future ashore suddenly looked as though it might turn out to be very different from the cold hard slog of duty he had been imagining. With Aimée at his side.

Already, coming to Bowdon Manor was not the ordeal it had been the last time around. Oh, the Dowager was still as obstreperous, her daughter still as irritating. But the way Aimée had faced the Dowager down, exactly as he would have wished…it was like having, as he had mentioned to her, an able lieutenant at his side.

She was quite a find! He had been right to advertise for a woman who was prepared to work for her living. He could not have stood being shackled to some vapid, decorative female who would dangle from his arm like some useless ornament. Who would have to be berthed in some safe harbour while he went out learning about his vast new holdings.

Much of his time from now on would be taken up with learning how to run all his newly acquired estates, finding men he could trust and putting them into key roles. He had already established she would not be a hindrance in his travels. She could pack and be ready to move out in the blink of an eye. She could manage without a maid. In short, she would make the perfect travelling companion.

Should he want to take her with him on his travels.

He grinned to himself in the dark. Why wouldn't he want to take her with him, wherever he went, so that he could enjoy more nights like this one? It was not as though a woman like her would be a nuisance during the working day. Given half a chance, he would not be a bit surprised if she did not roll up her sleeves and set to work alongside him.

Would it not be something, to have, encapsulated in the person of his wife, a true helpmeet, as well as a delightfully responsive lover? He would be glad of an equal to talk to. To share his hopes and dreams with. Discuss his concerns with. Confide in.

He had been toying with the idea of setting up some kind of refuge for sailors, like Jenks, who, for one reason or another, were finding it hard to make a decent living ashore. He had been lucky enough to have loyal men with him, who had found him a place to stay, then nursed him back to health, when he had been too weak from the fever that followed his injury, and too raw from Miranda's defection, to face his family. He had not wanted his mother or sisters to see him in that broken, wretched state. But there were others who had nobody. Poor devils left to decay in the various dock-yards of England with no friends, no family, no means to pay for their food, never mind a doctor's bills.

He could see her feeling sympathetic towards those poor wretches he intended to help. She must have been down on her luck, herself, to have applied for work as a governess.

And since she had already managed to charm the core of men who worked for him he could also envision her becoming an invaluable aid in taming some of the more severely damaged men he planned to drag, kicking and cursing, from the alehouses that offered them a dubious form of respite from their ills.

He sighed with contentment, settling back on to the pillows with Aimée held in the crook of his arm.

By heaven, he was glad she had answered his advertisement! She was a perfect fit. As if she had been tailor made for him.

He could scarcely believe his luck.

She was still sleeping when he woke next. Gently, he kissed the slope of one creamy shoulder. She pouted and rolled away from him, pulling the covers up round her ears.

It was not like her to be a slug-a-bed. But then, she was not accustomed to spending the night-time making love, either!

He grinned at the thought that it was his exertions that had left her so exhausted, then pushed himself reluctantly out of bed. He had a lot of work to do today. In any case, she might well be feeling somewhat tender this morning, given that she had been a virgin. Not that she had complained, during the night. Or given any indication that what he was doing caused her any discomfort.

But he would let her sleep on. And wait for tonight.

The anticipation would bring savour to the dreary grind of his day.

And all the days to come. He had tonight to look forward to, and all the nights to come, for the rest of their lives.

His smile took on a rueful cast as he took in the state of the room. Their clothing was strewn haphazardly all over the floor. Having been used to inhabiting the tiniest of spaces at sea, he disliked untidiness. But so intent had he been on getting her into bed last night, that he had cast his orderly habits to the four winds.

He chuckled as he picked up one of Aimée's stockings, pausing to run its silken length though his fingers before draping it over the footboard with a wicked grin. He next bent to retrieve her dress, shaking it out and spreading it over the back of a chair. Her petticoat lay in a froth of lace half under the bed itself.

As he retrieved the garment, it made a dragging sound, completely alien from anything he would have expected from such delicate material. It was far heavier than he had imagined a lady's petticoat would be, too. And when he shook off the dust it had gathered under the bed, there came a dull rattling sound.

Frowning, he ran his fingers along the hem, where a succession of distinctive lumps caught his eye.

Coins.

His wife had quite a collection of coins sewn into her petticoat.

But he was a rich man. He had told her he was a rich man. Why did she feel she had to keep money hidden about her person?

As he placed the petticoat on top of her dress, he recalled the lengths she had gone to, to avoid letting him handle any of her undergarments the night before. He had been charmed at the time, thinking she was attempting to show him just how ready she really was to make love with him.

But had she merely been intent on preventing him from finding out about this hidden cache of coin? There had been a glint of determination in her eyes as she had played with her breasts. Though he had not been able to tear his gaze from the sight, he had still been aware of her kicking her stays under the bed.

Muttering an oath, he dropped to his knees, and retrieved them. He noticed nothing amiss at first. Only after he had turned them over three times did he detect the crackle of paper. He stumbled to his feet, went to her dressing table and, after a brief forage, discovered a pair of scissors, which he used to unpick the edge of one of the half-dozen specially constructed panels that would encircle her waist when she pulled the garment on. And saw banknotes. A thick wad of them.

And if each of the other panels contained as much… His brows drew together in a quick frown. She had a small fortune!

He went cold inside. She had not done that erotic little striptease to prove how willing she was, how much she wanted him. She had merely been distracting him, clearly considering it worthwhile demeaning herself, if that was what it took to prevent him from finding out about her secret hoard.

The extent of her deception shook him to the core.

He had begun to think she was a woman he could trust. He had lain awake, looking forward to discussing his plans with her.

It was as though he had gone to bed with one woman and woken up with another. A complete stranger.

He suddenly recalled the way she had sat at his dining table that first night, and calmly told him she would consider his proposal, when all the time she had been secretly planning that mad dash into the woods.

Not so mad though, it occurred to him now, if she had all this money stitched into her clothing.

He felt foolish beyond belief, standing there, naked, with her stays in one hand and her scissors in the other. He was shaking, he realised. His heart was pounding as though he was in the grip of some kind of fever.

He turned and stared down at the woman who still lay calmly sleeping.

Who was she, really? What did he know about her? Only that she could look him straight in the eye and lie to him.

Could hold him in her arms, and make love with him as though he was all the world to her, so that he wondered if he was beginning to fall a little bit in love with her. He had almost believed it was safe to lower his defences, when all the while...

He shook his head, a sense of baffled rage welling up inside him. He wanted to shake her awake and demand an explanation.

He cast the scissors from him and strode to the bed, her stays clenched in his fists. Then stopped stone dead. He would look a bigger fool than ever if he started in on that angle. Love was not supposed to have been part of their bargain!

And if he showed her the stays stuffed with banknotes, shoved them in her face and demanded an explanation, what might she confess? That she was a thief? On the run from the law?

Was that why she had been so relieved to marry him? Why she had wept with relief on their wedding night? She felt safe, she had said. Well she would, under a new name! What better way to hide from the repercussions of whatever it was she had done to end up with all this money?

She could have done *anything*. Be guilty of any crime.

And if he forced her to tell him about it, and it turned out to be a hanging offence, what would he do then? Hand her over to the law? Hand his own *wife* over to the law?

His stomach turned right over.

Already, she had come to mean so much to him, he could not face the prospect of losing her. Not like that!

But perhaps she was not guilty of anything too terrible. Surely Aimée must have come by that money honestly? And was just being cautious, hiding it away like that. Who could blame her, a woman travelling alone?

So why had she not told him about it, and handed it over to him for safekeeping as soon as they were wed?

He discovered he did not want to know the answer to that question either.

With fingers that shook, he pulled the broken thread tight so that the money was hidden from view again, then knelt down and thrust the garment back under the bed. Leaving it exactly where she had wanted to hide it.

Feeling as though she had just made him her accomplice.

With a scowl, he seized the petticoat, screwed it into a ball and thrust it under the bed with her stays where he had found it.

Then he stormed out of the bedroom and into the adjoining dressing room, tugging so hard on the bell pull to summon the valet that the whole wire came away in his hand. It felt like an omen. The whole damn place was falling apart around his ears, just like his foolish dreams of a happy marriage.

God, he was such an idiot, he groaned, sinking on to a chair by his washstand and burying his head in his hands. How on earth could he expect a woman who had agreed to marry a perfect stranger to be trustworthy?

For some time, he just sat there, kneading at his hair and cursing himself for being seven kinds of a fool.

By the time Billy arrived with his shaving water, he had sponged himself down and pulled on a pair of breeches. And his scowl was no worse than the one that often darkened his brow first thing in the morning.

Billy poured his hot water and laid out his shaving things in his usual methodical way. It helped Septimus to calm down, somewhat.

As Billy lathered his face, Septimus shut his eye, leaned back and tried to consider his dilemma rationally.

So, Aimée had a great deal of money concealed about her person. Did that necessarily mean she had committed a crime? Billy made the first sweep of the razor across his cheek, cleansing him from the night-time's growth.

Bitterness settled over him like shrugging into a familiar coat. He was a grown man with one failed marriage behind him already. What kind of idiot fell prey to the same kind of feelings that had led him so far astray in his youth? He should have known Aimée could not possibly be as perfect as she would have him believe. Should never have let her creep under his guard.

He heard Billy rinsing his blade in the washbasin, and lifted his chin so that the man could attend to his throat next. Thank heaven he had found that money before he had fallen completely under her spell. Now he knew she was as deceitful as any other woman, he could write off those foolish feelings he'd had last night as a temporary burst of insanity, or something. Yes, he had got a bit carried away, after having the best sex he had ever had. But he was in command of himself again now.

As his man deftly swept lather and bristles from his face, he reminded himself that the very fact that he had immediately tried to search for reasons to exonerate her from any wrongdoing showed him how close he had come to following the same path as he had done with his first wife. He had seen only what he wanted to see, back then. Love was blind, so they said.

As Billy finished his task, and tidied away the shaving equipment, Septimus glared balefully at his clean-shaven reflection. He was not blind. He might have only one eye, but that would not prevent him from facing the truth head on. Facing reality was never pleasant.

But what he knew was this: Aimée had so much money on her that she'd not had any need to apply for that fictitious job. She had let him buy her any amount of clothes she could easily have afforded herself. Made him think she was utterly dependent on him.

She had made him consummate the marriage, so that he could not easily put her aside. She was using him for some purpose of her own that he had yet to discover. So he would have to watch her. Literally.

He accepted the towel Billy handed him, and patted his face dry.

He would not have time to do it himself, so he would have to set his men to watch over her, exactly as he had done from the first moment she had arrived at The Lady's Bower. That time, it had prevented her escape. This time… He shook his head. He had no idea what she was up to. What he did know was that he could not let his men know he had become suspicious of his wife. Not only had they all fallen under her spell, to one degree or another, but none of them was bright enough to fool her, should she discover he was having her watched.

No, he would have to let them think they were protecting her from some unknown menace. *That* would be the reason he gave for wanting to know where she was, and what she was doing, every hour of every day.

As Aimée yawned and stretched, she could not help smiling. Last night had been wonderful! It was strange to think that though she had feared intimacy all her life, she had instinctively known that with him she would be safe. Her mouth quirked into a saucy grin. Safe! That was not the word she could use to describe how Septimus had made her feel last night. Reckless, and wanton, and…oh, so lucky!

He had been so careful to see to her pleasure before taking his own. And she knew how rare that was. She had overheard plenty of conversations that she ought not to have done, which had given her a pretty good idea of just how disappointing men could be between the sheets.

She gathered his pillow to her, burying her face in it to inhale the scent that still lingered where her husband had been lying.

Her husband!

She hugged the pillow tighter, her smile growing wider.

He was everything she had ever dreamed of finding, all wrapped up in one handsome, vital package. Kind and decent and, yes, rich. She was not going to be hypocritical about it. She did not think she would be feeling quite so deliriously happy this morning if the man she had married did not happen to be so wealthy.

She would be able to buy as many gowns as she wanted, he had said! In which case, she was definitely going to need a maid, to do all her laundry and mending, so that she would be free to enjoy leisure pursuits, like… She flung herself back on to her own pillows, giggling aloud. What did wealthy, titled ladies do all day? Well, she would soon find out. Now that she was not going to have to go to market to haggle for bargains, and keep her rooms clean, and do her own laundry, and cook her own meals.

Her life, she sighed, now that she had married an Earl, was going to be just like a fairy tale!

The trouble with fairy tales, she soon remembered, was that there was always a wicked witch lurking in the background somewhere. In her case, it was the Dowager, who was sitting in the breakfast parlour where she had gone to search for Septimus.

'His lordship went out about his business, some considerable time ago,' the kindly butler informed her with what looked like a gleam of approval in his eyes.

'One thing to be said for him,' said the Dowager, around a mouthful of kipper, 'and that is that he takes his duties very seriously. Cannot fault the energy that he devotes to his new position.' She bit into a slice of toast. 'Even if he is often so misguided as to where his duties truly lie.'

Aimée ignored the thinly veiled reference to her marriage, walking across to the sideboard and making a selection from the tempting array of dishes she found there, as though she had not even heard. She took her plate to table and sat down opposite Lady Fenella, thinking that at least *she* was not averse to her presence.

But Lady Fenella barely lifted her head from her

plate, doggedly ploughing her way through her food and making no attempt at conversation at all.

'When you have finished,' the Dowager said with a malicious gleam in her eye, 'I have arranged for Mrs Trimley, the housekeeper, to show you around what you have become mistress of.'

'Oh. Well, thank you,' Aimée said, wondering what had prompted this apparent volte-face.

It was not long before she suspected that the Dowager's sole aim in insisting Trimley showed her *everything*, every last state room and porcelain collection, and attic and cellar and linen cupboard, was a deliberate attempt to overwhelm her. She certainly ended the tour feeling as though running such a vast and complex household was a task well beyond her capabilities.

After lunch, all she wanted to do was escape to her room and hide there until it was time for dinner, but Lady Fenella invited her to go to the flower room with her to help her with the arrangements for the hall, which, she said, were sadly in need of refreshing.

Septimus was still out somewhere, and Aimée was feeling a little lost. She had no idea how she was supposed to fill the long hours until dinner, and Lady Fenella was at least offering her some form of amusement.

'This will be such fun,' said Lady Fenella, once the door was closed behind them. 'We shall be able to talk and talk, and really get to know one another. Mama always goes for a lie down in the afternoons.'

That was what she should have done, said she needed a lie down! It was clearly an acceptable way for a lady to spend the hours between luncheon and dinner. Though even as the idea occurred to her, she dismissed it. She was used to being active. Lying down during the hours of daylight seemed such a criminal waste of time.

'Would you like to do the arrangement for the large stand?' Lady Fenella offered.

Aimée shook her head vehemently. 'I have never done any flower arranging before.'

'Oh?' Lady Fenella turned away, a blush staining her cheeks. She picked up some heavy-duty scissors, and became very busy chopping away at the stems of some rubbery-looking foliage.

'P-perhaps you would like me to show you how to do such things?' she said tentatively, after a prolonged and awkward silence. 'I mean, if *I* have learned to do it,' she said self-deprecatingly, 'I am sure you can.'

But somehow, in spite of following Lady Fenella's instructions to the letter, Aimée's arrangement looked as though a casually passing drunkard had thrown it into the vase. The Dowager was going to enjoy learning about this! Even if Lady Fenella had not managed to unearth any dark secrets about her past, through the incessant questions she had peppered her conversation with, she could at least report back that the new Countess of Bowdon was a stranger to the art of floristry.

'Oh, dear,' said Lady Fenella, standing back to assess the outcome of her tutorial. 'Perhaps if I were to just…' and with a few deft twists of her nimble fingers, a work of art sprang, fully formed, like Athena from the cloven head of her father Zeus.

Catching sight of Aimée's expression, she kindly said, 'You must not expect to be able to learn everything, all at once. Why, I have been brought up here, have spent my whole life learning how to do all that is required of a lady to run such an establishment. And

I still,' she added, casting Aimée a sideways glance, 'prefer to leave things to Mama.'

The hint that this was what Aimée ought to do, too, did not escape her.

And in some ways, she could see Lady Fenella's point. She was out of her depth here. A fish out of water.

And she missed Septimus.

Ached for him, to tell the truth. For the last few days, she had spent almost every waking hour in his company.

And she did not like the way he had just left her to her own devices all day. It felt as though a part of her was missing.

She frowned. She had been used to doing things on her own for years. She had never felt as though she missed having a man to lean on. But now, after knowing him less than a week, she was pining for the mere sight of him.

She sat down quickly when she finally managed to escape back to the sanctuary of her rooms, gripping the arm of her chair. Was she falling in love with him? Were these feelings that she was developing for Septimus the same kind that had made her mother run from the safety of her home and family? Lady Aurora had cast aside respectability and security because she could not bear to be apart from the charming, charismatic man who had inveigled his way into her heart.

She shut her eyes, shaking her head. There was no need to panic! Her case was quite different from her mother's. Her father had deliberately seduced her mother for the money he thought she would bring to the marriage. Septimus was the one in this relationship with the money. And he would always look after her. He had promised.

Even though he did not love her.

Her stomach seemed to contract as she remembered him warning her that he was not marrying for love. That after the way his wife had betrayed him, he had no intention of repeating his youthful mistakes.

She thumped the arm of her chair, rising to her feet and tugging on the bell-pull for the maid Lady Fenella had told her would be available to her from now on. It was time to change and dress for dinner.

She walked into her bedchamber, checking on the threshold at the transformation Nelson and his men had wrought in the space of one day. Clean and aired, it was no longer a gloomy, musty, oppressive space. It was bright and welcoming. They had somehow even managed to find some pretty, flowery curtains to replace the dusty velvet swags that had been hanging there the night before.

Yes, she thought bitterly, it was amazing how much could change during the course of just one day. Her mood, particularly, could not be more different from the way she had felt when she had woken up. In the afterglow of her first sexual experience, she had stupidly thought she was living in the middle of some great romance.

Silly, silly girl, she thought, giving the neatly made bed a contemptuous glance. She, better than anyone, should know how dangerous it was to trust a man you barely knew, and imagine you were going to live happily ever after. Her mother's fate should have been sufficient warning.

She flung her shoulders back and pulled open the door to her armoire.

So what if her husband did not love her! That did not necessarily mean he was going to break her heart. Not intentionally, certainly, for he was essentially a good, decent man. And, now she thought of it—and to tell the truth, she had thought of little else all day—it was not just she who had enjoyed their first night together. He had woken her up, gently yet insistently, and taken her a second time. He would not have done that if she had not pleased him the first!

Nor had he taken her swiftly, as though he was simply experiencing an animal urge he had to satisfy, but slowly, as though he was savouring every second of the encounter.

Her case was not hopeless.

She was the last one to reach the salon that night. She had never spent so much time fussing over her appearance. Or felt such a fluttering in her heart as she checked herself in the mirror, one last time, before going down. She so wanted Septimus to like the way she looked!

Silly of her, perhaps, but she could not help it. His opinion mattered to her. She wanted him to like, more than like, every single thing about her.

She lifted her chin and squared her shoulders as the footman opened the door and announced her.

She was going to prove herself a worthy bride for the Earl of Bowdon, see if she didn't! The Dowager might have succeeded in making her feel completely inadequate, for a while, but, as Lady Fenella had inadvertently pointed out, she was not an imbecile.

It was true, she had no experience of running a large household such as this, but there was no reason why she could not learn. She would just show the Dowager, and Lady Fenella, and all the household staff, who had regarded her with frank curiosity as she explored the furthest reaches of her new domain, and probably sniggered at the extent of her ignorance, that Septimus had not made an error in choosing her.

But most of all, she would prove it to her husband.

Chapter Ten

'Do tell me all about your family,' said the Dowager the moment they had taken their places at table. 'Your father was some kind of dockworker, was he not?'

Aimée looked across the table at Septimus, silently begging him to give some indication how he wished her to respond. To her consternation, he began to drink his soup as though he was completely indifferent to anything the Dowager might say or think.

Perhaps he was. He had said only last night that he did not care what they thought of him. It looked as though it was entirely up to her how much to reveal.

Admitting she was his second wife could be a bit awkward. He had not wanted Lady Fenella hurt, which was why he had not openly advertised for a wife. On the other hand, if she were to reveal her true parentage, it might take some of the pressure off him. At least the Dowager would no longer be able to complain that he had brought a commoner into the bloodline!

So she smiled and said, 'Oh, no. My father never soiled his hands with manual labour.'

The Dowager made an impatient gesture with her soup spoon. 'Ran a shop of some kind in the dockyards, then.'

'No, as a gentleman's son, he would have thought such an occupation entirely beneath his dignity,' she said a little wistfully. If only he had not been too proud to take up some honest work to support his wife and child!

'A gentleman's son?' The Dowager's eyes darted from her to Septimus, who was suddenly very busy trying to attract the attention of one of the footmen to refill his wine glass.

'He must have married beneath him, then.'

'On the contrary. My mother's family felt that *she* had married below her station.'

'How is this? I am sure I was informed that there was some kind of shopkeeper amongst your antecedents.'

At this point Septimus, who was now leaning back, sipping from his replenished wine glass, put in, 'You are thinking of my first wife's family. Her father, as you appear to have discovered by some means that did not involve asking me, is a ship's chandler.'

For once, he was not averse to the Dowager's tendency to pry into what was really none of her business. He wanted to find out more about his wife's past as much, if not more, than she did. But he had already decided he was not going to yield to the rampant curiosity she roused in him and beg her for details.

'First wife?' said the Dowager, her eyebrows rising so high they almost disappeared into her coiffure. 'You mean to tell me you have remarried? And this woman is your second wife?'

He would have liked to tell her that he meant to tell

her nothing, but it did not suit his purposes to cut her down to size just now.

'She is,' he said, turning to the butler and signalling that he should clear the table, since everyone appeared to have lost interest in the soup.

Aimée was relieved that he had paved the way for her to tell them all the truth, or, at least, as much of it as would not cause embarrassment to anyone. If he did not mind anyone knowing she was his second wife, *she* certainly did not! The Dowager, she noted with amusement, was quivering with barely suppressed curiosity throughout the bustle associated with the removal of one set of dishes and the introduction of the next.

'When did this marriage take place?' the Dowager demanded imperiously, the moment the second course had been set out. 'And why did his lordship not inform us of it before?'

'I really did not see that it was any of your business,' replied Septimus curtly.

To deflect the Dowager's curiosity from the details she knew Septimus did not want revealed, Aimée swiftly said, 'But I can, of course, see why you made the mistaken assumption it was *my* father who was some kind of a tradesman.'

The Dowager was still glowering at Septimus, and so Aimée added, 'But I can assure you, Papa would never have taken up a trade. He had a great deal of pride, even though he was only the younger son of quite an obscure family. Though my grandfather still did not approve of such an unequal match. Forbade it, in fact. Which was why,' she said, playing her ace card, 'in the end, I am afraid to tell you, my parents eloped.'

'Eloped!' gasped Lady Fenella, her eyes round with surprise. 'How shocking!'

Even the Dowager had stopped glaring at Septimus, in the wake of that announcement. She flapped her hand at her daughter impatiently, to silence her, which Aimée did not object to for once, not really. An elopement was a scandal best not discussed in front of the servants. Though she had no doubt the Dowager would quiz her about it when they had withdrawn from table.

And so she felt quite shocked when the Dowager pressed on. 'Who was your grandfather, then, if he objected to your mother marrying the son of what sounds like a perfectly respectable family?'

Aimée glanced furtively round at the footmen, before leaning forwards, and admitting, quietly, 'The Earl of Caxton.'

She glanced at Septimus to see how he had taken the news. She had not wanted him to learn about her background in this way, but at least she had managed to broach the topic of her heritage in a way that did not sound boastful. He must, surely, understand why she could not keep quiet about her background, not in the circumstances! But his face was so inscrutable that she could not tell what he was thinking.

The Dowager, however, left nobody in any doubt what she thought. 'A backstairs connection, I take it?' she said, with cold contempt. 'Your mother was the product of an affair with one of the maids.'

Aimée gasped. This was extremely rude, even by the Dowager's standards. Poor Lady Fenella did not know where to look.

'She was nothing of the sort!' she retorted, by now past caring what the servants were making of such inappropriate dinner-table talk. 'And if you took a moment to reflect, you would see for that yourself. Why, if my mother was that kind of person, it would have been my father's family who opposed the match!'

'Who do you claim she was, then?'

'My mother was Lady Aurora Vickery!'

'Lady Aurora!' the Dowager sneered. 'Do you take me for a simpleton? Lady Aurora was barely out of the schoolroom when she died!'

Aimée could not help flinching. Was that the story her grandfather had put about, to prevent people knowing she had eloped?

Septimus felt his heart sink as the Dowager tripped her up in one of her lies. For, no matter what he suspected, he could not permit anyone to publicly accuse his wife of lying, not without appearing to be completely lacking in honour himself. Furious that Aimée was forcing him to play along with her story, he said, 'Take care what you say, madam.' He raised his head, and only slowly turned to glare at the Dowager. 'Before you accuse my wife of anything else, perhaps it would benefit us all to hear a full account of the circumstances surrounding her mother's demise.' Then he turned to Aimée and said, challengingly, 'If you are willing to give it?'

Lifting her chin, and with a slight wobble to her voice, she declared, 'Of course I am. Lady Aurora *was* my mother. And whatever you may have heard, she died not quite ten years ago. In Rome.'

The Dowager snorted with contempt. 'You have learned to say your lines very prettily. But everyone knows Lady Aurora died the summer after her come out.'

'I th-think that must have been a story my grandfather put about, to conceal the scandal,' she said, as much to try to work it out for herself, as to explain it to the others. 'From what I have heard about him, he would probably have preferred people to think she had died than to know she had defied him and disgraced the family name by eloping. He cut her completely out of his life, for a while. Th-though he eventually made her a small allowance, which he paid directly to her, on the condition she went abroad and did not return to England with my father in tow.' Or her, though she would never divulge that to this harpy.

It was all very plausible, Septimus thought bleakly. She had already informed Jago, during the interview, that she had travelled all over the Continent in her childhood. And the cleverest part of it was that it would be almost impossible to ascertain if it was the truth. One could not go to the Earl of Caxton, and ask! But he could not give her story too much credence. If she was an orphan, as she was leading her audience to assume, and penniless, then how to account for the money she had in her possession? She must have come by it dishonestly, to be concocting such a far-fetched tale to cover her tracks.

At this point, as though sensing Aimée's growing distress, and desperate to restore some sense of normality to the proceedings, Lady Fenella put in, 'How interesting. Whereabouts did they live? I don't suppose you ever went to Paris, did you? I should love to visit Paris.'

Aimée turned to her with heartfelt gratitude.

'Yes, I have been to Paris, actually. Though we did not stay there as long as I should have liked.' They never did. It was never long before they outgrew their welcome, once her father's propensity for cheating at cards was discovered.

'So where did you go?' asked Lady Fenella, agog with curiosity.

'Oh, many places.' She mentally dismissed all the small towns of which Lady Fenella was not likely to have heard. 'Rome, as I have already mentioned. And Naples and Florence, as well as Marseilles, and Bordeaux…'

'Which must have been where you met his lordship!' Lady Fenella exclaimed. 'When his squadron was stationed there. Oh, but…' her brows drew down in confusion '…you could not have been very old then. Scarcely more than a child!'

Aimée swiftly stifled a small pang of jealousy upon hearing that Lady Fenella knew far more about her husband's naval career than she did. And darted him a beseeching look. She had no notion which, out of the list of places she had just named, Septimus might have been stationed in, nor in what year!

She was annoyed to find she could not catch his eye. He must know she was out of her depth with this one. Did he not care? If she began to admit she had only met him a matter of days ago, Lady Fenella was going to end up finding out about the advertisement.

Well, even if he did not care, she, at least, had no wish to hurt the poor girl.

'Well?' said the Dowager.

Her heart hammering in her chest, she said, as casually as she could, 'Scarce more than a child by your standards, Lady Fenella, perhaps. But because of my circumstances, I grew up faster than a lady as sheltered as yourself.'

Septimus marvelled at her facility for evading the truth. She had managed to couch her response so that people could make whatever they wished from that statement. What a deceitful creature he had married!

But the worst aspect of the case, to his mind, was that even as she sat there, spinning her outrageous tales, he was capable of admiring the dexterity of her mind. How could he? Why did her lies not make him despise her?

There, thought Aimée, taking a sip of her wine to moisten her mouth, which had been dry with nerves. That should cover any eventuality! No matter what year Septimus had docked at any of those ports she had mentioned, it would not matter how old she had been. She had made the question of maturity a moot point.

Besides, it was not beyond the bounds of possibility that he might, indeed, have been a visitor in her parents' home.

'My mother was always eager for news of England,' she elaborated. 'Whenever an English ship put into harbour, she would invite the officers to make free of our home.'

Septimus could well have been amongst their number. That she did not recall having met him was an insignificant detail that she could explain away, should it become necessary, in one of two ways. Either she had been too young at the time and therefore tucked away safely in her room, or old enough to have learned that it was better to keep out of the way when such men thronged the reception rooms, for while her mother clucked round them like a mother hen, her father, under the guise of genial host, would ply them with cheap local liquor, then fleece them at cards.

'So, if you were a mere child when his lordship visited those places, it must have been your parents with whom he became friends?' Lady Fenella persisted.

'Oh!' Actually, Aimée supposed that would be the logical conclusion to draw. 'Um…' In the end, she nodded, not feeling quite up to telling an outright lie.

'And his lordship had never forgotten you, though you were far too young to marry when he first met you. You see, Mama?' said Lady Fenella with a sentimental sigh, 'I said all along it was a love match.'

Septimus could not have looked less like a man in love at that particular moment, thought Aimée. She wondered what was the matter with him. The revelations about her background could surely not be upsetting him, could they? She had thought that learning they shared a common heritage, having both been nobly born, yet raised in less than luxurious circumstances, would have drawn them closer together.

Perhaps he was just preoccupied with estate matters? He had looked somewhat strained even before dinner. Yes, come to think of it, he had greeted her arrival in the gilded salon with an abstracted air.

She turned to Lady Fenella and gave a brittle smile. 'We took one look at each other, and knew there could never be anyone else for either of us.'

Out of the corner of her eye, she noticed Septimus was looking as though the beef he was chewing was made of leather, and he wished he could spit it out.

'I am so happy for you,' Lady Fenella said, drawing Aimée's attention back to the more friendly side of the table. 'To have found each other again, when you have both travelled so much, and might easily have lost each other for ever…'

'Nonsense!' the Dowager shouted, slamming the flat of her hand on the table. 'This is all utter nonsense! The Earl of Caxton has only one granddaughter. Lady

Jayne—remember her, Fenella? We met her at the Card-
ingtons' house party. That spoiled little madam with the
big blue eyes and an unnatural amount of gold ringlets.'

'Yes, I remember Lady Jayne,' said Lady Fenella.
'She looked just like a little fairy, I thought.'

'Oh, for heaven's sake!' the Dowager sputtered. 'The
point is that she looked nothing like this creature! No
family resemblance whatever!'

It was getting too much.

She did not really care what the Dowager thought of
her. But to learn, in this way, that she had a cousin, a
cousin that she had never met, with whom the Dowager
might have mingled freely...

To her chagrin, she felt tears start to her eyes.

Septimus got to his feet so swiftly the footmen had
no chance to draw the chair out for him. It scraped
noisily across the floorboards.

'I think we have had quite enough of this,' he said,
holding out his hand to Aimée. 'Come. It is time we
retired for the night.'

'Oh, but...pudding...' said Lady Fenella. 'You don't
want to miss pudding. It is apple charlotte...'

Hang pudding! thought Aimée. Thank heavens, Septimus had seen how upset she was becoming and had
come to her rescue. And not a moment too soon!

'Th-thank you for removing me from that unpleasantness,' she said, sniffing back a tear as they left the
room.

He shot her an irritated look. He was disgusted with
himself for feeling so protective towards her when he
had seen tears spring to her eyes, even after sitting
through that masterly demonstration of her duplicity.

'I am sorry that I did not stand up to the Dowager
better than that,' she said, misunderstanding the look.

'But it was hearing about Aunt Almeria's daughter. I had known, of course, that my grandfather has no legitimate male heirs of direct line, but until just now, I was unaware I had a cousin. A cousin, moreover, who is openly acknowledged. Spoiled, even. Whilst I am just the family's dark, d-dirty secret.'

He took her by the elbow and ushered her up the stairs, which was just as well. Her eyes were so blurred by tears she could not see properly which way to go.

'Your Aunt Almeria's daughter?' She looked so upset, speaking of these people as though she was really related to them, that he began to wonder if she actually believed what she was saying. He scowled. There had better be a grain of truth in it, somewhere. It was one thing listening to her telling stories to the Dowager and her silly daughter, but quite another for her to tell him barefaced lies. He would not stand for it!

'Yes,' she nodded miserably. 'My mother told me that her older sister had dutifully married the man their autocratic father had picked out for her. And been made utterly miserable. Aunt Almeria's fate bolstered Mama's determination only to marry for love, no matter how unsuitable the family considered her choice.'

'And so your parents eloped,' he said. For some reason, he did not doubt she had spent her childhood flitting about the Continent. She had told Mr Jago the same thing at her interview, before she had felt the need to impress anyone with her increasingly far-fetched tales!

'Why, exactly, did you return to England?' He had not meant to ask her anything about her past. To do so would imply that he cared, that her answers mattered. But now that the Dowager had stirred things up, it was only natural to bring this line of conversation to its natural conclusion.

'Well, you see, the allowance ceased when Mama died.'

'You said that was ten years ago,' he reminded her. The trouble with lies was that people nearly always forgot some salient point, which showed them up in the end.

But Aimée was looking down, rummaging in her reticule for a handkerchief, and so she totally missed the look of anger that flickered across his face.

'Yes, but Papa was in a terrible state for quite some time after that,' she replied, blowing her nose. 'He blamed himself for taking her to Rome during a season that was known to be unhealthy. It was a long time before it even dawned on him that there was nothing to prevent him from returning from exile.'

She had not missed a beat. No matter how closely he questioned her, she always had a ready answer. His heart began to pound. Perhaps she had been telling the truth. Perhaps she really was the offspring of a runaway match between the lady whatever her name was, and some swindler.

In any case, while they were on the subject, he might as well ask why she had applied for a job as a governess, when she had a small fortune in her keeping. There might be some perfectly simple explanation.

'And once here…' he prompted her, as they reached the landing, and turned towards their suite of rooms.

'I…' To his immense sorrow, she faltered for the first time in the fabrication of her fairy tale. Her eyes slid away from his face.

'I wanted a fresh start. A more settled existence…'

'And so you applied for the job as governess to a gentleman in Yorkshire?' he asked incredulously.

'Yes,' she said, with palpable relief.

She had no idea, of course, that he knew about the money. A sense of betrayal surged through him. He had given her a golden opportunity to confide in him, and she had fobbed him off. He could not believe how much it hurt.

'Go to your room, now, Aimée,' he said, barely holding himself in check. 'And compose yourself. I will be along shortly.'

She touched her handkerchief to her eyes one last time, shot him a watery smile and darted into her room.

Septimus strode along the corridor to his own door, rather than following her and accessing his room via hers. If he went anywhere private with her now, he did not know how he would prevent himself from putting her across his knee and giving her the spanking she deserved!

He gave vent to his anger by slamming his bedroom door behind him instead.

The lies had rolled off her tongue so glibly she almost had him convinced she was the long-lost granddaughter of some starched up old Earl.

Though why on earth had she come up with that tale about having a nobly born mother, anyway? He ran his fingers through his hair, striding up and down in his agitation. He had told her he didn't care what any of his newly discovered family thought of him, or her!

Perhaps she thought she ought to have that kind of background, in order to make some headway for herself, though. He had noted some of the servants looking askance at her, taking their lead from the Dowager.

He refused to countenance the possibility that what

she had told them could be true. He knew what came of believing a single word that slid from Aimée's treacherous little mouth.

Only a fool would keep on falling for her lies. To start with, she had made him believe she was accepting his proposal whilst, in her mind, she was already planning her flight from his house.

She had then convinced him that she had been weeping on their wedding night, out of gratitude for being rescued from life's hardships—though, he snorted, it had taken her almost a week to come up with that one.

And then, worst of all, last night, she had responded to him so sweetly, that he had almost been duped into opening his very heart to her! Which would have led to complete disaster.

But what sort of woman, he asked himself, striding across to the mirror and examining his reflection with disgust, would willingly ally herself to that? Only a woman like Aimée, a woman who had been brought up to think there was nothing wrong with lying and cheating, that was who.

He laughed hollowly. A woman like that was all he deserved. Any woman who was truly fit to be the mother of the next Earl of Bowdon would turn her nose up at the disfigured son of a country doctor and the local ironmonger's daughter.

He raised his hand to the patch he had worn to dinner, so as not to put Lady Fenella off her food, and tore it away. Let his wife suffer the sight of it!

She must be ready for bed now, surely? He had paced the floor of his room for what felt like plenty long enough for her to undress and hide the evidence of whatever crime it was she must have committed, to want to flee so far from London and marry a disfigured wreck of a man.

In the mood he was in, he almost did not care if he did catch her hiding her stolen money away from him. Perhaps it was time they confronted her past, got it all out in the open! He stormed into her room, spoiling for a fight.

But she was sitting up in bed, clad in one of the ridiculously expensive nightgowns he'd bought her in Harrogate, a shy smile of anticipation on her face.

It slipped as soon as she caught sight of his expression.

'Septimus?' she asked in that sweet, husky tone of hers that sent shivers of longing twisting his guts. 'Is there something wrong? Did I not tell them what you wanted them to hear at dinner?'

'What *I* wanted to hear?' So now she was going to make it sound as though she was lying to please him?

'If you wanted me to tell them a different story, why did you not prime me? I would have said whatever you wanted!'

She had the gall to look aggrieved. That did it. With a low growl, he strode across the room and took her by the shoulders.

'Would you?' His fingers closed hard down on her flesh. She looked back up at him with such an air of wounded innocence that it was all he could do not to laugh in her face. There was nothing innocent about her! Though the look in those eyes would have deceived anyone. Anyone.

He took her chin between his fingers, searching for some sign of treachery. He could see none. She looked straight back at him as though she had nothing to hide with those clear green eyes that so reminded him of the sea. And it struck him that you could never see far beneath the surface of the waves, either. You could never really tell how deep the waters were. Nor whether there were rocks lurking below that would rip a great hole in the hull. A mariner always sailed carefully in uncharted waters. Took nothing for granted. Only that way could he stay safe.

'Why are you angry with me?' she asked, those eyes taking on such a puzzled look that a man who did not know the crooked heart of her would have been taken in.

'I am not angry with you,' he said, realising that it would be pointless. Besides, right at this moment, most of his anger was directed at himself. How could he have allowed himself to be deceived into thinking he had married a woman he could be proud of? A woman who might become his friend?

A woman he could trust.

As well to trust the capricious seas not to blow up a tempest and swallow up ships and their entire crews whole!

She was breathing hard now, her lips slightly parted, her eyes wide with consternation.

'Then, why—?'

'Stop talking, woman,' he growled and stopped her mouth with a punishing kiss. If only he could stop her spinning such outrageous lies! If only she had not made him hope for something she would never be able to give him.

He felt her trying to end the kiss. She was taking a breath as though there was something she wanted to say. But there was nothing she could say that he wanted to hear. That he would believe. That would not make him so angry that he would not be responsible for his actions!

So he captured her face between his hands and deepened the kiss, until she stopped struggling, looped her arms about his neck and subsided back on to the bed, pulling him down with her.

This was the only truth they had.

Wasn't it?

Suddenly unsure even of this, he pushed up her skirts and ran his hands up between her thighs. Obligingly, she parted her legs and let him test her. His mouth twisted in derision. Of course she would let him test her. Because this was a test she knew she would pass.

For some reason, this was the one thing it seemed she did not need to fake. She was wet and trembling with wanting him.

He reared back and tore off his clothes. When he was stark naked, he stood quite still for a moment or two, just watching her. She licked her lips as she ran her eyes over his body, not flinching from examining his manhood as she had done the night before. Her eyes grew darker, her breath quickened. And her hands went to the buttons down the front of her nightgown.

'Aimée...' My God, the way she was looking at him!

If this was all an illusion, then, by God, he was not going to do anything to shatter it. If he demanded the truth, forced it from her, she might stop looking at him like that. Stop welcoming him into her bed, and giving him more nights like last night.

What the hell. With a feral growl, he strode to the bed and pulled the covers away from her, then thrust the flimsy nightdress up to her waist and plunged straight into her.

Her eyes widened with shock, but it only took her

a heartbeat to recover. She flung her arms round his neck again, and murmured, 'Oh, Septimus!'

'No,' he groaned, and buried his face in her neck. He did not want her to talk. She ruined everything with her lies!

'Wh-what…?' she panted. 'What is the matter?'

'What could possibly be the matter?' he replied sarcastically, before stopping her cheating mouth with a kiss.

She moaned in the back of her throat and wrapped her legs round his waist. She was hot and wet for him. And he was hard for her. He enjoyed the act. She enjoyed the act.

Why make it any more complicated than that?

Chapter Eleven

Aimée jolted awake the next morning with a feeling that something was wrong. She opened her eyes, realised that she was in her bedchamber at Bowdon Manor where she had every right to be, and not hiding in some dingy room behind a laundry, and heaved a sigh of relief. She sat up and rang for a maid to bring her hot water so that she could wash, but the vague feeling of disquiet persisted, niggling on the edges of her mind.

By the time the girl arrived, she could no longer deny what it was that was troubling her. Last night, Septimus had made love to her with a passion that had taken her breath away. Then he had shocked her by getting out of bed almost immediately after. She had lain there, too weak and languorous to move, watching him picking up the clothing that he had torn off and scattered all over the floor. He had bent over her, pressed a swift kiss to her forehead, said 'Goodnight. Sleep well.'

And gone to his own room.

If he had not stopped to kiss her, she might have thought he was angry with her. Or perhaps, not with her, but about something. He had been in an odd humour all evening, though he had never once taken it out on her.

Her spirits had recovered a little by the time she went down the stairs to the breakfast parlour. For, she reasoned, it was bound to take a while for her to get to know him properly and understand his odd humours. But the wonderful thing was that already, though she had seen him in all kinds of moods, not one of them made her think any the less of him.

The dreamy smile that had been playing round her lips, when she recollected the way he had made her feel the night before, dimmed a little when she entered the breakfast parlour, and encountered a look from the Dowager that put her in mind of a great black spider, waiting for some unsuspecting fly to get caught in her web. Repressing a shiver, Aimée turned away from her and went to the sideboard.

When she sat down, Lady Fenella, who had just finished a plate of ham, looked up and beamed at her. It was such a spontaneous, genuine smile of pleasure at seeing her that Aimée could not help smiling back.

Until Fenella said, 'What do you plan to do today?'

Aimée had no idea. She had wondered once before what titled ladies did with themselves all day. And she was no nearer finding any answers now.

'Lady Fenella,' said the Dowager, upon seeing Aimée's helpless shrug, 'adheres to a strict timetable. Her days are always filled with activity.'

'Really?'

'Yes, indeed. I am surprised your mother, Lady Aurora,' the Dowager said with a sneer, indicating she still did not believe Aimée's story, 'never taught you the importance of routine.'

There had never been the chance to form any kind of routine in the life they had led. Not that her mother seemed to have even attempted to establish any, as far as she could recall. On the contrary, she had clear memories of her mother giggling uncontrollably as they clambered out of a balcony into an alley below, where they had already thrown the bundles containing everything they could carry. She had looked upon every flit that filled a young Aimée with resentment as the start of yet another adventure.

'My mother had a love of spontaneity,' Aimée replied.

'Hmmph!' retorted the Dowager.

After breakfast, still uncertain how to fill the hours until the next meal, Aimée drifted down towards the offices. Septimus was not in the estate office, but Mr Jago was.

'His lordship?' he replied, when she asked if he knew where she might find her husband. 'Oh, he's ridden over to Endon today. To see about the roofs. There is a lot of neglect to put right,' he said, with a shake of his head. 'He is very busy.'

'Y-yes, of course,' she replied, backing out of the door, feeling like a child intruding upon adult's business, for Mr Jago had spoken with authority about subjects of which she was entirely ignorant.

In the end, she decided to seek out Lady Fenella. She, at least, would welcome her company. She discovered from a footman that Lady Fenella spent her mornings up under the glass dome of the rotunda, attending to her work.

Well, that sounded more promising. She disliked feeling redundant. She hoped she might be able to join in with Lady Fenella's work, and begin to do something that would contribute to the welfare of the manor and its people.

Lady Fenella welcomed her arrival with genuine pleasure. She always spent the mornings up here, she confided, when the light was good, but it was not yet too hot to work.

'Would you like to see my latest project?' she asked.

Aimée did not know what to say when she discovered that the project upon which Lady Fenella was engaged that morning was a piece of whitework. Lady Fenella had boxes and boxes of it. Handkerchiefs, nightgowns, napkins—all highly decorative, but too beautiful, the girl sighed, to actually be put to use.

She also had quite a collection of scrapbooks. Her pride and joy were the ones she had made of mementoes hoarded from her London Seasons.

'I am sure you could become quite adept at flower arranging, if you were only to persist,' Fenella said, as they descended the spiral staircase that led back to the upper floor of the house, much later. 'After lunch, you simply must come down to the flower room with me again.'

And since nobody else seemed to want her, she did exactly that.

That evening, she heard Septimus come in while she was putting the finishing touches to her *toilette*. The noises that came from his room then indicated he was taking a hasty wash and changing for dinner. When it sounded as though he must be almost ready, she went to the connecting door, thinking it would be pleasant to go down together. She had just set her hand to the handle, when she heard him leave his room by the other door, and the unmistakable sound of his footsteps hurrying along the corridor.

She let her hand fall to her side, a frown creasing her brow. It had not occurred to him to so much as glance into her room, though he must have known she was there!

Thank goodness, she thought, smoothing her gloves and walking slowly towards her own door, she had not actually got into his room. Knowing that he had no especial wish to be with her at the moment would have made her feel like a beggar, pleading for scraps of attention.

The odd analogy faded once she reached the gilded salon and saw how unutterably weary he looked. He had got back very late. Perhaps he had not, after all, realised she was upstairs, but had just hurried down so that dinner would not be held back on his account.

When he greeted her with that same abstracted look he had worn the night before, and she recalled Mr Jago saying how busy he was, she promptly decided she would not be the kind of wife who took offence at imagined slights. Who knows, he might even have rushed down here so that she would not be left on her own to deal with the Dowager.

And she smiled at him, with, she hoped, her heart in her eyes.

The Dowager was in a far less abrasive mood that night, so conversation at the table was desultory at best. But as the meal progressed through its various removes, Septimus, to her delight, looked at her more and more frequently. And with more and more heat until, by the time she had finished her dessert, she was in quite a froth of anticipation. Septimus had made love to her once cautiously, and later, lazily, and finally, ferociously. What new delight would he introduce her to tonight?

She made no demur when, once again, he announced that she would not be joining the other ladies for tea in the withdrawing room, for she could hardly wait to get upstairs!

Outside her sitting-room door, he paused, and said, 'Go and prepare yourself for me. I shall join you in a few minutes.'

She felt a bit let down at first, but only until she began to remove her clothes. Then she remembered the money she had stitched into her undergarments—she was going to have to find a better hiding place for it, somewhere the servants would not find it. She did not want to cause any more speculation than there must already be, after the way the Dowager had forced confessions from her the night before.

She had got into bed and been sitting there, watching the connecting door with eager eyes, for what seemed like an age before he came in.

But his reaction was everything she could have hoped for. He halted on the threshold, gazing at her hungrily.

'You are so damned beautiful,' he said.

He made her feel beautiful, the way he stalked across to her, his gaze fixed hungrily upon her as she flicked the sheet aside so that he could join her. He sat on the edge of the bed, reached out and ran his fingers through her hair.

'I have been thinking about doing this all day,' he said.

Aimée was puzzled by what sounded like a note of

irritation in his voice, but then he kissed her so passionately, her momentary qualm was banished.

'I have been thinking about you, too,' she confessed shyly, when he broke off the kiss, reared back and tore off his dressing gown.

Perhaps this…whatever it was that had flared so hot between them was as much of a puzzle to her as it was to him, he conceded. And remembered the decision he had taken the night before, not to question what they had here, in bed, but just to enjoy it while it lasted.

With fingers that shook, he removed her nightgown and, for a moment or two, just knelt above her, drinking in the delectable sight of her. She bit down on her lower lip, a little nervous at being naked, he guessed, but also aroused by it, to judge by the way her breathing quickened, and her hips were making impatient little gyrations.

'You want me,' he said, stroking his hand along her side, watching her rise into his caress.

She nodded, her eyes dark with longing. The colour of them had always reminded him of the sea—which reminded him he needed to beware, especially now, when he felt the tug of wanting her pulling him under.

'I cannot resist you,' he admitted, settling over her. Every time he took her, his hunger for her only increased. How was he to do this, night after night, and not drown?

There it was again, Aimée noted, that faint note of resentment in his voice. But then he kissed her again, and his hands upon her body were so urgent, the faint misgivings in her mind were drowned out by the glorious clamour of her body. Tonight, it appeared he intended to kiss and caress every inch of her, as though he would lay claim to her entire body.

If he was going to drown, he vowed, then he was taking her down with him. He deliberately drove her to the edge, then brought her back, time and time again, until she was clawing at him, begging him for release. When they finally went down, they went together, in a wild thrashing of limbs, and gasping for breath, as though they had both been sucked into a whirlpool of need that was stronger than both of them.

And, at last, he smiled. He was not her slave, not in this. And he would not be. He had the experience to ride the storm, to steer her through it, and make her totally dependant upon him for her passage through. He was her captain.

He gazed down at her with satisfaction as she lay sprawled naked amidst the twisted sheets, exhausted and spent. She did not notice when he left the bed. He took a moment to cover her with a sheet. It was one thing to have the victory, quite another to humiliate her. He would not do that to her. She could not help what she was, any more than a river could help flowing into the sea.

She woke the next morning alone again. Septimus had come to her, and reduced her to a quivering mass of satiation, then left to sleep in his own bed.

She was beginning to suspect that this was the pattern he would always follow. He must just have taken particular care of her, that first night, because that was the kind of man he was. Kind and considerate. But in a way, she sighed, she supposed she ought to be glad that he preferred to sleep alone. It certainly made it easier to preserve her guilty secret about Lord Matthison's money.

But surely there ought to be more between a husband and wife than just this? She knew he was busy,

but could he not spare a few moments to tell her how
his day had gone and ask her what she had been doing?
Was he not interested?

That night, when he came to her bed, she scrambled
away when he reached for her. She was determined to at
least try to get to know him better. She was sure there
must be some way she could be of help, if things on the
estate were in such bad shape.

'How have you spent your day, Septimus?' she asked
him, when he frowned at her evasive manoeuvre.

'Aimée…' he sighed, running his fingers through his
mane of tawny hair, 'I have spent all day in discussions
with stewards, tenants and local bigwigs. And then I
came in to dinner, to find the Dowager chattering at
me too. Please, don't expect me to talk any more. I am
done with talking. I just want some peace and quiet.'
He gathered her into his arms and kissed her until she
had almost forgotten why it was important that they
talk to each other. 'Let me find solace in this. Your
soft, warm embrace…'

Flattered that here was something only she could
give him, she yielded.

But, after only a few more days, she began to wonder
if his attitude really was very flattering after all. Whenever she came across him during the day, which was
not all that often, he disliked it if she tried to show
any signs of affection. Surely there was nothing wrong
with a wife giving her husband a kiss on the cheek, or
a hug, was there? He never actually reprimanded her,
but his discomfort was plain. His mouth flattened, and
his shoulders visibly tensed.

Since she had determined to be the kind of wife

he wanted, she checked her natural urge to demonstrate her feelings of delight whenever she saw him and merely curtsied politely, though she hated being so reserved when what she wanted was to... She shook her head impatiently.

This was a convenient arrangement. Her marriage to Septimus was only the same as very many others entered into by the aristocracy, where the husband dashed about all day being important, whilst the wife stayed within doors, recouping her strength for her main duty. The breeding of an heir.

She shivered.

When she had agreed to such a marriage, it had not sounded quite so...demeaning as she was now finding it.

She took herself to task. What did she have to complain about, really? On the face of it, she had everything she had thought she ever wanted. Respectability and security. A husband who demonstrated both enthusiasm and expertise every night in her bed.

Why complain because...she pushed herself to face it...he did not love her?

It need not matter. It *should* not matter. She had not married for love either! She had agreed to marry Septimus because she had seen he could provide her with the stability she had craved all her life. Because she had thought marrying a man who could provide all the material things she had always longed for would make her happy.

Instead, she was becoming increasingly *un*happy, because she was learning that there was more to life than having food on the table, and a roof over your head that did not leak, from which nobody could evict you.

She could even see, for the first time in her life, why

her mother had run away from her sheltered, indolent existence with a man who had whispered sweet nothings in her ear.

What would she not give, to hear Septimus whisper words of love?

As the days passed, and became weeks, Aimée felt increasingly useless.

She supposed she could climb on her high horse and insist that the Dowager and Lady Fenella moved to the Dower House—which was what they should have done voluntarily, the moment Septimus had brought her here—and take up the reins of household management herself.

Only she felt that would be an extremely cruel thing to do. Running Bowdon Manor was the Dowager's *raison d'être*. She would not know what to do with herself occupying a more restricted sphere. Aimée could see her expending all that pent-up, unused organising ability upon hounding poor Lady Fenella. The timid girl seemed content enough, keeping to her little routine. Having that torn away from her, and exposing her to the full force of her mama's displeasure, would distress her.

And what did she care about any of it anyway? She had never had any ambition to be mistress of such a vast and complex establishment, nor to cut a dash amongst provincial gentry by throwing lavish dinner parties, or county balls. It was no great hardship to leave all that sort of thing to the Dowager, to whom it meant so much.

Besides, she did not want to take any sort of stand, unless she was sure it was what her husband wanted her to do.

Though the longer she was married to him, the more she began to think that he simply did not care what she did with any part of her day, as long as she welcomed him into her bed at the end of it.

By the time she had been at Bowdon Manor three weeks, even Lady Fenella's pleasure in sharing her company was beginning to pall, in spite of the fact that during her lonely childhood she had dreamed of being able to stay in one place long enough to make a friend.

The truth was that she and Lady Fenella had nothing in common, apart from their love of good food. Last night, as she had been undressing for bed, she had noted how this was affecting her figure. The reflection she saw in the mirror no longer had hollow cheeks. There was a layer of satiny smooth skin covering her formerly protuberant hipbones, and she could hardly make out her ribs at all.

'I am putting on weight,' she said to Lady Fenella, whose head was bent over her latest piece of whitework. 'When I got dressed this morning, it was all I could do to fasten the buttons.'

Lady Fenella's brow furrowed. 'Well, you really ought not to be attempting to fasten your own clothes. It is high time you settled upon a lady's maid.'

Aimée shrugged one shoulder. She did not want to admit it to Lady Fenella, but she had not felt able to trust any of the Bowden Manor girls who had professed an interest in filling the position. Mrs Trimley had trained all of them, and, she was convinced, they would be expected to report her every movement. On the whole, she would rather manage for herself until she could hire somebody who did not owe any allegiance to the Dowager. If Septimus would agree.

She thought he would. He had been very generous with her so far. And had he not promised she should have servants? She could have anything that money could buy.

But not his love.

She sighed heavily and pressed her face to the window-panes. The view from up here was marvellous. If she walked around the inside of the cupola, she could see the entire estate. There were formal gardens close to the house, giving way to shrubberies intersected with winding paths, and, further afield, a wooded hillside that looked incredibly inviting. And it was a lovely sunny day.

'Do you never go out for walks?' Aimée asked Lady Fenella. 'Apart from those little strolls we take through the gardens, to select the blooms to arrange for the house?'

Lady Fenella tilted her head to look at the sky and shook her head.

'Far too sunny,' she observed. 'I should ruin my complexion.'

'Well, I need some exercise,' Aimée declared.

'Well, if you cannot fasten your dress, what does it matter? You look much better for putting on a little weight. When you arrived, you looked as though you had been unwell. I know!' she said, looking genuinely pleased with herself. 'We must go into town, and choose some material and have some new gowns made up. There are one or two dressmakers I know of that are quite capable. Oh, not up to London standards, of course, but adequate for making things for you to wear while you are in the country.'

'But I *like* going for walks,' Aimée protested, hoping she could make Lady Fenella understand that it was not the fit of her clothes that troubled her.

She sat down on the chair opposite Lady Fenella's, and tried to explain how bored she was. 'I am hopeless at the kind of stitchery you do. And I have no souvenirs to paste into scrapbooks. Nor can I sketch very well.

'I hope you do not think me rude in leaving you on your own, but I am going to go outside and explore a little. I want to make the most of the privilege of living in such beautiful surroundings.'

Lady Fenella put her work to one side. 'Oh, but…' she faltered and blinked, then lifted her chin and took a deep breath. 'That is, I do not know what habits prevail abroad, but I could not let you go out without warning you that in England, titled ladies do not go wandering about on their own.' Her face was turning crimson, but she gamely persisted. 'I am only saying this because I am your friend, and I do not want you to give Mama any more reasons to criticise you. And she would think it most odd if you did not have a footman in attendance.'

'A footman?' Aimée nearly burst out laughing. When she thought of the places she had lived, it was absurd to think she now needed to have a footman accompany her for a walk on private land!

But, since she had no wish to wound Lady Fenella, who was, after all, only trying to shield her from the sharp end of her mother's tongue, she decided not to argue on that point.

'Very well, I shall try to find one.'

'And a parasol?' called Lady Fenella anxiously as Aimée strode to the door.

'Yes, if that will make you happy.' Aimée twinkled over her shoulder.

It was a great stroke of luck that just as she reached the foot of the spiral staircase that led back to the upper floor of the house, she spied Jenks, strolling up and down with his shoulders hunched, and a pained expression on his face. He always seemed to be hanging about the place, looking as though he did not know what to do with himself.

She knew exactly how he felt!

'Ah, Jenks! How would you like to take a walk up to the top of the hill to the east of the park?' He was not exactly a footman, but she thought it would do him the world of good to feel useful for once.

'Me, miss? I mean, my lady?' He turned beetroot red. 'Well, I don't know as how I ought to...'

'Apparently, it is not safe for ladies to venture out of doors in these parts without the presence of a footman,' she quipped. 'Would you not like to be a footman, just for an hour or so?'

The perplexed creases in his face turned to a look of resolution. 'I ain't no footman. But I can keep a weather eye out for trouble, my lady.'

'Excellent!' She was glad to see her request had put heart back into this simple-minded fellow.

He waited outside her room while she put on her boots with the daisy motif picked out on the sides. They made her smile just to look at them. But actually lacing them up and taking them out for an airing lifted her spirits no end.

She had thought that Mrs Trimley had shown her all over the house, but Jenks led her downstairs via a back staircase that was clearly only used by servants. It brought them out right next to the flower room, which was only a few yards from the kitchen door.

He did not stop talking as he led her through the

kitchen gardens, and then through a gate that took them into the park. She realised she could not have hit upon a better choice of escort. The poor man was as eager for occupation and companionship as she.

'Is there no proper post for you to fill here?' she asked him.

He snorted in derision. 'Every job as I could mebbe learn to do is filled by some toffee-nosed youngster, wot's related to one of the higher-ups.'

Her empathy for the man redoubled. There was no real position for her here, either. She was feeling more and more like one of those silhouettes that Lady Fenella had pasted into a page of one of her London scrapbooks. Except that it was Septimus who had pasted her into the corner of his life. Just a shadowy outline of the Countess of Bowdon. Without discernible features, or any real depth.

She pushed her own concerns to the back of her mind, by suggesting to Jenks a number of jobs she thought he might be able to do. It quickly became evident that he had no skills that could provide him with gainful employment on land. Not even in the stables.

'Not many sailors do know much about horses,' he pointed out. 'Even some of the officers can barely stay in the saddle. Capting's different, o' course. His pa learned him to ride as a nipper. And soon as he wor big enough to hold the reins, his grandfer learned him to drive his delivery wagon. Can handle a team like one of them Four-Hand Club nobs.'

That snippet of information instantly wiped the smile from her face. It hurt to hear about his childhood from one of his crew. They should be discussing things like this together. Getting to know each other!

'Anyhow,' said Jenks, brightening, 'it ain't as if I'll be kicking my heels here for much longer.'

'Oh, are you leaving us, then?'

'We'll all be leaving, won't we? Capting's going to start looking round all his new houses, to see if he can't fit one of them up as a kind of refuge for old sailors. I'm to help run it.'

'Is…is that so?' she managed to squeak through the shock of hearing such news from a man like Jenks. The crew member all the others seemed to hold in least regard. It had not taken her long to see why Septimus had kept the other four men. Mr Jago had book learning and brains, Nelson had brawn. Billy had a great deal of medical expertise, and the cook…cooked. But Jenks was the living embodiment of the phrase 'good for nothing'.

Her stomach clenched into a knot. Septimus had told her she would make an able lieutenant in his new life. She had looked forward to becoming a valued member of his crew. Yet while he had made sure even Jenks knew what his future held in store, he had not bothered to keep *her* informed of his plans.

'This is a grand spot!' Jenks was saying, as they reached the crest of the hill. 'You can see for miles and miles. Just like being up in the crow's nest, it is. Only without the swaying.'

'Crow's nest?' she gasped stupidly, clutching at a cold pain that had sliced right across her midriff.

The crow's nest, Jenks explained, oblivious to her discomfort, was the vantage point at the top of the mast, from where a man with a telescope would be sent to keep a lookout.

She stood there, only half-listening, as Jenks droned on about things he had seen when he had been on lookout duties. She did not think anything would help her to recover from the blow this man had just dealt her. She had finally run out of excuses to account for the way Septimus treated her. She could not put it down to the strain of taking up his new role in society. Or the fact that he already had so many demands upon his time and energy that he just wanted to relax with her. Her husband could not feel even the smallest scrap of respect for her if he could manage to find time to confide in this, the lowliest member of his crew, but not her!

'Did you ever see a view so grand?' Jenks said now.

She joined him at the crest of the rise, and took in the vista spread below them. It was very different from the view she had seen from the rotunda. She could see the stone walls that marked the border of the park, the lane that ran along its length, and the turning to the main road that went into Burslem. Beyond that were fields, and beyond them, darker smudges staining the valley bottoms that indicated the presence of industry. Turning round, she could just see the glass dome of Bowdon Manor, rising like a crystal island from the deep green woodland they had just traversed.

She sighed. From up here, she had a different perspective. Of the land, of the manor.

Of her marriage.

Not three weeks ago, she had decided she would do her utmost to be the best wife she could be. Since then she had poured herself out for Septimus, in countless ways. Whatever he wanted, she gave without stinting. Whatever he decreed, she obeyed without complaint.

Because she, she realised with shock, had fallen in love with him. When had that happened? The night he had reined in his anger to tend to her injuries, and she had marvelled at meeting a man with such self-control? Or their wedding night, when she had realised that in giving her his name he had truly rescued her, and would for ever keep her safe? Or was it the nights he had spent at Bowdon, reducing her to mindless ecstasy, over and over again? Or the cumulative effect of all that? What woman could possibly guard her heart against such overwhelming odds?

But she would be naïve to think anything would move him from the stance he had taken right from the start. Septimus had no need for the sentimental kind of love she was, she had finally admitted, craving with every fibre of her being. He would never let her close. Would never love her back. His heart might as well be hewn from the solid oak of the ships he'd served in all his life.

Jenks, she realised, had finally shown her that she had no excuse for clinging to any sort of romantic fantasy involving her husband.

Seeing her shiver, he said, 'It is a bit blowy up here, ain't it, my lady? Do you want to head back now?'

With a nod, she turned back towards the luxury of Bowdon Manor.

And as they headed down the path, and gained the shelter of the woods, she wondered how she would cope with this new insight into her future. She knew she had promised herself to Septimus for better or worse. But somehow, she had imagined the 'worse' would perhaps consist of financial hardship.

Not the sheer loneliness of falling deeper in love every day with a man who had no intention of doing anything so feeble as loving her back.

Her mother had often said that it was better to go

hungry sometimes than to be shackled to a cold intolerant man, which had been the fate of Aunt Almeria.

She shook her head at herself, angrily. Septimus was not cold and intolerant. He was good and kind and…

She sighed. He was good and kind to everyone, indiscriminately, that was the trouble. She was not special to him. He had advertised for her in a newspaper, for heaven's sake! She could be anyone. Anyone at all! She had to face facts. All Septimus wanted from her, all he had ever wanted from her, was her name on the marriage licence and her body in his bed. Anything else was surplus to his requirements.

It was a long walk back to the house. Far longer than it had seemed coming out. For she was tired now, and cold, and dispirited by the bleak vision of her future as an unloved wife. Every time he offered her some slight, either real or imaginary, it would take on immense significance, because of the tender state of her heart, while he would remain completely impervious to her misery. How was she to bear it?

Though she had no right to complain. She had agreed to his bargain. It was not his fault that his convenient bride had fallen headlong in love with him. He had not even done anything to encourage her! No, any misery she experienced would be all her own, stupid fault.

They went back into the house by means of the mud-room, where they both left their boots. They were just passing the flower room, when Lady Fenella, who was fiddling with some foliage at the sink, looked up and said, 'Oh! I am so glad to see you. Do you have a minute to help me with this periwinkle?'

She looked really worried. Aimée was not sure how on earth she could be of any help with a flower-arranging crisis, but she smiled, dismissed Jenks and went into the little room.

'Oh, thank heaven I caught you!' Lady Fenella cried, the moment Jenks had sauntered off in the direction of the kitchens. She shut the door firmly, and whirled round, her hands clasped before her.

'Once Mama hears you are back, she will be sending a footman up to fetch you down to the gold sitting room, as though she needs to tell you something. But she has someone there from London. Someone who knows you!' She went across to the workbench, and fumbled in her reticule for a handkerchief. 'Oh dear, oh dear!' She blew her nose and dabbed at her eyes.

Someone who knew her. From London.

'I do not know who he may be, or how she found him…indeed, she says it took some time to run him to ground, but that all the trouble was worth it.'

If that was what the Dowager was saying, it was obvious she had managed to dredge up somebody who knew that her own father had attempted to auction her off. Lord Matthison, most likely, since it was his money she had absconded with. It was amazing to think of the Dowager inviting a man like Lord Matthison into her house. It meant that her hatred was so intense it even overrode her reluctance to mix with any but the most socially superior.

Lord Matthison's reputation was such that he only skirted the fringes of society. Her father had met him in the very lowest sorts of gambling hells where they whispered that his luck at the cards was so phenomenal, he must be in league with the devil.

'She said he will expose you for the f-fraud you are…' She hiccupped.

Fraud? Then she might have found out about the

forged references too. Her connections to Hincksey and his criminal fraternity. She went to one of the stools by the sink and sat down heavily.

'Oh, Aimée, I am so sorry! Is there anything I can do? You know, I hope, by now, that I am your friend? If there is any way I may help you, any way at all…'

Aimée covered her face with her hands. It was over. It was all over. Unless…

Her mind began to whirl. And as her plans took shape, she felt new life flowing through her veins. During these past weeks, while she had been trying so hard to fit in to the mould of English society, attempting to become more like dear, sweet, childlike Lady Fenella, she had been steadily withering away inside. That was why she had been feeling lost and insubstantial as a shadow.

While she had been falling in love with Septimus, she had lost sight of who she really was. Though she wore the clothes her husband had decreed made her look like a Countess, bore the title that qualified her to mingle with the greatest in the land, she would never truly be a docile, indolent, conventional English lady. She was the daughter of two outcasts from society. One of whom had looked upon life as a grand adventure, and the other, a series of opportunities to be seized with both hands.

She lifted her head and gazed up at Lady Fenella, who was hovering over her anxiously.

'You have done me a great service by warning me of impending danger.'

Though, bizarrely, she welcomed the very danger itself, because her heart was beating now with the purpose and resolve she had lacked since setting foot in Bowdon Manor. No, before that, she reflected with a curl of her lip. Since giving herself up into a man's keeping!

'Oh!' cried Lady Fenella. 'Then it is true? This man will expose you for a f-fraud?'

She nodded. In all likelihood, the man in the gold sitting room was Lord Matthison. She had always known it was dangerous to take money from a man with his reputation, without yielding up what he thought he had paid for. But using it had been her only means of escape!

'Oh, dear! And I did like you, so very much!' Lady Fenella wailed.

'I like you, too, Lady Fenella,' said Aimée sadly. 'Thank you for warning me about…this man. And for being a friend to me, while I have lived here.' She stood up. 'I deeply regret the necessity for deceiving you.'

Lady Fenella gave her a look of reproach as she continued, 'And I wish you all the happiness you deserve, in your future. I will always remember you with fondness.'

'You are going to run away, then?'

Aimée smiled ruefully. It was the only solution. She had tried so hard to live respectably. But the truth was that the staid life of a pampered lady, chained down in a marriage of convenience, did not suit her. She was bored, lonely and miserable. And had just realised that she was only going to grow more miserable with every day she spent shackled to a man who was determined he would never fall in love again, particularly not with his own wife.

Besides, she was not going to tamely walk downstairs and let the Dowager win the day!

'I know I have no right to ask you, and I will understand if you refuse my request, but it would be an immense help to me if you could somehow contrive to conceal from your mama that I have returned from my walk. I need a little time to…'

'M-make your escape?' Lady Fenella's eyes bulged in alarm. 'Oh, dear! I do not know how I may do that! Mama said I was to tell her the moment I knew you were home…'

'You could quite easily stay in here and close the door,' Aimée said challengingly. 'Nobody need know you have spoken to me at all. And afterwards, when all the fuss has died down, I am sure nobody will blame you for having tried to avoid what will, inevitably, be a most unpleasant scene.'

Because everyone knew how much Lady Fenella hated the sound of loud, angry voices. Or, indeed, any form of confrontation.

Lady Fenella still looked dubious. So Aimée ruthlessly aimed her next dart at the girl's tender heart.

'It will help his lordship, too,' she said softly. 'You know, none of this is his fault. I withheld several pertinent facts about myself when he agreed to marry me.'

And he had never been sufficiently interested in her to make any attempt to find out so much as one detail of her former life. Why had it taken her so long to see that? Why had she put up with being treated with such a lack of respect? This was what love did to a woman. She became a man's plaything. When she thought of how she had let Septimus treat her like a…a doll, to take out and play with when it suited him, she wanted to hit something!

'Oh!' gasped Lady Fenella, eyeing her clenched fists with trepidation. 'Mama maintained from the very first that you were an actress!'

Aimée did not bother to correct her misapprehension. What did it matter now? Besides, it only went to show how easily her flight could be explained away with no suspicion of any wrongdoing falling upon her husband.

'Then surely,' she said, 'you must wish to help to spare him the embarrassment my exposure would bring him?' And embarrassment, she was sure, was the strongest emotion he would feel. A man had to love his wife for his heart to be touched by anything she did. And Septimus was impervious to the gentler emotions. She should know! She had been pouring herself out on him, ceaselessly, without making the slightest impression. Passing every test he set her, she reflected bitterly, and yet never quite measuring up.

'I promise you,' she pushed on relentlessly, 'it will be far better for him if I simply…disappear.'

Oh, yes, he would carry on with his duties as Earl of Bowdon and commence upon his charitable work, without missing a beat. Ironically, it was the very strength of purpose that made her admire him so very much which would enable him to carry on perfectly well without her.

She had played her part. He had needed a wife. Any wife. And it had been just her misfortune that she had stumbled into his path and fallen in love with him, when that was the last thing he had wanted.

She supposed it ought to be a comfort to know that she had enabled him to take up the role he had inherited, in the way he wanted to go about it.

He would be a good landlord to his tenants, just as he had been a good captain to his crew. He was so capable, and so diligent, that it would not be long before he made all his long-neglected estates prosper.

It would be as though she had never existed.

Pain ripped through her. And it occurred to her she ought to be grateful that Lord Matthison had turned up to denounce her for a thief. She had come perilously close to spending the rest of her life dashing herself to pieces against the unyielding rock that was her husband's heart.

'Oh, dear,' said Lady Fenella. 'I do hate the need to employ subterfuge of any sort!'

'I know,' said Aimée. 'But once I am gone, there will be no more need for it, I assure you. And everyone will be far happier.'

'I shan't!' gulped Lady Fenella, her eyes filling with tears. And then, with a little sob, she turned to the sink, picked up her scissors and set about a bucket of greenery with surprising savagery.

Aimée knew she did not have much time. Somebody was bound to have spotted her return. Or Jenks would announce it, in all innocence, and somebody would be sent to fetch her.

So she hurried up to her bedroom, and, having glanced briefly about to make sure nobody was lying in wait for her there, went to her wardrobe. On the floor lay a prettily embroidered cotton bag. Lady Fenella had given it to her, after Aimée had showed her the flowers she had pressed. 'You may use it for collecting more specimens,' she had said. 'I have no use for it,' she had added, with a timid smile when Aimée had hesitated to accept it, because she was not really interested in pressing flowers, as a hobby.

But even then, she thought with a wry smile, she had seen that it would make an excellent overnight bag. There was a broad strap that went across one shoulder, and several little inside pockets that were supposed to be used for holding scissors, or string, or other little necessities. She went to her dressing table, tugged open the drawers and filled those handy pockets with a couple of pairs of stockings, a nightdress, some tooth-powder and a toothbrush.

There was only one other item she was determined not to leave behind. Once she had that in the larger, central compartment of the bag, she scooped her brush and comb from the dressing table and did up the button that fastened the bag shut.

She had no need of further preparations for flight. She had not yet taken off her bonnet and coat from her walk. Her petticoats were heavy with guineas and her corsets stuffed with banknotes. There was nothing left to do but walk out.

Head bowed, and finding it hard to breathe through the mingled pain and anger that felt as though it was solidifying where her lungs ought to be, she made use of the back way that Jenks had just shown her. When she reached the corridor that ran past the kitchens, she paused, to make certain that the staff were busy enough not to notice one small, lone female scurrying to the back door. Though what would they think if they did see her? All she was carrying was one little satchel, which everyone knew Lady Fenella had given her for the purpose of collecting botanical specimens. She looked as though she was just going for another walk. They would have no idea that this was a flight.

Her daisy boots were still in the mudroom where she had left them. She stamped her feet into them. How on earth could she have been stupid enough to think that marrying somebody would save her from the lecher-ous lord her father had sold her to? Or running away to Yorkshire to work as a governess? She marched out into the kitchen garden. France, that was where she should have gone! Yes, she ought to have put the width of the Channel between herself and her tormentors.

It took her several attempts to fumble open the latch to the garden gate. But at length she was through it, and out into the formal gardens. She did not take the path Jenks had led her down earlier, but struck out across the lawns towards the copse, which she had seen from high up on the rise, that divided the park from the lane. She was going to take the lane to the main road and head for the town. She could find a room in an inn, and then discover the best route to the coast, without having to go back through London.

It would be harder, in many ways, to make a fresh start as a woman alone. But she had connections in Paris. And Amiens, come to think of it. And at least she could be herself. Free to make her own decisions, and live exactly as she pleased.

Yes, free, she sniffed, wiping at her eyes. She did not know why she had ever thought marriage would be the answer. Respectability was not all it was cracked up to be.

And love most definitely was not. Not when the man you loved felt nothing for you in return. No, that was the most painful state of affairs. Worse even than knowing your own father saw you only as a means of saving his own hide?

Yes. Much worse. Her father's betrayal had shocked and hurt and angered her. Having to flee from the parent who should have protected her had left her scarred.

But staying with Septimus would destroy her.

She did not look back. She had no wish to have any further memories of Bowdon Manor. Particularly not seen through a watery haze of despair.

It was bad enough knowing she would never see Septimus again.

She stumbled on an obstacle that, had she not been crying so much, she would certainly have avoided.

'Pull yourself together!' she muttered angrily. Now was not the time to give way to self-pity. Tonight, in whichever inn she managed to reach, she could weep for the man she had loved and lost. And mourn the life that might have been hers if not for her shameful past...

She wiped her face with the back of her hand. Stupid! Stupid! There had never been any chance of making a success of her marriage to Septimus. And it was better to end it now, while she was young enough and still mentally strong enough to recover. If she had stayed, enduring his indifference, while she kept on loving him, it would have torn her to pieces.

Flinging her shoulders back and lifting her head high, she strode out with renewed resolve.

She needed to look like a Countess, going out for a walk.

Not a weak, snivelling, pathetic, broken-hearted girl, fleeing from the shattered remnants of her brief and ill-advised marriage.

Never, she vowed. She would never let anybody know that her heart had been broken.

And she would never let anybody touch it, ever again!

Chapter Twelve

'Gone out again? What do you mean, gone out again?'

'Like I said, Cap'n, I mean, my lord, sir,' stammered Jenks. 'I just went to the kitchen to get a jug of ale, and when I come out, she was running out the back door. Watched her set off across the park again, but not the same way we went before.'

Why should she do that? Go straight out again, not minutes after coming back from a lengthy walk?

Something cold twisted into a knot deep inside him. She was leaving.

He just knew it. She had been growing more and more unhappy with every day she was married to him. At first, she had put a brave face on things. Done her utmost to fit in with what he wanted, without asking anything for herself.

And he had never asked her what she wanted. All he had thought about was resisting her, so he had rebuffed any attempt she made to show affection. And because she took her cues from him, because she was desperate to please him, she had stopped. He could not believe how much he missed seeing her face light up when he walked into a room. Or the little hugs and kisses she would give him. He had told himself it was just as well he had nipped all that sort of thing in the bud, if he could miss it so much after so short an exposure to it.

Though he could not help feeling a twinge of conscience as he noted that with each passing day she withdrew further and further into herself.

The men he had set to watch her said she just moped about in Lady Fenella's wake all day.

He should have taken her out with him, in a carriage if she could not ride. Should have shown her off to his tenants. She would have been wonderful with them. Not haughty or patronising, but genuinely interested in them and their problems.

Instead of which he had deliberately excluded her. Forced her into the idle, useless role of the very kind of wife he had gone to such lengths to avoid marrying! He knew there would have been dozens of women only too keen to marry a relatively young, and wealthy Earl. Society women who would be content to just drift about all day, like Lady Fenella, sewing, and such.

But Aimée was not that kind of woman.

And she had finally reached the end of her tether.

She must have realised that she could not continue in the kind of loveless marriage he had decreed they should have.

She needed affection. And he had deliberately starved her of it.

When he thought of the way she had used to look at him, when they first became lovers, he felt his stomach curdle. During those early days, he had been aware of her burgeoning feelings for him. He attributed it to the fact that he had given this little waif more than anybody had given her in her entire life. Now he saw that with a little effort he might have coaxed her into believing she loved him. What would it have cost him? A few soft words? A little kindness? Dammit all, he had vowed in church to cherish her! He had meant to, at the time.

But what had he done instead? Kept her at arm's length, because he did not want to get hurt again, the way Miranda had hurt him. But God in heaven! If Aimée had left him, it would be far worse than anything Miranda had done to him. Miranda had been trouble from the start. If he had not been a green boy, he would not have been dazzled by her beauty, or hoodwinked by her wiles. He would have kept a wide berth from such a duplicitous creature!

He had been lying to himself when he had used the discovery of that money as a proof that Aimée was not trustworthy. The truth was that he had been afraid of the power she might have over him if he let himself love her.

Yes, it was true that she was concealing something from him. But she was such a good person that she must have some compelling reason for holding on to her secrets.

Could she simply be afraid of the consequences of revealing what she had been involved in? He only had to think of the state she had been in when they had met. Jumping at shadows. Running off into the night because she was used to men trying to take advantage of her, when all she wanted was to be respectable.

Aimée was nothing like Miranda. She was sweet, and kind, and brave, and…

And what the hell was he doing sitting here, working out where he had gone wrong, when with every pass-

242   *Captain Corcoran's Hoyden Bride*

ing minute Aimée might be getting further and further away from him?

He ran to the stables. He had not got back from Endon so very long ago, and, as he had suspected, the lad had not finished unsaddling his horse. It was a work of moments to get his mount readied and then he was galloping out of the yard, pounding along the drive for all he was worth. And it was only then that he realised he was in his shirtsleeves. He had taken off his jacket and draped it over the back of the chair, because he was about to launch into some paperwork and did not want the ink to stain the fine fabric.

If she was not leaving him, but only going about some innocent activity, he was going to look a complete fool, galloping up to her like this and pouring out all his doubts.

He did not care. He had not made a very good fist of being her husband, up till now, but he had to tell her that it would all be different. If she would just forgive him for his stupidity, and give him another chance...

And that was when he saw her. She was not yet off Bowdon land, thank God. She must have heard the beat of his horse's hooves because she glanced over her shoulder...then darted into the trees.

A fresh shaft of pain seared right through him. His gut instinct had been right. She was trying to hide from him. Probably thought he was about estate business, and might not have noticed her. She would have no idea he was looking specifically for her. Because he had let her think he did not care!

He put the horse straight at the trees. She could not have got far into them.

His horse reared up on to its hind legs as he drew up far too close to the tightly packed trunks for the creature's liking. He kicked his feet free of the stirrups and leaped down. He would be better on foot amongst the dense growth, anyway.

To his astonishment, she had not run very far at all. She was peeping out at him from behind the bole of a slender beech tree, looking, if anything, a little shame-faced.

Then she stepped out into full view and lifted her chin as she faced him. The same way she had lifted it after the Dowager had insulted her. He felt the gesture like a slap to the face. She was expecting him to hurt her and bracing herself for it.

Why would she not? All he had done since they had met was hurt her!

'Don't leave, Aimée,' he pleaded. 'Whatever I have done that makes you want to walk away from our marriage—'

She gasped. 'It is not *you*!'

He laughed bitterly and indicated the bag she had over her shoulder. 'What is that, then? What have you got in there?'

'Oh, this…' Her eyes darted from his, and she laid a protective hand over the flap. She did not want him to see whatever it was she had in there.

So he grabbed hold of it, meaning to open it and just look. She stepped back, in consternation, and the thing was so flimsy, the strap broke. The contents went tumbling on to the beech mast. As he had suspected. Brush and comb, stockings, nightdress and…

'Oh, no!' she cried, as the wind riffled through the pages of the *History of the Present War in Spain and Portugal*, sending the flowers she had preserved from her wedding bouquet swirling away into the under-growth.

He sank to his knees, clutching the book in his hands as she darted off after her treasures, braving brambles and getting her bonnet knocked off by low-hanging branches. For the sake of a half-dozen papery-thin flowers and a scrap of material she had cut from her wedding dress. He had recognised the pattern as it fluttered across the ground.

It felt like a reprieve. There was still hope for them if she could want to take things like this with her, wherever she had been planning to run. A book he had given her. Because *he* had given it to her. He could not imagine her actually wanting to read such stuff.

'You don't really want to leave me, do you?'

'What?' She was intent on retrieving just one more flower, though it was no mean feat, what with tripping over her skirts and pushing her straggling hair out of her face. When her bonnet had come off, it had dragged her hair down with it.

She looked at him warily over her shoulder.

He raised the book, drawing her eye to it. 'You ran upstairs and were back down again in the time it took Jenks to down a jug of ale. You only grabbed a few essentials. And this. To remember me by.'

'What of it?' she snapped, folding the three blooms she had managed to salvage into the carefully hemmed scrap of printed cotton she had cut from her wedding dress. 'It makes no difference now.' She tucked the lot into a pocket of her skirts. 'I will not be bothering you with my unwanted emotions any more.'

'Perhaps I want you to bother me with them,' he said, getting to his feet.

'No,' she said grimly. 'You told me from the start you did not want this marriage to be about love. You have made it perfectly clear you will not change your mind about that.'

'Oh, but I have,' he said, wishing he dared take a step towards her. He was half-afraid that she was on the verge of running. She had that look about her—an air of subdued desperation.

Flinging up her chin another notch, she said, 'Get back on your horse, Septimus, and pretend you have not seen me. It will be better if you claim ignorance of my doings today. It would have been better...' She glanced ruefully at the book, as though mentally bidding it farewell. 'Better if you had not come after me at all.'

'Better for whom?' He shook his head. 'Certainly not for me. Not any more. At first, it is true, I thought it would be best to marry a woman I hardly knew, rather than one I thought I loved. Like a fool I thought if I went into marriage with a clear head, I would not get hurt. Miranda, you see, my first wife, she did not...well, she did die, eventually. But she had left me before that. She swore that she loved me, that she could not live without me. That,' he said bitterly, 'was how she got me to propose to her. I sent her all my pay, and she spent it going to places where she could meet someone else. When I came home wounded, when I needed her the most, she took one look at my face and ran off with another man. And I swore I would never trust a woman's word again.'

'No, how could she?' It was Aimée who closed the distance between them, Aimée who reached up and cupped his face with her hand. She had heard the facts from his men, but never truly seen the pain his wife's behaviour had caused him.

'Because she was nothing like you, Aimée. She had

no heart, no notion of loyalty. I should have seen it
from the start, but I was so busy trying not to fall too
deeply for you… I got all tangled up in wanting you,
yet wanting to stay free of you. I have been thrashing
about, inside—' he tossed the book aside and tugged
her hand down to his chest '—like a fish in a net. Night
after night, I had to come to your bed. And day after
day I grew angrier and angrier with myself for needing
you. Kept myself busy sorting out everyone else's problems, to stop myself thinking about you. And nothing
worked. Nothing.' His heart was beating so fast it was
making him shake. 'I don't want to live without you,
Aimée. My life will not mean anything to me if you
go.'

'I…I do mean something to you, after all?' she said,
searching his face to see, he expected, if he was telling
her the truth.

'Everything,' he said simply. 'I love you.' And felt a
great weight rolling off him. He had thought it would
chain him down, if he ever said that to a woman again.
But instead, he felt freer than he had for a long time,
because he was no longer fighting himself.

'Please come home.'

She took a step back, shaking her head, tears welling
in her eyes.

'I c-can't,' she whispered. 'Septimus…I told you
it was nothing you have done. Oh, why did you have
to tell me you love me? It makes everything so much
worse!'

'How can it?' he said, releasing her hand reluctantly.
'I know I have been harsh with you thus far, but you
still feel some affection for me, or you would not have
tried to keep a memento of our time together. Don't
you see? It will all be different now. Give me another

chance, and I swear, this time, I will be all you want a husband to be.'

But her eyes shifted away from his, and her hand went to her waist, where he knew she kept all that money hidden. And he suddenly wondered if there was more to her flight than just running out of patience with him. Yes, there must be! A woman like Aimée would never just give up on her marriage. She had too much pride.

'Look, I know you were in some kind of trouble before we met. But I do not care what you may have done, or what you have been involved in—that is all in the past.'

And as he said it, he recalled the way she had craved respectability so much, she had fled out into the night, rather than give herself to a man she feared would debauch her. Married him, when she was still a little afraid of him, rather than return to whatever life she had known before. And, he realised in a blinding flash, applied for work as a governess rather than use the money that might have given her an easy life.

She was not a criminal. Not by nature. She would never willingly return to whatever she had been mixed up in, whatever she had done to come by so much money. He almost laughed. He already loved her so much that he had come chasing after her before he had even worked this much out. 'Whatever it is you fear, whatever it is you are fleeing from, it will not make me think any less of you. It could not.'

She looked back at him then, and he could see hope flickering to life within her.

'Just come home with me and I will protect you. Stand by you. That is what a husband is for!'

But then she shook her head, fresh tears welling in her eyes.

'No,' she whispered. Her lips trembling with the effort it was taking her not to break apart, she said, 'You must just go back to the house, and meet who-ever it is the Dowager has summoned from London to expose me, and pretend you know nothing about any of it! There is no need for anybody to know you were complicit in my crimes. Just tell everyone that you were completely taken in by me,' she said desperately. 'Let them blame me for it all, I shan't care. I won't be here to face it.'

Crimes? 'The Dowager?'

She turned then, intending to retrieve her bonnet, but he caught hold of her arm and spun her back.

'It is about time you did face up to things, instead of always running away! For once in your life, woman, can you not stand and fight?'

'No amount of fighting will get me what I want,' she said bitterly.

'And just what is it you want, Aimée?' he urged her. 'Tell me.'

She shrugged off his hand, and looked away.

'I thought I wanted you to love me. I thought if you loved me...' She tailed off, looking confused. 'I truly thought you never would. Ever. And since our whole farce of a marriage is ab-bout to be blown out of the water, I stupidly thought the last thing I could do for you was to arrange things so that the scandal would f-fall on me, not you! I don't want,' she said, raising woebegone eyes, 'to bring you down with me.'

'You are trying to tell me that you are leaving it all behind, the safety, the security, the respectability you have craved all your life, to save me from scandal?'

She nodded. 'The only way for you to get clear of the sc-scandal that is about to erupt is for you to l-let me go. P-please, Septimus,' she begged him, 'go back to the house, and act surprised when you hear…' She laughed bitterly through her tears. 'No need for you to act. You have not the remotest idea where I came from, or what I went through to get out of London, have you?'

'No, but you can tell me,' he said, grasping her by the shoulders. 'Whatever it is you fear about this man who has come here, just tell me, and we can deal with it. You do not have to fight him on your own! I won't turn away from you, I swear.'

Aimée pushed the straggling hank of hair off her face for the umpteenth time and swallowed down a sob. The expression on her face was so desolate, so…humiliated, that he could not help putting his arms round her and drawing her close. She bowed her head, slid her arms about his waist, and, for a few moments, she just clung to him.

But after a while, he felt her stiffening, drawing away. He let her go, knowing that at last she had drawn the courage from deep within herself to tell him the worst.

'My father is not dead, Septimus.'

It was the last thing he would have expected her to say. While he was still wondering where she was going with that piece of information, she hurriedly added, 'I may have led you to believe that, by saying I am all alone in the world now. I…I did not tell you an outright lie. Not once!' She hung her head. 'Though I have skirted round the edges of the truth very often.'

He nodded. 'I know.'

'What?' She looked up at him, consternation all over her face. 'That my father is not dead, or…'

'That you are economical with the truth.'

A look of hurt flickered across her face.

'Sometimes,' he amended. 'But it does not matter, Aimée. I still love you. I cannot help it. I do not think anything you could say or do would make me stop loving you. Believe me, I have tried, and it is like trying to swim against the tide.'

But her beautiful face was all closed up like a coffin. Her eyes diamond bright with tears she was valiantly holding in check, she said, 'He betrayed me. My father. He was in some gambling hell, losing heavily as usual. When somebody offered to clear his debts in return for my virginity, he auctioned me off, Septimus...' She drew in a ragged breath. 'Sold me to the h-highest bidder!'

'What?' How could a man do that to his own daughter? It was appalling.

When she saw the shock written all over his face, she stepped smartly back.

He reached for her, but she shook her head. She was trembling now, her cheeks fiery red.

'You wanted me to tell you! So let me speak!' Head high, fists clenched, she said, 'One of the men at that table, a man who claimed to be my friend, ran to warn me. And then Lord Matthison's servant came with an enormous sum of money...' a shudder of disgust shook her slim body '...for apparently the virginity of a lady with my antecedents is worth a great deal! And a message that in future he expected only to deal directly with me. And after that, as far as I was concerned, my father was dead to me. How could he have done that?'

For a moment she looked so lost, so bewildered and alone that it was all he could do not to pull her into his arms again and stop her confession right there. But as he moved towards her, arms outstretched, she took another step back, holding up her hands in front of her to ward him off.

'No,' she hissed. 'You wanted this! You shall not stop me until I have told you the whole story! I took the money and ran. Yes, as you say, I am good at running!' She laughed a little hysterically. 'I learned that from a master. All my life, whenever things got too hot in one town, we would run from Papa's creditors and start out again somewhere else. A new city. A new country.'

Her heel came up against her bonnet then. She stooped to pick it up, avoiding seeing the expression on his face by making herself busy brushing off the leaves.

'And hiding! I knew all about that, too. I moved from one lodging house to another after I fled Papa, never staying more than one night in each of them, until the day I saw your advertisement. It was like a sign— that I could have a new life, a new sort of life, doing honest work. I did not care that technically I would be somebody's servant. Mr Jago said he would give me tickets for the stage. I had been too afraid to go to the booking office myself, in case they were watching out for me. But this way, all I had to do was pick up the tickets minutes before I boarded the coach. Even if they saw me, they would not have time to stop me. Only—' she twisted the bonnet round and round in her fingers '—only Mr Jago said I had to provide charac- ter references. And I had never worked before. Had no previous employer to vouch for me. So I contacted some people…people I'd already had dealings with, in my efforts to keep Papa from debtors' prison. They supplied Mr Jago with a set of fake references, which as you know I sent to him along with my letter of acceptance. Which is probably a criminal offence. Buying and using a set of forged references.' She glanced up at him anxiously. 'Quite apart from misappropriating the funds Lord Matthison sent me…'

He looked furious. Her heart quailed. But when he spoke, it was to say, 'You have been the victim of wicked men, or almost their victim. You did what you had to do. No more, no less. If anything, it makes me admire you all the more.'

'Th-then you don't…?'

He never knew what it was she had meant to say, because she had flung herself into his arms, was clinging to him and sobbing. But the sobs were of relief, not anguish. And even when she stopped, she still clung to him. It was one of the sweetest moments of his life.

'You have not told me anything that convinces me you have any reason to run away from *me*. Or what made you take to your heels today, of all days.'

'It is because of that man,' she said, tilting her head back so that she could look into his face, without moving away from him. 'The man the Dowager tracked down!'

'Damn the woman!' he said. 'I suspected she was investigating Miranda's background. She must have sent some of her minions to find out more about you.'

'Lady Fenella warned me that she sent for him so that he could expose my f-fraud, she called it. And I knew it would all come out. What my father tried to do must have been the talk of the gentlemen's clubs. And they might have found out how I cheated to get the means to live and work away from London. How you…you have married a woman who is no better than Haymarket ware!'

He shook his head. 'How can you say that? When you went to such lengths to preserve your virtue?'

'Septimus,' she said, looking up at him in wonder, her fingers kneading the silk of his shirt sleeves. 'Septimus, you…' Then she shook her head, a frown pleating her brow. 'You cannot ignore the fact that the Dowager has found somebody who was involved in that disgusting auction. Most probably Lord Matthison. He has the reputation of a devil! He would not let such a massive amount of money go, I am sure. He is bound to want revenge for being balked of his prey.'

'No, I do not think it can be him,' Septimus replied. 'At about the time you answered my advertisement, he was creating another scandal by claiming some seamstress was his long-lost fiancée—the woman everyone thinks he murdered several years ago. I would think he is far too busy trying to clear his name of that crime, to bother hunting you down, Aimée. Not for any reason that we cannot deal with.'

'Deal with? We?' Her fingers dug into his sleeves so hard he could feel her nails through the silk. 'Even if you do stand by me, Septimus, my shame and disgrace is going to be noised abroad. I will never be able to look anyone in the face ever again!'

As if to illustrate how she felt, she covered her face with her hands. He could feel, from the convulsive movements of her shoulders, that she was crying again.

But at least when he hugged her to himself, she leaned into him. He could almost revel in the fact that, finally, his independent little wife needed to feel his arms about her.

Only he could not stand to see her this upset.

'God,' he groaned, 'if only I had made you tell me

where you'd got that money from when I first found it.
I could have stopped the Dowager in her tracks.'

She jerked in his arms. Looked up at him in shock.
'You knew about it? Why did you not…when…?'
Understanding dawned on her. 'That is why you would
not sleep with me again. Why you always let me dress
and undress in private after that first time.'

He nodded. 'Forgive me? I was so afraid of what you
might have done. It was not until today, when I thought
I had lost you, that I realised you would never willingly
commit a crime.'

She bit down on her lower lip, worrying at it with her
teeth. Then, with a sigh, she said, 'I wanted to tell you
about it so many times, but I was so afraid of having
to tell you…'

'And I made it even harder for you than it already
was.' He kissed her brow tenderly, and tucked her hair
behind her ears. She blinked up at him, her expression
wary.

'What woman could have spoken freely about such a
sordid incident, orchestrated by her own father? It must
have shattered you. Ah, Aimée, Aimée, I am sorry I
made you feel you had to keep your past concealed from
me. You see, from the start, I had thought you were too
good to be true, and when I saw the money, I thought
I had unearthed your one flaw. You were a thief. And
perhaps you were keeping that money hidden, so that
you could run away at a moment's notice, just like you
did today.'

She looked appalled.

'What kind of woman do you think I am?'

'The kind that could not possibly love me,' he said
urgently. 'What gently bred woman could love this?'
He indicated the scarring on his face with a grimace.

'I could,' she declared. Then she took a deep breath, flung up her chin, and said, 'I do. Septimus, I have met genuinely ugly men in the past. Men who did not have any scars on the outside at all. You are, without doubt, the most handsome man I have ever met!'

His great frame shuddered. 'I have wanted you so badly. But from the first moment I saw you, I thought you were so beautiful that you must surely flinch from a wreck like me. That night, when you ran away, I feared it was because you could not stomach me...'

'Septimus, no!' She reached up and stroked his cheek. 'It does not matter. It has never mattered to me. This...' she ran her fingers gently over his eyepatch '...is only on the outside of you. It is not what you are.' Briefly, her face hardened. 'That Miranda person has a lot to answer for!'

'She does,' he agreed. 'When she left me, to live openly as another man's mistress, I had to rely on my men to nurse me through all the fevers and the pain that followed. And I thought, only men know what loyalty means. At least, men who have lived and fought on board ship together. But women...' He shook his head ruefully.

'I do not deserve you,' he continued. 'I kidnapped you, seduced you, forced you to put up with my abominable relatives, spoke not two kind words together to you. Still, you would have sacrificed yourself today, in order to salvage the remnants of my own reputation. That is real loyalty. You...' His voice lowered to little more than an incredulous whisper. 'You have shown me today that you really do love me. Don't you?'

Tears filled her eyes and spilled down her cheeks. 'Yes,' she whispered. 'I have often wished I did not, but...'

'Ah, Aimée,' he growled, hauling her up against his chest so hard that she could scarcely draw breath. 'I know. I did not want to love you, either. It hurts so much. Love. Doesn't it?'

And then he kissed her with such passion, she felt it right down to her toes. He was still clutching her so hard it was painful to breathe. But she did not care.

She tore her mouth free. 'It does not hurt any more, Septimus. Not now I know you love me too.'

For a few moments they just stood there, searching each other's faces, to see if it could really be true. And then, as it dawned on each of them that all their behaviour made complete sense, they moved into each other's arms again and clung together. The moment was too poignant to kiss. They just stood there, rocking gently, breathing hard.

At length, Septimus said, 'We have both made mistakes. Misjudged each other. Because we married whilst we were still strangers. And because both of us had learned, through the vilest sorts of betrayal, to distrust the opposite sex. But, Aimée, we have the rest of our lives to learn each other.'

'Yes.' She sighed, but then pulled back far enough so that she could gaze up into his face. She looked worried.

'Septimus, what are we going to do about that man who is waiting for us back at the hall?' A frown pleated her brow. 'It might not be Lord Matthison himself. It might be someone to arrest me over the money I made off with. Or those forged references...'

He grinned. 'You don't know how good it is to hear you say *us*, like that.' He gripped her round the waist and twirled her round, laughing aloud.

'No, Septimus, put me down. We have to be serious for a minute...'

'I am serious,' he grumbled, but he did set her on her feet. 'Stop worrying about those references, sweetheart,' he said, kissing the tip of her nose. 'Nobody but you and I, and Mr Jago, know aught of them, anyway.'

'And Hincksey,' she pointed out. 'And whoever forged them. And whichever lad hopped in through an open study window and stole the sheet of headed, embossed notepaper…'

He reached down to smooth away the deep creases between her brows. 'Nobody can start any kind of action against you if I burn the wretched things. And deny all knowledge of them.'

'Y-yes,' she agreed shakily, 'but what about the money I took from Lord Matthison? I spent quite a bit of it, clearing the worst of Papa's debts, and renting rooms, and getting those references forged, not to mention paying for food and clothes…' she said, her fingers kneading at his shirt.

'Have you completely forgotten that you are married to a rich man? Whatever sum he demands, I can easily pay…'

'I still have quite a bit of it.' Her expression cleared. 'We can manage it between us. Oh,' she breathed, 'you have no idea how good it will feel to be able to fling it all back in his face!'

'That's my girl!' he said, then kissed her. Another of those toe-curling kisses that left her breathless, and shaken, but feeling, oh, so very happy.

'Now,' he said, taking her hand in his, 'let us return, and face the music together!'

She hung back for a moment. 'A-are you quite sure? It is all very well talking about flinging his money in his face, but if we go back now, it will all come out. Every sordid detail. Of my father's vile bargain, and our arrangement, and how you put an advertisement in the papers for a governess so that you would not get saddled with a society miss for a wife...'

'So?'

'B-but you cannot want it all to come out! What will people say? What will people think? You have a position in society now...'

'Aimée, so long as I have your love, I do not care what anyone else may think. I only kept quiet about you answering that advertisement because I thought you might not like people to know how low you had been brought. Also because I suspected there was something in your past you needed to keep concealed.'

'And I only went along with that silly story about meeting years ago, and never forgetting each other, because I thought you did not want Lady Fenella upset!'

In trying so hard to please each other, they had only succeeded in bolstering the sense of mistrust each had for the opposite sex.

'I do not give a rap what Lady Fenella may think about our marriage. Nor anyone else, either. I am the Earl of Bowdon now, and there is nothing anyone can do to alter that. If they do not like the way I am going to run my life, and my estates, they can go hang! And if they do not approve of my choice in wife, they can... well, I won't pollute your ears with what I was about to say.' He laughed.

'God, I love you!' he said, crushing her to his chest, and burying his face in her hair. 'And your feelings, and your happiness, mean more to me than anything else in this world. If things get a bit unpleasant here after we have faced down the Dowager's mysterious visitor, we never need to come back. I have estates and smaller properties all over the place. Probably all equally run down, and in need of attention. I have been planning to visit them all and assess the situation. You shall come with me and tell me which of them you like best, and we can settle there.'

'Oh,' she said very quietly. If only he had said that yesterday. How much hurt he could have spared her!

And how much hurt she could have spared them both, if she had been able to trust him, to begin with. He had said he had fought loving her, but in her turn, had she not distrusted the feelings he evoked, as well? Though she had spoken to him of love, she had done no better than him, not really.

When he would have stood by her, dealt with her problems, lifted her burden of guilt…

Solemnly, she placed her hand in his. Finally, she knew she had found a man she could trust. She had not thought such a person existed. But here he was. And knowing it brought peace, something she had never known before, settling over her like a mantle.

'I am ready to go back now,' she said. 'And deal with whatever we may find waiting for us there. Together.'

A lump came to his throat.

'I won't let you down again, Aimée,' he vowed.

She smiled again. 'I know. I trust you.'

And he could see it in her face. She did.

Hand in hand, they left the shelter of the trees.

The horse had long since grown tired of standing about with nothing to do and had trotted back to its stable where it knew the long-overdue food and water were to be found.

So they walked back to Bowdon Manor. Pausing

every now and then to kiss. Or to hug. Or to just simply stand there, looking at each other.

As if they could still not quite believe how fortunate they were.

Chapter Thirteen

Aimée had sneaked out of one of the back doors of Bowdon Manor, head down, in floods of tears.

Now she was climbing up the steps to the front door, hand in hand with her husband, and her heart was singing with joy.

Septimus handed her satchel, which he had been carrying, to the supercilious upper footman who had smoothly opened the door just as they had reached the top step.

'Take this up to her ladyship's room, would you?' he said. 'She will not be needing it again today.'

'Not ever,' she confirmed, squeezing Septimus's arm, and rubbing her cheek affectionately against his shoulder.

Far from rebuffing her, as he had been wont to do until now when she attempted to be demonstrative, he hauled her into his arms, and kissed her full, and lingeringly, on the lips.

The scandalised footman cleared his throat. 'Begging your pardon,' he said in a repressive tone, 'but the

Dowager Countess has asked me to inform you there is a visitor for you, my lady. They are waiting for you in the gold sitting room.'

Aimée's stomach lurched uncomfortably. She knew that whoever, and whatever, awaited her in the Dowager's lair, Septimus would not let her down. But it was not going to be a pleasant business. The Dowager would gloat. Septimus would be shamed by association with her. And as for poor Lady Fenella…how was she going to feel upon learning that the woman she had befriended out of the goodness of her heart, had narrowly escaped degradation only by consorting with criminals and fleeing with her ill-gotten gains?

'Septimus,' she said as they began to mount the stairs, 'are you sure we need to meet whoever it is? Could we not just—?'

'Thinking of running again?' he said, with a disapproving frown.

'N-not really, it is just that…'

He paused on the landing, gently took her by the shoulders and turned her so that she was facing him.

'I know this is not going to be easy for you. But once it is settled, you will be free of the shadow that has been hanging over you ever since…we first met,' he finished, conscious that the footman was still within hearing.

'And *then* we can leave, if you do not think you can bear to stay within the Dowager's orbit. In fact, I shall not be sorry to see the back of this place.' He raised his head, scanning the long corridor off which numerous doors led to the many reception rooms, all of which were showing signs of decay through disuse. 'It would take an army of staff to refurbish and run this place, and even then, it will never make a comfortable home.' Then, suddenly, a wicked grin lit up his face. 'I tell you what, though—it would make a wonderful asylum for crippled sailors. Just think how many we could house on this floor alone!'

The footman came to an abrupt halt and swung round to stare at them. The expression on his face was so appalled that, in spite of her best efforts, Aimée could not help giggling. The servants here had not accepted her as their new mistress, thanks to the Dowager's lack of discretion. They probably all believed she was an impostor, who was about to be ousted.

And so it was that when they entered the faded glory of the Dowager's sitting room, she was not clinging to her husband's arm like a frightened criminal brought up before her judge, but flushed from his kisses and giggling.

The look of utter disgust on the Dowager's face sobered her, though. Suddenly Aimée was very conscious that she had abandoned her bonnet somewhere in the woods, and her hair was half-up and half-down. Since she had been crying, and wiping her tears away with her gloved hands, her face was probably quite dirty. Her boots were muddy, the hem of her skirts was damp, and there was a rent where she had braved the edge of the bramble patch to rescue one of her treasured pressed flowers.

She flung up her chin. Yes, she might look a bit dishevelled, but a kinder woman would have asked if some mishap had befallen her. The Dowager was always ready to judge, but never to forgive. It was a miracle she had managed to produce a daughter as gentle as Lady Fenella.

Instinctively, she glanced up at Septimus for reassurance. And it occurred to her that he looked no better than she did. In his shirtsleeves, breeches and riding boots, with his windswept tawny hair, the eyepatch and the grim expression, he looked for all the world like a pirate!

A pirate and a hoyden. A well-matched pair!

Yes, she thought, giving his arm an affectionate squeeze, at last she could believe that they truly belonged together.

He did not care about her past. So nothing could blight their future. Nothing!

No, it was the Dowager who would suffer the most as a result of the hornet's nest she had stirred up. The story that was about to come to light today was the stuff that would keep gossip buzzing for a very long time. This would not bother either her, or Septimus, since neither of them had ever moved in that kind of society. But the Dowager would hate it. She would not be able to show her face anywhere for some considerable time.

And if Septimus truly did turn this house into a refuge for sailors, then she would be obliged to remove to the Dower House. She would spend the rest of her life almost afraid to go out of doors, lest she run into one of the rescued seamen walking about the grounds she considered belonged to her. In some ways, it would be a just punishment for her spite.

But how would poor Lady Fenella bear it?

She took a half-step towards her, hand outstretched. 'Please, madam, will you not reconsider...?'

The Dowager's eyes flashed with malevolent triumph.

'You may well beg me for mercy! But I have one here who will expose you for the cheating hussy that you are!'

She pointed to a chair to the right of the door, upon which an elderly man was sitting, one leg crossed over the other. He placed the teacup he had been holding in his slender fingers upon a conveniently placed side table, and got to his feet. He was looking at her so intently that Aimée got the impression he must have had his eyes fixed upon her from the moment she entered the room.

Like a hawk, preparing to swoop down on its prey.

She drew a little closer to the solid strength of her husband's body. Even though she knew this man could do her no real harm, it helped to remind herself that she was not going to have to face him alone.

Whoever he was. For she felt positive this was not Lord Matthison at all. From what she had heard, *he* was quite a young man. Besides, Septimus had already convinced her that he was too preoccupied with clearing his own name to bother with her.

Then who could he be? The Dowager had boasted that he had come to expose her as a hussy. There were only four men who could say with any degree of certainty what had happened at that card table in the Restoration. Lord Matthison she had already ruled out. Mr Carpenter she knew by sight. Besides, in spite of the way he had deserted her, she was sure he would never willingly denounce her. The only other man at that table, apart from her father, had been one Lord Sandiford.

In fact, now she came to reflect, it had been that very Lord Sandiford, a man Mr Carpenter had described as an ageing lecher, steeped in vice, who had first put the idea of staking her virginity into her father's drink-addled mind. And, although he looked like a perfectly respectable gentleman, she knew just how deceptive appearances could be and decided this man had to be Lord Sandiford.

Her lip curled with contempt. What kind of man egged another on to sell his own daughter's virginity, then strolled into a respectable household, and looked upon his potential victim with open hunger?

'I believe you wished me to meet this person, my lady?' she said coldly. 'Though I cannot imagine how such a man has the nerve to show his face in polite society. Or openly admit to the events he set in train.'

The Dowager's jaw dropped.

The elderly man turned white and dropped back into his chair.

'I knew it was unlikely you would forgive me,' he grated, through bloodless lips. 'But I had hoped...' His trembling hands clenched at the arms of his chair.

The Dowager was pulling herself together, visibly swelling with outrage.

'How dare you speak so rudely to his lordship! Especially since you claim he is your own grandfather!'

Aimée gasped and whirled back to the elderly man, whose eyes were still fixed upon her, not with hunger any longer, but with despair.

'Aha! You may well look shocked!' the Dowager continued. 'For the truth about your fraudulent claims to kinship with the Earl of Caxton are about to be shown for what they are! The whole world will know that you are nothing but a lying hussy!' She swivelled her upper body towards the elderly Earl. 'You have only the one granddaughter, is that not so, my lord? The lovely Lady Jayne.'

Aimée looked really closely at the elderly man. His voice bleak, he said, 'I am still not sure. I had hoped that today I would find that I have two granddaughters. But I fear that my stubborn pride, my rigid refusal to back down from the stand I took over your father, may have robbed me of you for ever.'

'Who…?' Aimée took a step towards the old man, feeling as though her whole world was turning upside down. 'Who are you?' Could this frail, unhappy-looking old man really be her grandfather? He did not look anything like she had imagined the domestic dictator who had ruined the lives of both his daughters would look.

And yet, there was something about his features…

'This,' declared the Dowager triumphantly, 'is the Earl of Caxton himself! The man you claim is your grandfather! There! What do you have to say now?'

'That he is the last person I had expected to find here,' she admitted frankly.

'Naturally!' the Dowager gloated. 'Now we shall see what we shall see!'

Aimée walked unsteadily across the room and dropped into the other chair that was pulled up to the tea table.

'Are you really the Earl of Caxton?'

Even before he nodded, Aimée knew it must be true. The Dowager had spoken of having some acquaintance with him. She would not have invited anyone but the Earl himself here today. Because she wanted to expose Aimée's 'fraud'. With profound relief, she saw that the Dowager had not investigated in at all the direction where she most feared the danger might come from.

No, it was her claim to kinship with the Earl of Caxton alone that the Dowager had sought to disprove.

Well, she could understand why the Dowager had invited the Earl to come here, but not why he had travelled all the way up to Staffordshire, when, as far as she was aware, he had never wanted anything to do with her before.

Though, from the expression on his face, the hesitantly spoken words of penitence, it sounded as though he might have undergone a change of heart.

'Why did you come here?' she managed to whisper.

'To expose you for the fraud you are!' hissed the Dowager. 'He cannot stand idly by and let nobodies wander round the countryside, claiming to be his granddaughters!'

The Earl took his eyes off Aimée just long enough to shoot the Dowager a coldly contemptuous look.

'That is why this vulgar person wrote to me, to be sure. But when she gave me the particulars of what she said you had told her, I had to come, to see if it could really be you.'

Aimée's heart thudded against her breastbone. It took her a few attempts before she managed to say, in a voice that sounded forced, even to her own ears, 'You need me to confirm my identity, is that it?'

He stretched out one trembling hand. 'No...no, there is no need. I can see her in you...' The Earl's face contorted with pain. 'I thought she would come home,' he said in a voice that quivered with regret. 'Your mother, that is. I thought that cutting her off would expose Peters for the grubby fortune-hunter that he was. When he did not immediately cast her off, I let her have enough money so they would not starve, but I thought it could only be a matter of time before she came to her senses. How could she stay with a man like that? A gambler, a wastrel, a drunkard? How could she...?'

'Keep to her marriage vows?' replied Aimée ruefully. 'To keep faith with him, for richer or poorer. In sickness or health. For better or worse.' She reached out blindly and felt Septimus grasp her hand firmly. Though her attention had been focused on her grandfather, she had been aware of the moment Septimus came to stand beside her chair. As he would stand by her, she now knew, whatever life might throw at them.

'Unto death,' she whispered, turning to place a kiss on the back of his strong, brown hand.

The Earl seemed to shrink from her words as from a blow, and though she would not have believed it possible, turned even more pale.

'I never thought she would defy me to the end! I always thought something would happen to effect a reconciliation…'

'Why did you not then acknowledge my birth?' Aimée said sorrowfully. 'Surely that would have been the perfect opportunity…'

'It would have, if only you had been a boy,' he groaned. 'That would have given me a reason to recall my daughter to England. Nobody would have thought I was weak for acknowledging my only legitimate heir, no matter what had gone before. Peters was, after all, the son of a gentleman. And they were legally married. I could have established them in one of my smaller properties, and gradually, so that I did not look as though I was backing down, I could have restored my relationship with her.'

'But I was merely a girl.'

He hung his head. The proud old aristocrat actually hung his head in shame.

'I have been guilty of making every mistake a man could make. Anger, pride…' He shook his head ruefully.

'And cruelty,' she said, tears coming to her eyes. 'I know I was only a girl, but when she died, you turned a deaf ear to my father's pleas for assistance! We were distrtaught. And destitute without the allowance you paid her. How could you have done that? Do you know how we had to live without that money? Can you even begin to imagine the hardships I have endured—?' She broke off as a spasm of pain crossed the old man's face.

'I never meant to punish you for the sins of your parents,' he said hoarsely. 'It was just such a shock when I received news of Aurora's death. And the tone of your father's letter…' He grimaced. 'It infuriated me. By the time I had calmed down somewhat, and acknowledged the justice of what he had said, it was too late. You had left Rome. There was no trace of either of you. And then I thought that if I ever did find you, it would be too late.'

He looked up at her, his eyes bleak. 'Is it too late? You must have grown up hating me. I dare say you want to repudiate me, as I once repudiated your father. You are in a position to do it,' he said, flicking a look at Septimus. 'You have no need of me. And perhaps it will be some consolation, to take this revenge on me.'

Revenge? Aimée was angry with this man, but she did not have it in her heart to hate him. She could tell, just by looking at him, that he was the one who had suffered most from the rift with his daughter. Her mother, from what she remembered of her childhood, had not seemed unhappy with her lot.

And if she was honest, she would be no better than the Dowager if she persisted in maintaining hostilities when there was a chance to make peace. Had she not just been thinking that the past should stay in the past?

'Grandfather…' she began hesitantly.

But the Dowager shot to her feet, screaming, 'No! You are no relation to this man! You cannot be! You are some actress this vile man has brought into my home to humiliate us all!'

And she flew at Aimée, her fingers curled into claws.

Such an uncharacteristically energetic attack took Aimée completely by surprise, for she had been sitting sideways on to the woman, with her attention fixed firmly upon her grandfather. But the elderly Earl had been keeping a watchful eye on the Dowager over Aimée's shoulder. At first she had looked only bewildered that the scene was not playing out exactly as she had envisaged, but her mounting fury had become increasingly apparent as the revelations piled up.

He leapt to his feet with remarkable agility for a man his age, and prevented the Dowager from knocking Aimée to the ground by flinging himself in her path.

The talons that had been aimed at Aimée's face scored the Earl's cheek instead. The Dowager screeched with fury and tried to thrust the old man aside, but he steadfastly interposed his body between the women, letting all the blows aimed at his granddaughter rain down upon him.

Septimus entered the fray then, separating the two elderly combatants by the simple expedient of lifting the dumpy Dowager bodily off her feet, whirling her round, and depositing her none too gently back on her sofa.

She bounced straight up and launched herself at Aimée again.

This time, Septimus grabbed her flailing arms and sat down next to her on the sofa, holding her wrists firmly while she struggled, and kicked, and screamed insults indiscriminately at all three of them.

The Earl of Caxton sank back into his chair, clearly as shaken as Aimée felt by that appalling development.

Bright blood was trickling down his otherwise ashen cheeks from the three deep scratches the Dowager had inflicted on him. He reached up to touch the wounds, then began to fumble in his pocket for a handkerchief to staunch the flow.

'Here, sir, let me help you,' said Aimée, coming out of her stupor to render him assistance. She took the handkerchief from his trembling hands and pressed it to his cheek.

'Thank you, my dear,' he said, raising his hand to cover hers. Their eyes met, and suddenly Aimée saw, not the ogre of her childhood imagination, but a spent and weary old man. A man whose pride had been crushed, whose hopes had never borne fruit, and whose last years would be filled with sorrow if she did not put the past firmly behind her. A man who had made mistakes, yes, but who bitterly regretted them.

And who was she to judge another? Or to refuse to take the olive branch he was extending to her by coming here and abasing himself before her?

Had she not made mistakes, criminal mistakes, in her own efforts to live the life she chose?

She lowered herself until she was kneeling on the floor at his feet. 'Think nothing of it…' she took a deep breath '…Grandfather.'

Hope lit his eyes. Some colour returned to his cheeks. His entire body seemed to pulse with renewed vigour.

He turned towards the Dowager, who was still grappling with Septimus upon the sofa, cursing and kicking in a most unladylike manner.

'That will do, madam!' His voice cut right through her display of hysterics, as nothing else had managed to do. She stopped fighting Septimus and gaped at the sight of Aimée kneeling at the Earl's feet, with her hand clasped firmly in his.

And identical expressions of contempt on their faces.

Even the Dowager could no longer deny Aimée's origins. It was written in the set of their determined chins, the proud tilt to their heads, the way they both elevated one eyebrow slightly, to convey reproof. Even though she had not been brought up in his orbit, even though she bore no resemblance to the Earl's other grand-daughter, there was no doubt that Aimée had inherited several of her grandfather's features and mannerisms.

With a wail, the Dowager flung herself back upon the cushions and burst into tears.

Aimée got up and went to the bell pull. 'I think we had better send for the housekeeper, don't you?' she said rather shakily. 'My lady,' she said in a firmer voice, 'I think you had better go and have a lie down. You are clearly unwell.'

An uneasy silence prevailed in the room, punctuated only by the Dowager's increasingly feeble moans, until the moment Mrs Trimley arrived. Her eyes widened at the scene that met her. The Dowager slumped on the sofa, her cushions scattered all over the floor. The Earl of Bowdon sitting beside her, scowling in a way that made him look even more piratical than usual, and the young Countess in a state that could only be described as dishevelled!

'Your mistress needs to go and have a lie down,' said Aimée. 'She has had a very nasty turn.'

'Yes,' the Dowager agreed feebly. 'I am not well. Really, it is all too much for a woman my age...'

She allowed Trimley to assist her to her feet, and, leaning heavily upon her arm, tottered from the room, still muttering complaints.

'What the deuce,' remarked the Earl of Caxton when she had gone, 'is the matter with that woman?'

A curl to his lip, Septimus replied, 'Been used to getting her own way for far too long.'

'It had crossed my mind,' replied the Earl of Caxton drily, 'that if she were forty years younger, I should have described that as a temper tantrum and had her sent up to the nursery without any supper.'

Then something like a spasm of pain flashed across his face. Perhaps he was remembering how harshly he had treated both his daughters.

Septimus made for the sideboard. 'I don't know about either of you, but I could do with a drink.'

Now that the Dowager had gone, it felt as though a storm had passed, leaving the air washed fresh and clean. The sun was already beginning to peep from behind the clouds. As if to confirm her impression, the Earl said, with the ghost of a smile, 'If it were up to me, I would call for champagne.'

'Well, my love?'

His love. Hearing the open affection in his voice as he employed that endearment made her certain that her future would be brighter than anything she had ever dreamed of.

'Just this once,' she admitted, 'I would not object to having a drink. I feel...' she sucked in a breath to prevent her voice wobbling with all the emotions she was feeling '...as though I have cause to celebrate.' Septimus had made her face up to her fears, had given her the assurance she could face anything, with his support.

Because of Septimus she had made peace with her grandfather. And she now had a cousin, too. That Lady

Jayne the Dowager had said was the complete opposite of her.

He had restored her family to her.

She walked across to her husband, leaned up and kissed him full on the lips.

'I would have missed out on this—' she indicated her grandfather, who was sitting regarding them with a fond smile '—if it had not been for you. Thank you.'

She gazed up at his rugged, slightly damaged face and counted herself the most fortunate woman in the world.

She had her security, at last.

And it did not come from having money, or status, or a big house to live in, but from realising that at last, she had found a man she could trust. Septimus would never let her down. He would not repudiate her, or neglect her, or try to sell her to pay his debts. Whatever fate flung at them, this man would be beside her. Dealing with her troubles as if they were his own.

Because he loved her.

Epilogue

Aimée started nervously as she heard the front door slam. She had been on edge ever since Septimus had brought her to this property in Surrey, knowing that he meant to ride over to Kingsmede, which was scarce one day's ride away, to settle things with Lord Matthison.

'I won't have you worrying about him any more,' he had growled before setting out just after dawn that morning. 'I will make him take all the money back, and let him know just what he will have to face should he ever speak of his part in the affair.'

She got to her feet as Septimus strode into the room.

'You did do it, didn't you?' she managed to say, just before he swept her into a crushing embrace and stopped her mouth with a passionate kiss.

'You won't have any trouble from that quarter, that is certain,' he said, tugging her to the sofa, and pulling her down onto his lap. 'But it was not quite as you thought, my lovely wife.'

Hearing him address her so affectionately, and acting so demonstratively, after despairing she might never find a way to reach his heart, instantly put paid to the slight qualm his cryptic comment had roused.

'To start with, he denies outright that he had any thought of making you his mistress.'

'What? But—'

'Just hear me out, sweetheart. He claims that he was disgusted that any man could auction off his own daughter to a man of Sandiford's stamp. That he only took part in the bidding so that he could ensure you would be safe. He says he sent you all the winnings from that accursed table, to provide you with the means to escape. He says that he told his manservant to make that very clear.'

Aimée cast her mind back to that night. The servant had said she was not to let her father know about the money. That it was not for him, but for her. But she had assumed…because of what Mr Carpenter had said, about all those lechers bidding for her…

'I s-suppose I might have misunderstood. I was so frightened, and alone…'

'And suspicious of every man, I know. You fled from me, just because I made a mull of proposing to you, remember?'

When she blushed, he kissed her until she felt better. Then she said, 'So, he has taken the money back then, and it is all over.'

'Ah, well, not exactly. The fact of the matter is,' he said, looking a bit sheepish, 'he refused point blank to so much as touch it. He told me that now he has found happiness at last with his new wife, he dare not risk offending Lady Luck by taking it back. Cora explained it in such a way that I saw it all made perfect sense to Lord Matthison. He is very superstitious. Gamblers often are, you know.'

'Cora?'

'Lord Matthison's wife. Remarkable woman,' he said. 'You know, I went to Kingsmede planning to call the devil out and make him pay for what I thought he'd done to you. And he squared up to me, breathing fire and brimstone for daring to accuse him of such villainy, and then in walked this tiny little woman, with red hair and freckles, so slight you would have thought a puff of wind would blow her away, and within seconds she managed to have the pair of us feeling like guilty schoolboys.'

Aimée blinked in surprise. The sight of Septimus in a cold fury would have made many women swoon. And Lord Matthison had such a terrible reputation that people trembled when his shadow fell on them. Yet this Cora had made them both mind their manners. She had a sudden vision of this tiny woman, quelling the rage of two such men as Lord Matthison and her Septimus, and felt a rising urge to giggle.

'I think I shall like her.'

'Well, I very much hope so, because I seem to have invited the pair of them to come and stay with us when we open up Bowdon House,' he admitted, colouring up.

'You have done what?' She had agreed, after much persuasion from both her husband and grandfather, to go to London and enter society. The Earl of Caxton had sworn that his other granddaughter would help to smooth her path. And even though she still felt nervous about meeting Lady Jayne, who sounded so very polished and self-assured, in the end, a mixture of curiosity about her cousin, and her ingrained pride had made her agree. But now he expected her to entertain guests as well!

'We got to talking, you see, about the money. After

he refused to tempt fate by taking it back, I swore I would not risk offending my own wife by keeping hold of it. It was Cora who suggested we find some worthy cause, and donate it to that. So naturally I thought of my plans to open up homes for ex-mariners. And she was so interested, so enthusiastic, that before I knew it I was inviting her to stay with us.'

'She sounds like a remarkable woman,' said Aimée, much impressed.

'Yes, that is just what I thought,' said Septimus with relief. 'She has something of your spirit. She openly admitted she has spent the last seven years working as a seamstress, quite unaware of her true identity. And with you having lived the same sort of hand-to-mouth existence, she seemed to think you would both become friends—'

He broke off suddenly, as she stiffened in his arms, aware that she could only have heard about Aimée's background from him.

'And you know, my darling,' he said cajolingly, nuzzling her neck, 'you will find London society a sight easier to deal with if you have a friend at your side. It struck me that you will not have many friends, just at first. And nor will she.'

She promptly forgave him. He was doing his best to deal with all her worries the best way he could. And, to be honest, it would be good to have a friend who would completely understand the feelings of inadequacy that were bound to assail her as she entered her new sphere of life.

Besides, Cora would also be finding her own way in a society that would look askance at any girl who had previously worked for her living.

And she had shown wisdom in suggesting they put

the disputed money to a good use. She sounded like a person who was determined to use her influence to benefit others. A kindred spirit indeed.

'In a way,' Aimée admitted, 'I owe my happiness to her husband. If Lord Matthison had not sent me that money, I would never have taken fright and run away. But because I did, I now have the best husband in the world, as well as a new family, and, oh, everything I could ever want. The least I can do is stand friend to his wife.'

Septimus heaved a sigh of relief. 'Best husband in the world, hmm?'

'Without a doubt,' she declared. And kissed him.

* * * * *

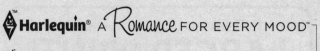

The series you love are now available in

LARGER PRINT!

The books are complete and unabridged—
printed in a larger type size to make it
easier on your eyes.

Harlequin *Romance*

From the Heart, For the Heart

Harlequin
INTRIGUE
BREATHTAKING ROMANTIC SUSPENSE

Harlequin *Presents*

Seduction and Passion Guaranteed!

Harlequin *Super Romance*

Exciting, emotional, unexpected!

Try **LARGER PRINT** today!

Visit: www.ReaderService.com
Call: 1-800-873-8635

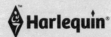

Harlequin

A *Romance* FOR EVERY MOOD™

www.ReaderService.com

HLPDIR11